NOBLE CONFLICT

www.malorieblackman.co.uk

NOBLE CONFLICT

malorie
blackman

CORGI

NOBLE CONFLICT
A CORGI BOOK 978 0 552 55462 6

First published in Great Britain by Doubleday,
an imprint of Random House Children's Publishers UK
A Random House Group Company

Doubleday edition published 2013
Corgi edition published 2014

5 7 9 10 8 6 4

The Random House Group Limited supports the Forest Stewardship Council®
(FSC®), the leading international forest-certification organisation. Our books
carrying the FSC label are printed on FSC®-certified paper. FSC is the only
forest-certification scheme supported by the leading environmental organisa-
tions, including Greenpeace. Our paper procurement policy can be found at
www.randomhouse.co.uk/environment

MIX
Paper from
responsible sources
FSC® C016897

Set in 12.5/15pt Bembo

Corgi Books are published by
Random House Children's Publishers UK,
61–63 Uxbridge Road, London W5 5SA

www.**randomhousechildrens**.co.uk
www.**totallyrandombooks**.co.uk
www.**randomhouse**.co.uk

Addresses for companies within The Random House Group Limited
can be found at: www.randomhouse.co.uk/offices.htm

THE RANDOM HOUSE GROUP Limited Reg. No. 954009

A CIP catalogue record for this book is available from the British Library.

Printed and bound in Great Britain by CPI Group (UK), Croydon, CR0 4YY

For Neil and Lizzy,
with love as always.

Dulce et decorum est pro patria mori
(It is sweet and fitting to die for one's country)

Quintus Horatius Flaccus, Ode III, 2: 13

All war is deception.

Sun Tzu

*Crusade – a vigorous movement or enterprise against poverty
or a similar social evil; a personal campaign undertaken for a
particular cause*

Oxford English Dictionary

Nearly two centuries ago, the region on our Eastern borders was not the volcanic wasteland it is today. It was a land as beautiful as our own, but inhabited by another culture, the so-called Crusaders, whose very nature was intemperate and undisciplined. While we in the Alliance lived in harmony with the land, valuing and living at one with nature, their highly skilled scientists sought to control and subdue nature through their technology. While we lived in peace and were tolerant to all, they were aggressive and expansionist and viewed our lands with covetous eyes. While we respected nature, they sought to modify the very face of the continents, shifting the tectonic plates beneath their feet to create more territory for their ever-expanding population by triggering nuclear explosives deep within the Earth.

But in their hubris they over-reached themselves. Their nuclear devices deployed, triggering a massive outpouring of lava which turned their homeland into a barren desert. They very nearly annihilated themselves – and those few who survived lived as nomads in the volcanic wasteland they had created, a wasteland which came to be known as the Badlands. But in time, their numbers began to increase, and a group of their deadliest fighters – the Insurgents – turned avaricious eyes towards us once again, dreaming of the day when they would take our land by force and make it their new home.

Extract taken from 'The Origins of the Insurgency' by Brother Telem

1

'I'm here. I actually made it!'

Kaspar Wilding shouldn't have been grinning, but he couldn't help it. In full dress uniform, he stood to attention with his fellow graduates of the Guardian Academy. Seated dignitaries, selected visitors and family members surrounded them on three sides, but none of them were there specifically for Kaspar. Uncle Jeff, the only family Kaspar had left, couldn't make it.

'I can't just up and leave the farm, not when there's work to be done,' said Uncle Jeff's holo-message in response to Kaspar's invitation. 'I haven't got the time to spare to attend your . . . ceremony.' Uncle Jeff had spat out the last word as if it burned his tongue.

Kaspar didn't even bother to argue. Conclusive proof – not that any was required – that Uncle Jeff still hadn't forgiven him for leaving the farm and signing up to be a Guardian. Kaspar doubted that his uncle ever would. But was he about to let that ruin even one minute of his big day? No way.

Brother Simon stood with his back to the graduates as he made his speech. It was a real honour to have a member of the High Council officiating over the graduation ceremony and it was the first time Kaspar had seen anyone from the Council up close and personal like this. This was meant to be a solemn moment full of import and gravity, but for the life of him, Kaspar just couldn't keep a straight face.

Keeping his eyes front, he whispered through rigid lips like a ventriloquist to the tall, red-headed girl with dark blue eyes on his left, 'Hey, Janna, if Brother Simon waves his arms any harder he'll take off.'

'Shut up,' Janna hissed in reply. 'Or Voss will kick you so hard *you'll* be the one who leaves the ground.'

Voss was not only one of the most senior Guardians at the Academy, but also their formidable new boss. At well over two metres, their commander was a lean, mean fighting machine. He'd regularly taken them through a number of exercises during their training and the man took no prisoners. No way would Kaspar like to get on his bad side. He was bald as an egg, the only hair on his face being his jet-black eyebrows which framed his piercing brown eyes. His laser-beam gaze was renowned for missing nothing. Kaspar quickly stowed his smile and resumed his fixed stare at the horizon.

'. . . such a fine body of young people who have sworn to protect our way of life here in the Alliance and our communities from those misguided Insurgents who would seek to deprive us of everything we hold dear . . .' Brother Simon droned on, still watering his dry words with the frenzied flailing of his arms. Kaspar found it more

4

interesting to concentrate on the High Councillor's active limbs than his arid words.

'I still can't believe they made a melon farmer like you Honour Cadet,' whispered Dillon from Kaspar's right. 'You must have compromising photos of someone very important doing something really embarrassing with barnyard animals.'

'Jealousy. Pure jealousy,' replied Kaspar, but his grin was back with a vengeance.

Dillon had a point, though. To think that until eighteen months ago, Kaspar had been working on his uncle's farm on the edge of the Badlands. But after brooding and stewing and agonizing about it for months, he'd applied to be a cadet at the Academy behind his uncle's back . . .

He remembered every moment of his interview . . . 'Congratulations on making it this far,' the Inducting Officer had said. 'But I warn you now, I'm not here to rubber-stamp your application. We only take those with the potential to become the best, the elite. So what makes you think you could be a Guardian?'

The IndO's unexpectedly brusque manner threw Kaspar for a moment. He took a deep, steadying breath. 'As you can see from my medical report, I'm fit. I regularly run and swim. And I'm strong. I'm used to hard work on the farm. Plus I scored nine hundred and eighty-four on the aptitude test,' he answered, prickles of heat lancing his skin as he spoke.

He wanted to join the Academy so badly he could taste

it sharp and sweet on his tongue, reach out his hand and almost touch it. *Almost.* If he were to fail at one of the first hurdles . . .

'It takes more than that,' the IndO continued, distinctly unimpressed. 'I see from your application that you've spent most of your life on your uncle's farm. Even visits to Capital City have been rare. To put it mildly, you lack experience of anything but farm life.'

'That's true, sir, but I'm a very fast learner, I think quickly on my feet and I'm eager to serve,' said Kaspar.

'Blah, blah, blah! You seriously think you could face a mob of homicidal terrorists intent on death and destruction and still keep it together? Well, farm boy?'

The IndO turned away before Kaspar could even reply, his finger heading for the REJECTED icon at the bottom of the data screen.

'Runs in the family, sir,' Kaspar shot back defiantly. 'My father was R. J. Wilding and my mother was Kristin Jaeger.'

The Inducting Officer froze momentarily before slowly turning to face Kaspar. For the first time since he'd entered the room, Kaspar had the IndO's full, undivided attention, just not the way he wanted to get it.

'Rob and Kristin were your parents?'

Kaspar nodded.

RJ and KJ, as they were known, had been paired up straight out of the Academy. Two years of stellar performance had followed as they had gelled into one superb unit that protected and served along with the best of the veteran Guardians. Their name and fame had spread

6

further and faster when they'd saved Sister Elena, one of the High Council, from an assassination attempt. Less than two years later they had got married, and Kristin became pregnant – but on the night she went into labour, RJ had been killed. Ironically, Kaspar knew it had been an accident – on his way to the hospital to be with his wife, a truck had slammed into RJ's car and he'd died immediately. After Kaspar was born, Kristin had returned to work and successfully juggled being a mum and an Academy Instructor for seven more years until she too died. That death *hadn't* been accidental. A terrorist attempt to sabotage a nuclear power plant had led to a release of lethal radiation. Kristin, her partner and two of the terrorists had been so badly irradiated that it hadn't even been safe to recover their bodies. The Radiological Protection team had just poured in tonne after tonne of concrete and entombed them all together. After that, Kaspar had been sent to live with Uncle Jeff.

The Inducting Officer's hand returned to his side as he sat back in his high-back chair and scrutinized Kaspar. 'That's quite a pedigree to live up to.'

'Yes, sir.' Kaspar tried desperately to keep his expression neutral. He sighed inwardly. So much for his promise to himself not to use his heavyweight parents as a battering ram to open doors. He had barely warmed the seat he was sitting on, before his famous parents were practically the first thing out of his mouth.

'You seriously reckon you're up to the task?' the IndO persisted.

'Absolutely, sir. I know I am. I've never wanted to do anything else or be anything else. All I need is a chance.'

The officer gave Kaspar an appraising look, then turned back to Kaspar's application. 'Congratulations, Cadet Wilding. You're in.' He stabbed at the APPROVED icon decisively.

Kaspar should've been happy, but he wasn't. He headed for the door, but then lingered. The IndO was scrolling through Kaspar's application. Kaspar could see his own 3D image projecting from the screen, turning slowly through three hundred and sixty degrees.

'Sir?'

'Yes, Cadet Wilding?' asked the IndO, turning to face him.

'Sir, could you not put down who my parents were on my application form?' asked Kaspar.

'Why ever not?'

'I'd like to do this on my own merits, no one else's,' said Kaspar carefully.

The IndO studied him for several seconds. 'Have you thought this through? Your parents' names could open a lot of doors.'

'Sir, if I can't open those doors for myself, I'd rather they stayed closed.'

'Cadet Wilding, your mother was a very good friend of mine. I see you have inherited her . . . spirit of independence.' A trace of a smile tugged at the IndO's lips. 'Very well. If you're sure that's what you want.'

'Yes, sir, it is.'

'Good luck, Cadet.'

'Thank you, sir.'

And the IndO had been as good as his word. Not once had his famous parents been mentioned in the entire time Kaspar had gone through Guardian training.

Today, gazing over the heads of the assembled crowd to the northern mountains in the distance, Kaspar could actually see the hydroponic towers of his uncle's farm and of the neighbouring ones. The afternoon sun glinted off the tinted glass panels and the computer-controlled aluminium shutters. Uncle Jeff's farm was only about fifteen kilometres beyond the Capital City boundaries, but it was light years away in attitude.

And now look at me, Kaspar thought with satisfaction. Nearly nineteen years old, a fully fledged Guardian – and Honour Cadet to boot.

'No more skulking in the agric shelters at the first hint of trouble,' he muttered.

He was ready to fight for what was right, just like his parents before him.

'What?' asked Janna.

'Nothing. Sorry. Just thinking out loud.'

Only then did Kaspar notice Voss glaring at them. Both Kaspar and Janna clamped their lips shut.

What was that?

A sudden movement off to his right caught Kaspar's eye. Nothing specific, no obvious threat – just a few casually dressed latecomers emerging from the woods and

9

starting across the lawns. Keeping his head straight but his eyes trained, Kaspar watched them advance. Visitors cutting through the woods wasn't unusual. It was the fastest route from the road to the ceremonial grounds at the Academy. Taking the official route more than doubled the journey time. But somehow the pattern of their movements was wrong, simultaneously furtive and purposeful. They moved like hunting snakes.

Not good.

At the Academy, cadets were taught to trust their instincts, but Kaspar hesitated. He was on parade at a very formal occasion. He wasn't even officially on duty yet and he certainly didn't relish the idea of launching his military career by interrupting Brother Simon's speech to cry wolf. Another group emerged on the other flank. Same movement, same feeling. Definitely not good. Insurgents? His mind made up, Kaspar started to move, but the decision to interrupt Brother Simon was taken out of his hands. A soft whooshing sound filled the air.

'THERMAL GRENADE! TAKE COV—'

A colossal explosion and a licking tongue of flame erupted in front of the platform before Kaspar could finish his warning. The heat from the blast seared his face and the backs of his hands. Both ears felt like they'd been simultaneously hit by a wrecking ball.

Lucky for my eardrums that I had my mouth open, he thought fleetingly.

But hearing loss wasn't the biggest problem right now. He and everyone around him still had an excellent chance of being killed. Kaspar hurled himself at Brother Simon, flattening him behind the limited safety of the podium just as another grenade exploded close by.

Kaspar rolled onto his feet. 'Janna, Dillon, with me,' he bellowed at the other recruits, wanting them to follow him.

He knew he was shouting, but his voice sounded muffled and far away. It was like trying to hear underwater. Some of the recruits were still standing on the platform looking around like tourists, not even seeking cover. Did he have to draw them a picture?

'It's an attack. Take cover,' Kaspar yelled. At least he hoped it was yelling. His voice still sounded stifled.

But the warning did little good. Another thermal grenade landed near the left-hand end of the reviewing stand. The colossal boom that followed was probably heard in the Badlands. Shock waves rocketed through Kaspar's head, their intensity threatening to split his skull open. He shook his head several times to try and clear it. Shrieks and screams resounded. But now at least some of the other recruits were getting organized. Kaspar had Janna and Dillon with him and could see on the other side of what used to be the platform that Voss was leading another group across the lawn towards the trees.

Kaspar had already stripped the ceremonial cover off his rifle and now, as he thumbed off the safety catch, he shouted to his colleagues to do the same.

'Targets at Green-Two, by the lake.'

He scanned the grounds through the telescopic sights

and immediately saw a man crouching in the middle of the lawn, reloading a grenade launcher. Kaspar took careful aim, inhaled sharply, held his breath and squeezed the trigger. There was a powerful crack and a brilliant blue bolt shot out of the gun, striking the man in the chest, dropping him twitching to the ground. Hitting actual people was far more dramatic than when using the simulators. Far more satisfying too. One down. Kaspar swept the sights across the lawn, looking for more targets. He caught sight of another running past the memorial and tracked him with the rifle scope.

'Wait for it,' he told himself. 'Don't fire too soon. Wait for the full charge to build.'

The 'max charge' tone sounded in his headset and he immediately fired. The running man was instantaneously bathed in a blue glow; his legs folded beneath him and he violently somersaulted into a heap. Another one out for the count. Off to his right, Kaspar saw Janna and Dillon bring down a couple more. He could hear the fizzing crack of more firing from the other flank too. Kaspar took out another Insurgent who was running in an erratic pattern hoping it would make him harder to take down. It didn't. Voss and his group had forced what was left of the attackers back towards the edge of the woods. Now that the explosions had stopped, Kaspar snatched a glance at his watch.

Three minutes? He couldn't believe it. All this had happened in only three minutes? Kaspar turned to peruse the injured around him. The walking, sitting and lying wounded surrounded him. The occasional groan, moan and anguished cry split the otherwise stunned silence. With his hearing returning, he looked around again, more slowly this time. Though there were a number of injured, he couldn't actually see any prone bodies that weren't moving. Could it be that, by the grace of some divine power or pure luck, no one had been killed? If so, then it was certainly no thanks to the terrorists. And to attack here, at the Academy, when the place was swarming with Guardians, was a new level of bold and stupid combined.

Fury, hot and devouring, flared within Kaspar. The full import of what had happened hit him now that the adrenalin coursing through his body was beginning to subside. The ones who had done this were nothing more than low-life, cowardly scumbags. Kaspar's grip on his rifle tightened as he found himself wishing that it could do more than merely stun.

But his job wasn't over yet. Nor would it be over until the last of the Insurgents had been hunted down. The Insurgents were a small but deadly force of terrorists made up of the fighting elite from those living in the Badlands – *the Crusaders*. The number of Insurgents who had based themselves among the Alliance population, within the pockets of Crusaders allowed to live in Capital City, were limited. Less than one hundred, according to the last official estimates. But they believed in making their presence felt, to say the least. Another look around and

Kaspar made himself a promise. He wouldn't rest until every last one of them had been rounded up and held accountable for their actions. He owed it to his mum if nothing else.

This was turning out to be one hell of a first day.

2

On the other side of the building, a black-clad figure crouched down between the trees, waiting. Once he saw the Guardians running round to reinforce the efforts of their colleagues – the diversion working as planned – he slipped out of the shadows and darted for the back of the main building, heading towards the Admin annexe. More skilful than the assailants at the main building, he reached the security fence unseen, dug into the small rucksack on his back to remove a thick but narrow rolled-up mat, which he threw over the razor-wire, and nimbly hauled himself up and over. Each step, each movement, betrayed expert precision as he made no sound. Now inside the secure compound, he used the available cover to approach the Admin building. Unholstering a climber's dart-gun, he fired a steel piton into the frame of a third-storey window. It pierced the window frame with a dull *thwack*. He rapidly climbed the spider-wire attached to the piton, his skill barely causing it to sway more than a few centimetres in any direction. At the second-floor window, he began to disarm the electronic window lock.

Two Guardians came running round the corner of the

building, about twenty metres from where he was hanging. He froze, holding on with one hand and pointing a pistol fitted with a silencer with the other. But good quality spider-wire was nearly invisible and neither Guardian looked up as they ran by.

He swung his legs through the now-open window and dropped lightly onto the floor of the caretaker's storeroom. So far, the intelligence he'd been given had been spot on. He opened the door quietly, but as expected the building was deserted. Through the door, turn ninety degrees right, fifteen metres true, ninety degrees left, second door, fire stairs, two flights up to the footbridge that led to the main Admin building. Two Guardians manned the footbridge as he had anticipated, but they were deep in conversation and he slipped past them without incident. Then down six flights of stairs to sub-basement B – the computer core. A deep breath later, he input an eight-digit code on the keypad by the door. The door slid open with a hiss. A blast of ice-cold air rushed out to meet him. His stance alert, his gun drawn, he took a quick look around but the place appeared empty. He entered the cavernous room that housed the local data hub. Steadying himself, he took another strong, deep breath. So far, so good.

But everything up until then had been the easy part.

The attack had worked brilliantly to divert the Guardians. And he had made it into the core and set off no alarms. But now that would change. As soon as he accessed the network, he knew he would be detected and they would come for him.

So be it.

He would have enough time.

He sat at the operator's console and began to search, his hands moving rapidly as he flicked through data screen after data screen.

3

The last attacker outside was now desperately trying to escape back behind the curtain of trees. He zigzagged while firing blindly behind him. Kaspar dropped to one knee, took aim at the terrorist's back and squeezed the trigger. As he did so another bolt of electricity lanced out from slightly behind him, to his left. Both bolts hit their target. The fleeing man was sent sprawling into a flower bed. Kaspar looked around for the source of the second shot and saw Voss breaking out an unsanctioned second weapon, both hands now loaded. The commander ran over, still scanning for any remaining enemies.

'Nice shot, kid. What's your name again?'

'Wilding, sir,' replied Kaspar. 'Kaspar Wilding.'

Voss looked at the man twitching in the flowers. 'Double stunned. He is going to feel real rough when he wakes up.' He laughed. 'Serves him right. Bastard.'

Kaspar nodded his agreement, feeling not the least bit sorry for the terrorist. He steadied himself to look around again. Moans and weeping still filled the air. He pressed his thumb and index finger together in an effort to try and bank down his feelings. If he lost it now, who would that help? As silence slowly descended, an ear-splitting siren went off.

'Better late than never,' he said drily. The alarm had certainly taken its time in going off.

'Damn it!' Voss spat. 'That isn't the general alarm. This was just a diversion. Someone has breached the computer core!' He started running towards the Admin building. 'Come on, Wilding,' he shouted over his shoulder. 'Or d'you think you've done enough for one day?'

Kaspar sprinted to catch up. They arrived at the same time as eight or nine other Guardians, including Dillon and Janna, who charged up the steps to the main entrance.

'You two.' Voss pointed at Dillon and Janna. 'Secure the rest of the building. The rest of you head down to the computer core and don't let anyone slip past you or you'll answer to me.'

Kaspar went to follow, but Voss caught his arm.

'Not that way,' he said, dragging Kaspar away from the entrance. 'I have a better idea.'

Voss tore off, leading the way to a series of four backup air-conditioning vents around one side of the building, each of which measured at least two metres in diameter. He keyed the transmit switch on the CommLink located at his throat.

'229 Voss to Maintenance. Shut down the power on vent 9H.'

'I can't, sir. It's against regul—' That was as far as the duty engineer was allowed to get.

'*This is Commander Voss. Kill the power on vent niner hotel. NOW.*'

If the engineer still had doubts, he kept them to himself. With a loud clunk, the fan blades of the vent began to slow down.

'What do they want with the computer core?' asked Kaspar as they waited for the fan to stop. 'Can they get access to our defence systems through there?'

'No,' replied Voss. 'As soon as the alarm goes off, all comms are severed. No data is going in or coming out of there now.'

'How about via CommLink or a radio? Can the assailant transmit what he finds to Insurgents elsewhere?'

'No, that place is shielded against all EM radiation,' replied Voss as he started to unscrew the access panel with his Guardian utility knife. 'It doesn't matter what he does. He's caught like a rat in a trap.'

'Maybe they don't know they can't transmit from there?' said Kaspar.

'Oh, they know all right. I'd put money on it,' Voss replied. 'All of our data nodes are shielded against electromagnetic radiation, so why would they think this one will be different?'

'So it's just sabotage?'

'That won't do them any good either. All the data is duplicated and all the computers have multiple, multi-site backups. The stupid sods can't achieve anything except minor nuisance value.' Voss lifted the access panel and started to squeeze into the narrow air-conditioning duct.

'Leads down to the core,' he explained. 'Hope you ain't claustrophobic?'

'No, sir,' replied Kaspar.

'It'd be tough if you were,' Voss called back.

Kaspar peered after Voss into a pipe that rapidly narrowed until it was barely a metre wide. Well, if he wasn't claustrophobic before, this experience could very easily change that. The AC duct ran horizontally for a couple of metres then disappeared. A deep breath later, Kaspar followed his boss into the conduit. It didn't take him long to discover why the duct just seemed to disappear. It turned downwards at a ninety-degree angle. Voss had already jammed his feet against one side of the shaft and his back was wedged hard against the opposite side as he started to edge downwards. Kaspar let him get down a couple of metres, then followed. Dust flew up around them like an angry insect swarm.

Descending, however, was easier than it looked, and both men were soon crouching in another horizontal pipe. Kaspar reckoned they were now nine or ten metres below ground. It was certainly dim, but not completely dark. Voss placed his finger against his lips, then started crawling as quietly as he could towards a patch of light about twenty metres ahead. A dust storm swirled around them, far worse than before, and Kaspar struggled not to sneeze. He'd already applied a finger to his nose three times as they made their way towards the light. He opened his mouth slightly to take in air that way instead of through his nose. The dust left an ashy aftertaste on his tongue, but better that than sneezing or coughing and alerting the enemy to their presence or, worse still, incurring Voss's wrath.

At the end of this passageway, Kaspar was able to peer through an air-conditioning grille right into the computer core. Row upon row of servers, patchers and communications equipment lined the room. Some of the monitors were set into the various panels. Most of the data was designed to be projected at eye level. A huge screen dominated one wall. The only door was directly across the room from the vent where Kaspar and Voss were hidden.

Not three metres away sat the terrorist.

Kaspar wasn't sure what he had expected – maybe someone bigger, more threatening, possibly ranting and perhaps planting bombs. In fact, the guy he spied was his age or only slightly older, was lean to the point of being positively skinny and was at least a head shorter than Kaspar from the look of it. He sat in an office chair, calmly reading the data off the screen before him, looking uncannily like a student simply relaxing in a library. He wore a close-fitting black outfit like a scuba suit. The terrorist had taken off his hooded mask and left it on the desk to his left next to his rucksack. He reminded Kaspar of the historical ninjas he'd read about in some of his graphic novels. To the terrorist's right lay a pistol with a silencer attached, and beside the gun was a dagger with a wicked-looking twenty-centimetre black blade that had been plunged into the desk, tip first.

Kaspar frowned and cast a glance at his boss. If any of

the Guardians had done that to a knife, Voss would've had seven fits. His boss turned so that he was facing the terrorist with his feet pressed against the grille. He unslung his rifle and pointed it into the room between his feet, signing to Kaspar to do the same. At that moment, the rest of the Guardians arrived outside the door. They obviously weren't operating in stealth mode – Kaspar could hear them from across the room. Voss held up three fingers. The keypad on the other side of the room beeped as the eight-digit code was entered.

Two fingers.

The door across the room clicked as the magnetic locks disengaged. The terrorist stood up, and with a swipe of his fingers dismissed the screen he'd just been reading. He snatched up his knife and faced the door, his back towards Voss and Kaspar.

One finger.

The door slid open. Kaspar tightened his grip on his weapon. A nod from Voss and both men kicked as hard as they could. The grille flew off its mountings. The terrorist spun round, the knife in his hand already moving upwards, but too late. Kaspar and Voss fired simultaneously and the terrorist slumped to the floor, convulsing. Then the juddering stopped. The rest of the Guardians swept into the room, looking a little bit disappointed that the action was over.

'Nicely done again, kid,' said Voss as he slapped Kaspar on the back. Hard. 'You have the makings of a first-class Guardian, like me.'

Voss laughed at his own joke as he made his way over to the terrorist, who lay on the floor, his knife discarded beside him. The rest stood around, lightening the tension by swapping stories about who had shot whom, and what morons the terrorists were, though quickly shutting up when Voss glared at them, his face stern again.

Kaspar walked over to the terrorist and squatted down to check for bugs and other devices. The guy had no pockets, no gadgets, no devices of any kind, not even a watch. Kaspar straightened up to examine the rucksack on the desk. There were no transmission devices in there either. Just some spider-wire and climbing equipment. He leaned over to examine the assailant's gun. Unlike the guns of the Guardians, this was an automatic projectile-weapon, loaded and lethal. Kaspar wanted to pick it up, but he knew better than to touch it – his training had taught him about contaminating evidence. While the others were securing the area, Kaspar turned to the computer and accessed the history list, flicking through a couple of the virtual screens that had so held the Insurgent's attention.

What on earth . . . ?

Why was the terrorist looking at data about Calliston Water? It was a lake several kilometres away from Capital City. No one went there as it was too isolated; you could see that much from the image on the screen. It didn't supply Capital City with water or food and there were no dwellings or industrial bases around it – just a whole heap of nothing. Why risk breaking into the Academy's computer core merely to find out more about it? It didn't make sense.

Janna and Dillon came running into the room.

'The rest of the facility is secure, sir,' Dillon announced.

He and Janna spied the terrorist still lying unconscious on the floor, their expressions betraying their disappointment at not being part of the takedown. Kaspar used the opportunity to take another look at the terrorist. His initial assessment wasn't far off the mark. This guy was only a couple of years older than him, if that, with buzz-cut hair and a sallow complexion that spoke of his life in the Badlands. Kaspar was struck by just how ordinary he looked. No horns or tail, no fangs, just nondescript. The kind of guy you'd walk past in the street without sparing him a first glance, never mind a second one.

'Wilding, when you've finished staring holes through the Insurgent, perhaps you'd like to get back to work,' Voss snapped.

'Sorry, sir.' Kaspar snapped out of his reverie.

'Spraining your arm from patting yourself on the back, are you?' Janna asked without malice.

'No, my arm is still working just fine. But thanks for asking,' Kaspar replied with a grin.

'Kas saved the day!' someone across the room announced to the raucous laughter of those present.

Kaspar accepted the congratulations and the teasing of his friends with equal embarrassment, his face burning.

'Not bad, Kas,' said Dillon, slapping him on the back.

'Thanks.' Kaspar rolled his shoulder, trying to ease the ache in it.

'What's wrong with you?' asked Dillon. 'Did the bad guy manage to get one or two licks in first?'

'No, but you did! Dillon, mate, you're built like a tank transport,' said Kaspar. 'Could you not pat me on the back 'cause it hurts every time.'

'Wuss!' Dillon said without a trace of sympathy.

Kaspar looked up at Dillon and shook his head. The trouble was, Dillon didn't know his own strength. He was as tall as Voss but a lot beefier. His best friend spent every spare minute in the gym working out and had the muscles on his muscles to prove it.

'Anyway, well done for not making a complete twat of yourself today,' smiled Dillon.

In truth, Kaspar couldn't help feeling relieved over exactly the same thing. At least he hadn't given Voss a reason to kick his butt or, worse still, kick him out. Dillon booted the unconscious terrorist, which Voss chose not to see. Kaspar watched with a frown as Dillon kicked the saboteur's knife further away from him, just in case.

'People, it doesn't take all of us to guard one unconscious lowlife. Kaspar and Dillon, stay put till the criminal investigation forensic unit and the medics arrive to take this piece of garbage away. The rest of you are with me,' Voss ordered. The commander headed for the door, not bothering to look back to make sure his instructions were being followed. He knew they would be.

'Kas, what's up with you?' said Janna as she drew level.

'I don't get this,' replied Kaspar.

'What's to get?' asked Dillon. 'Bad guys make trouble, good guys kick their arses. Bad guys go to hospital, good guys go and drink beer once their shift is over. Simple.' Dillon didn't do nuances.

'Yeah, but why?' Kaspar persisted. 'Why did they arrange a diversion to get this man into the core when he didn't even try to escape or do any damage? And he was so calm, he didn't seem the least bit deranged or fanatical. He was just *reading*, about Calliston Water, of all places. What's that all about?'

'They're all intellectually challenged, my hero, so why worry about it?' Janna offered as explanation. A smile later, she slapped his butt and headed for the door.

'Yes, but why go for his knife and not the gun?' Kaspar asked.

But Janna was gone and Dillon wasn't listening.

The savagery, the brutality, the sheer inhumanity of the Uprising was like nothing that had gone before. When the Insurgency first started, we in the Alliance had no choice but to fight as they fought. Nothing less than our very survival was at stake. We became worryingly adept at killing them, but we were paying for our new expertise with the loss of our humanity. We came to realize that we were destined to become just like them — constantly plotting, rejoicing in enemies slain, keeping score by counting bodies.

We had to adopt a new ethos or lose our very souls.

With our technical ability, we put our minds to the development of non-lethal weapons. Thus came the stun rifle, immobilizing gas and the glue-guns, amongst others. Renouncing killing was our salvation. Though the battle may continue, let us never return to those dark days of long ago where killing was seen as the first, last and only solution.

Ours is a noble conflict.

Extract taken from 'Towards a New Morality' by Sister Madeleine

4

By the time Kaspar got back outside, the front lawn looked like a medical convention. Non-wounded guests and dignitaries had long since been escorted off the premises, leaving behind only the wounded friendlies, who were being triaged by one junior doctor, a guy in his mid-twenties with light brown hair and a permanently creased forehead. He had assessed each casualty and split them into three groups – 'beyond hope', 'non-urgent', and the third vital category, 'serious but saveable'. Only one person was in the first category: a middle-aged woman who'd had a heart attack when the assault started and the terrorists began lobbing thermal grenades. Either bad luck or bad judgement on the part of the terrorists meant that the 'beyond hope' category contained far fewer people than Kaspar had first feared.

It was so damned unfair that none of the terrorists was 'beyond hope', because he and the other Guardians only used non-lethal weapons. Each terrorist casualty was allocated their own team of medics. The unconscious ones were put on spinal boards, had central lines inserted and were wired up to heart monitors. Those still conscious were handcuffed. Then everyone was carefully loaded into transports and flown to the Clinic – Capital City's trauma centre.

Watching the way the terrorists were being handled made Kaspar slightly ashamed of his previous wish that his weapon might do more than stun. His first real-life confrontational situation, and what was his reaction? To wallow in anger and yearn to dish out the same as the Insurgents. It was just as well that the High Councillors set the rules about the Guardians using only non-lethal techniques and weapons, not him. He'd have to watch that in future. In combat, he needed to make sure that he kept his emotions on lock-down.

'This is surreal,' he said.

'What is?' said Janna.

'The way we treat the bad guys just the same as our own. In fact, better,' replied Kaspar. 'I always knew that was the philosophy, but it's weird – and kind of wonderful – to see that we actually practise what we preach.'

'Pardon me if I'm less than impressed,' hissed Janna. 'My arm hurts like a bastard and some pointy-nosed heifer with a stethoscope ran right past me to get to a terrorist with an ingrowing toenail.'

'Let's have a look,' said Kaspar.

Janna rolled up her sleeve to reveal a vicious-looking raised blister covering at least a third of her left forearm. The area around the blister was an intense, angry red.

'You should get that looked at,' said Dillon.

Kaspar shook his head at Dillon. Winding up Janna

when she was already puce with anger was like cheating at Solitaire – a guaranteed win but hardly worth the effort.

'You think? Try telling that to the medicos. These Insurgents come at us with thermal grenades, we defend ourselves with stun-guns and then the doctors give them priority for treatment.' Janna was spitting nails. 'How messed up is that?'

'It's the price we pay for being better than them,' chipped in Dillon. 'Though I must admit, I wasn't think-ing particularly charitable, non-lethal thoughts when it all kicked off. I would've happily killed them all and screw what the Council say. My mum was in the audience.'

'Is she OK?' Kaspar frowned.

'Oh, yeah. She's gone home now. I didn't get much of a chance to speak to her, to be honest, so I'll have to CommLink with her tonight. She's going to worry about me even worse than before now.'

'Amen to happily killing them all,' said Janna. 'Con-sidering what those animals do, stunning them just isn't enough. Maybe we could go back to using some of the early non-lethals that the first Guardians used, like the quick-setting plastifoam that often caused death by suffocation.'

'Or the infrasonic generators that were meant to cause nausea but actually burst your eardrums,' said Dillon with relish.

'How about the mood-altering drugs that caused madness and suicide?' Janna's eyes lit up at the thought.

'Or my personal favourite, the spray that incapacitated by causing diarrhoea,' laughed Dillon.

'Ooh, that must have been nasty.' Janna's nose wrinkled at the idea. 'At least stun rifles require less clean-up.'

In an attempt to change the subject, Kaspar pointed out that not everyone flitting about the lawn was a medic.

'Wow, they've got a TV crew here. That was fast.'

Vivian Sykes, veteran of a hundred bloodbaths, picked her way through the carnage, stopping every few steps to deliver some words of on-camera wisdom.

'. . . yet another illustration of why they won't win. In spite of their provocation, their relentless nihilism and their savage attacks on our people, we in the Alliance hold tight to our principles: that we can defend ourself without descending to the level of animals, that a war can be conducted rationally and without losing our essential humanity, no matter how evil the enemy. This is Vivian Sykes for Daily Report, at the Guardian Inauguration Ceremony outrage.'

Later, in the barracks, Kaspar and the other Guardians sat drinking beers in front of the TV in the recreation room as they watched the rest of Vivian Sykes' special report. The Guardians who had saved the day received barely a mention, fifteen seconds if that. The rest of the ten-minute report was filled with commentary and images of transports arriving at Capital City's Clinic, the hi-tech trauma centre where Insurgent prisoners were always taken for treatment. Unconscious terrorists were carefully unloaded before being whisked away to operating theatres,

34

or tucked into neat beds in brightly decorated high-dependency units.

'Oh, please,' snapped Janna. She threw a beer can at the TV and leaped to her feet.

Kaspar watched as she stormed out of the room. And a major part of him couldn't blame her.

5

Kaspar lay in bed; he was exhausted but his mind was buzzing too much to allow him to sleep. He was a low-grade Guardian, a rookie, a grunt. What did he know about issues and causes? He'd joined up to serve and protect the Alliance, plus he loved the idea of no two days panning out exactly the same. The prospect of working on his uncle's farm, where one year was pretty much the same as the five years that had gone before, had filled him with dread. Hell! His uncle's idea of excitement was to grow a larger than average melon that he could display as a 3D holographic image on the farm's website.

'What do we do if we are attacked?' Kaspar had once asked his uncle when he was about seven or eight years old.

'We activate the emergency alarm and we go to the shelters,' had been the reply.

'Is that it?' Kaspar had puzzled. 'We just abandon the farm to them and hide?'

'Better than getting killed.' That had ended the discussion as far as Uncle Jeff was concerned, but even at that young age Kaspar hadn't been at all convinced that his uncle was right. Surely if that was the case, then they were all just victims-in-waiting? And as he grew older, Kaspar couldn't shake the feeling that he was meant to be more, *do* more than just be an agric walking around with a virtual target painted on his back.

Uncle Jeff was full of tall tales about the Insurgents and what they did to their captives.

'Kaspar, don't argue with me,' he snapped with exasperation one night over dinner when Kaspar had questioned another one of his incredible stories. 'The Insurgents are evil incarnate, and those who associate with them can't help but become evil themselves. Why d'you think the Council have ordered that no one should ever touch them using bare hands except specially cleared medical staff? They are unclean and just one touch could infect us with God alone knows what.'

'But, Uncle, how can someone just touch you and . . . ?'

'Kaspar, are you calling me a liar?' Uncle Jeff asked softly.

'No, sir,' Kaspar said hastily. He knew from bitter experience when to back down – like now.

'You're a smart boy, but you don't know everything,' said Uncle Jeff. 'The Council know better than most what the Insurgents are capable of.'

'Yes, sir.'

'We don't question the Brothers and Sisters of the Council in this house. Do I make myself clear?'

'Yes, sir.'

Uncle Jeff allowed himself a smile now that his point

had been made. 'We are farmers, Kaspar. That is all we are and all we need to be. It is not our place to question the High Council. They are wiser than we will ever be.'

Kaspar didn't answer.

Uncle Jeff regarded him for a moment, then sighed. 'Kas, I know that sometimes this life must seem . . . mundane compared to the lives your parents led. But both your parents asked me to keep you from harm if anything should happen to them, and I intend to keep my word.' Uncle Jeff placed a hand beneath Kaspar's chin to raise his head. 'Your mum and dad wanted nothing more than to keep you safe. Your mum even made me promise to only let you eat food grown or produced on this farm and to drink only the water from my well. As a child she wouldn't drink anything else. I've kept my word all these years and I'm not going to break it now. So I will teach you everything I know and you will take over the farm when I'm gone. OK?'

'Yes, Uncle,' Kaspar replied, lowering his gaze in feigned obedience.

But that was on the outside.

Inside, Kaspar's mind was racing. Uncle Jeff obviously derived pleasure from drawing ice-cold water from his very own well at the back of the farmhouse and preparing meals made entirely from produce grown on his own farm. Not that Uncle Jeff ever drank just water himself! During the day, he drank fruit juice – usually melon, or whatever he could whisk together from leftover fruit and vegetables each morning. With and after dinner, Kaspar's uncle drank melon brew, which was so potent that his breath after one glass could blister wood. Kaspar had only tried it once. It was like putting pure acid in his mouth. After that he'd been happy to stick to well water.

Uncle Jeff prided himself on his self-sufficiency. The highlight of his year was finding a cheaper alternative nitrate-rich fertilizer for his melon crop. But those highs weren't anywhere near high enough for Kaspar. Kaspar wanted to *serve* the Alliance, not *feed* it. His uncle might be happy to be a farmer until the day he died, but the thought of following in Uncle Jeff's footsteps made Kaspar break out in a cold sweat.

'That's not going to happen. I'm going to make something of my life,' Kaspar had promised himself.

Looking back, he now understood that with his tall tales and his scaremongering, Uncle Jeff had, in his own unique way, been trying to protect him. But it had backfired spectacularly, making Kaspar ever more determined with each passing day not to grow up to be a reflection of his uncle. Every thought and action Uncle Jeff had was reactive, never spontaneous. His uncle never put a foot wrong because he never put a foot out. Kaspar wasn't going to live like that. He was going to be pro-active, make his own choices. He was determined to make a difference.

Ironic really that his uncle should so revere the High Council and the ideals of the Alliance but not want to personally defend those ideals. And because Uncle Jeff didn't want to directly defend their way of life, he thought that Kaspar shouldn't either. Well, luckily the law stated that Kaspar was his own person from the age of sixteen. It was unusual to be accepted onto the Guardian training programme so early, but not unheard of.

He'd made it and there was no turning back.

The day after the attack was hell. Pure hell. It was as frenetic as the previous day's combat had been but without the option of firing back at your tormentors. It started when Vivian Sykes was granted a rare interview with Brother Simon for breakfast TV.

'Brother Simon, it must have been terrible,' said Vivian earnestly, in her best 'voice of the people' tone.

Brother Simon nodded. 'That the Insurgents would try to attack me at the Guardian Academy just shows a new level of desperation on their part. It also proves that we in the Alliance are winning this war,' he said, his practised smile reassuring.

'You were pulled to safety by a Guardian – Honour Cadet Wilding.'

Hoots and cheers filled the mess hall. Kaspar barely looked up at the screen across the hall. He tucked into his breakfast of bacon, eggs and toast, his cheeks flaming.

'You got a name-check,' Janna called from across the table. 'You're famous!'

'Yeah, right,' Kaspar murmured, just before a bread roll hit him on the side of his head. He ignored the blow and carried on eating. It was just Kaspar's luck that the mess hall was full to overflowing with Guardians wolfing down their breakfast before their daily duty assignments were given out.

'Guardian Wilding was magnificent,' said Brother Simon. 'From out of nowhere, he flew across at me and pushed me behind the parapet. He definitely saved my life. He was very brave, a credit to the training all Guardians receive. Guardians of his calibre are the reason why the Alliance will prevail and the Insurgents will fail.' Brother Simon was now in full flow.

Kaspar's cheeks burned as Dillon, who was seated next to him, smacked him heartily on the back, nearly pushing his spinal cord through his chest in the process. Kaspar glared at an unrepentant and grinning Dillon.

'Hear that!' said Dillon. 'You're a credit to the Guardians.'

'Someone pass me a sick bag,' said Mariska.

'Make that two,' agreed Dillon.

'Guardian Wilding is certainly a chip off the old block,' said Vivian, her smile filling the screen.

Kaspar's head snapped up. His blood ran cold. No . . .

'I don't follow,' said Brother Simon.

'Guardian Kaspar Wilding is the son of the famous guardians RJ Wilding and Kristin Jaeger,' preened Vivian.

Shit! Kaspar stared at the TV screen, stricken. His heart plummeted. He might have used his parents' names in his Guardian application interview, but he'd made damned sure not to mention them to anyone else since – not even

Dillon. No way did he want special, or even different, treatment because of his parents. But now that cat had well and truly clawed its way out of the bag.

Brother Simon's acutely surprised response went unheard as the Guardians in the mess hall burst into ironic cheering. Some dropped to their knees and started 'worshipping' Kaspar with cries of, 'We're not worthy, we're not worthy.' Ford and Ian began flailing their arms around and shouting, 'Save me, Kaspar. Save me!' Pauling fluttered his scraggy eyelashes at Kaspar and asked, 'Can I have your babies?' and Bryan and Dillon dropped their trousers and asked him to autograph their backsides.

'And thus it begins,' Kaspar muttered sourly. How he wished that Vivian Sykes could've kept her colossal mouth shut.

And that *was* just the start.

A request for a photoshoot with Brother Simon and a one-to-one interview with Vivian Sykes came through within the hour.

'Aw, c'mon, sir. Do I have to do this PR crap?' Kaspar protested.

'Hell, yes! You better believe it,' replied Voss. 'TV laps this stuff up. The good citizens of the Alliance get to see what vicious bastards the terrorists are and what selfless paragons of virtue we are. It reminds them to support us and to give us information. It boosts recruitment too. So if Vivian Sykes asks you to do naked juggling while riding a unicycle, you'll bloody well do it. Are we clear?'

After that, the rest of the day's events left the sight of

Dillon's hairy buttocks as the highlight. The joint interview with Brother Simon was painful, to say the least. Kaspar only spoke when directly addressed, but even so Brother Simon was overly deferential. Brother Simon gushed, Kaspar squirmed. Vivian Sykes flattered and oozed. Kaspar tried to be self-deprecating, but that just made her ooze more. By 1500 hours, he was praying for some fresh terrorist outrage just so he would have an excuse to leave.

By the time Kaspar hit the sack later that night, his image was plastered all over the place and, as Voss had predicted, they had rushed out a new recruitment advert featuring the reluctant superstar. Kaspar lay in bed, exhausted, and dreamed of Vivian Sykes – but not in a good way.

7

After one week of being a Guardian, Kaspar was feeling rather nostalgic for melon farming. While the rest of his squad were deployed on regular duties, he was doing his eighth school visit.

'Oh, come on, sir. *Please?*' he pleaded with Voss over the CommLink. 'I've already missed two intelligence briefings and a civil defence exercise. Everyone else is getting up-to-speed tactically and I'm attending coffee mornings and talking to school kids about my combat experience. All three minutes of it.'

'Suck it up, Wilding,' replied Voss, sympathy entirely absent. 'We all have our assignments and yours is currently Public Relations. You should be pleased. Media Affairs say that you are really wowing the crowds, particularly the old and ugly demographic.' The commander laughed heartily at that.

Kaspar wasn't going to give up, not without a fight, or a severe whinge at any rate. 'Sir, they've even taken away my gun,' he complained. 'They said carrying a real stun rifle into schools was too dangerous, so they issued me with a realistic replica that I can let the kids handle.'

Voss laughed even harder. 'You are reaching new heights in the pursuit of non-lethal law enforcement,' he cackled. 'They may well offer you a seat on the High Council.'

Kaspar closed his eyes and visualized giving Voss a stun-rifle suppository.

'Listen, Wilding,' said Voss, finally getting his laughter under control. 'It's temporary – and it *is* useful. Keep flying the flag for a few more days and I'll make sure that we keep you in the loop. I've already arranged to have a summary of the Intel and Tactical briefings sent to you each evening. Don't worry, the media circus will tire of you soon enough and there will still be plenty of lunatics with grenade launchers when you get back.' And with that he disconnected the call.

Kaspar closed the CommLink and plastered on a smile when he saw Sara, his press nanny, approaching. Another school visit coming up.

'Are we all set for Loring Primary?' she asked brightly.

'You bet!' he replied with as much simulated enthusiasm as he could manage. It was all right for Sara – public relations was her job. But for Kaspar, another two hours talking to kids and answering their questions was going to be torture. PR was worse than watching melons grow.

Initially, Loring Primary School wasn't as bad as Kaspar had expected. It was worse. The school didn't seem to have as many resources as some of the others he'd visited and the building was shabby and definitely showing its age.

Plus, instead of talking to the older kids as he'd been promised, Miss Ackles, the Head, asked him to lead an assembly for the infants.

'I'm a Guardian,' Kaspar protested, aghast. 'I carry a gun and shoot at people – that's the beginning, middle and end of it. I don't have the first clue how to lead a school assembly.'

'Well, I'm sure you can beef it up and tone it down for our students,' said Miss Ackles.

Kaspar's eyebrows shot up to practically touch his hairline. How on earth was he supposed to do that?

'You can beef up the goodwill and protection messages and what you Guardians do for us,' explained Miss Ackles. 'But tone down the gung-ho violent aspects.'

Kaspar was insulted. 'We Guardians take our job seriously and we are *never* gung-ho.'

'Then there should be no difficulty,' said Miss Ackles. Her tone indicated that the subject was closed as far as she was concerned. As the Head led the way into the hall, where wall-to-wall ankle biters were already seated cross-legged on the floor, Kaspar looked to Sara for backup. No luck there. Sara just shrugged and leaned against the wall by the door. Kaspar swallowed hard. He'd never spoken to an audience this young before. He could barely remember even being that young, for heaven's sake. The kids were four-, five- and six-year-olds. As he stood on the raised platform, with at least one hundred pairs of eyes trained on him, he swallowed hard. Help!

'Hi, everyone. My name is Kaspar Wilding and I'm a

47

Guardian. I . . . er . . . I . . . erm . . . my job is to help keep you and your families and friends safe from the Insurgents.'

Hell! Now what should he say?

Beads of sweat prickled Kaspar's forehead. A hand in the front row shot up.

'Yes?' Kaspar indicated the girl whose hand was now raised. Her black hair was a riot of curls and her green-brown eyes were strikingly huge.

'What does detergents mean?' asked the girl.

'Huh?' said Kaspar.

'Insurgents,' Miss Ackles provided from behind him.

'Oh!' Kaspar smiled. 'It means the bad people who want to harm us to get what they want.'

'Oh, you mean terrorists,' said the girl. 'At home that's what we call them.'

'Yes, that is another word for them,' said Kaspar.

'What do they want?' asked the girl. 'I asked my mum that but she didn't know.'

'Er . . . to disrupt . . . to mess up the way we live.'

'Why do they want to do that?'

That made Kaspar blink. 'Because . . . they don't like the way we live and they want to change it.'

'Why?'

'Gnea, that's enough,' Miss Ackles thankfully interrupted.

Another hand shot up. 'How many people have you killed?' asked a boy with a small head and big eyes.

'None,' Kaspar replied vehemently. 'We don't do that. We only stun Insurgents. It's the code each Guardian lives by, our first rule. We will not take a life, any life.'

'Why is your gun so big then?' The question was called out.

'Is it heavy?'

'Can I hold it?'

'Why're you so tall?'

'What's your favourite colour?'

Kaspar was rapidly losing control. Miss Ackles stepped forward and the noise in the hall immediately died away. Kaspar glanced at her, and her thunderous expression had him taking half a step back himself.

A familiar hand went up. It was the girl with the unusual name. What was it again? Ny-ah? It was something like that.

'Yes?' said Kaspar, desperation setting in.

'Do you like your job?' she asked.

Kaspar breathed a sigh of relief. Safer ground. 'I love my job,' he said. 'I get to do something worthwhile, something useful. I get to protect special people – like you.'

Gnea smiled at Kaspar. He smiled back. 'Can I give you a hug?' the little girl asked.

'Of course you can,' Kaspar replied, surprised and un-expectedly moved.

'Now, Gnea . . .' began Miss Ackles.

But Gnea ignored the Head and was already making her way to Kaspar. Kaspar slung his gun over his back so it would be out of the way and squatted down. Gnea's arms were immediately around his neck.

'Thank you for protecting me,' she whispered.

'You're welcome,' Kaspar whispered back.

'My name is Gnea – with a G. G-N-E-A,' she spelled it out. 'It's pronounced *Ni–ah*! Everybody always gets that wrong.' Gnea spoke to Kaspar as if they were the only two in the hall. 'May I hold your gun?'

'It's a bit too big and heavy for you,' said Kaspar with a smile as he straightened up.

'I'm five and three quarters. I'm sure I can hold it. Can I try, please? *Please?*'

Kaspar glanced at Sara, who was nodding vigorously at him. She was not one for letting a public relations moment or a photo opportunity slip past her. Reaching behind his back, Kaspar pulled his gun forward and slipped it off his shoulder. And still he hesitated. Giving a kid a gun just didn't sit well with him, even if it was only a replica. He glanced at Sara again, who was glowering at him. Impatient, she nodded even more forcefully this time.

Oh well. Kaspar had been told to do whatever the PR woman said. Besides, where was the harm? After all, it wasn't as if Gnea could do any inadvertent damage with it.

'Be careful, Gnea,' he warned. He reluctantly held it out towards her. 'Don't hurt yourself.'

Somehow it just didn't seem right to see a stun rifle in the hands of someone so small. But Gnea loved it. Once he said she could touch it, she took a couple of steps back, bunny-rolled over to him before grabbing the gun, targeting imaginary terrorists and making zapping noises as she took them out. The girl reduced the whole hall to peals of laughter, including Kaspar.

50

'I'm going to be a Guardian when I grow up,' she announced, handing back the replica.

'Like me?' smiled Kaspar.

'Oh, no. Way better than you!' Gnea replied.

'Good for you, Gnea,' laughed Kaspar. 'Aim high!'

'Gnea, that's quite enough,' said Miss Ackles.

With another smile at Kaspar, Gnea made her way back to where she'd previously been sitting. Kaspar looked around the hall. A forest of arms had now sprung up. And just like that, Kaspar relaxed. Maybe this wouldn't be so bad after all.

Later, as they drove through leafy suburbs on their way back from a very successful school visit, Kaspar tried to read some of the intel that Voss had sent him while Sara wittered on about stuff he really didn't give a damn about. As the driver waited at an intersection to merge into traffic, Kaspar realized from the expectant silence in the car that Sara was waiting for a response from him. He replayed in his mind the last couple of things she'd said.

'Of course, Sara,' he replied. 'We are all fully committed to this PR mission. My boss was just explaining the crucial importance of a tight law enforcement media cohesion. But I do have concerns – it didn't seem appropriate for a little girl like that to be handling weaponry.'

Jeez! He was even starting to talk like her.

'You let me worry about that,' Sara told him. 'It was an amazing Guardian recruitment photo opportunity and you almost blew it.'

And a hearty sod off to you too, Kaspar thought sourly.

Just as the driver found a gap in the traffic and pulled away, Kaspar spied something out of the corner of his eye. He turned and craned his neck to see, but Sara was in the way. He leaned across her, squashing her back into the seat in his effort to get a better look.

'Sorry,' he offered quickly as he tried to confirm what he had seen out the window.

'That's OK,' replied Sara brightly, taking his body leaning across hers in her stride. 'I don't—'

But Kaspar wasn't listening.

'Hey, Alun, isn't it? I need you to do something. Could you turn us round, take us back the way we just came and park at the intersection?'

'Kaspar, we really don't have time,' Sara countered. 'We're a bit behind schedule and we should—'

'Alun. Do it. Now. And make it smooth. No drama.' Kaspar's PR voice had vanished. This was his imitation Voss 'voice of authority' and – surprise, surprise – it worked. The driver did as he was asked and turned.

Sara's brow furrowed. 'What's the problem?' she asked.

'I'm not sure yet,' replied Kaspar. 'That's what we're going to find out.'

Alun slowed to a chauffeur's stop about fifteen metres back from the intersection.

'OK, that's good. Now could you get out and ask a passer-by for directions to somewhere complicated.'

'Sorry?' said the driver.

'We have a functioning satnav,' added Sara helpfully.

'We need an excuse to sit here for a minute. Go on, Alun, act like a lost tourist.'

'It's not . . . dangerous, is it?'

'Not at all,' Kaspar replied, in what he hoped was his most reassuring tone.

Alun nodded and climbed out. Moments later he had button-holed some pedestrian and was pointing in a number of different directions. Kaspar's attention was on the Old Bob's produce delivery truck just in front of them. Shielded by the tinted windows, Kaspar watched the two men in farm coveralls who stood chatting next to it. One was really tall, over two metres high, with light brown wavy hair. The other man was black, slightly shorter and much stockier.

'Why are you suddenly so interested in fruit deliveries?' asked Sara. 'Are you looking for a taste of home?'

Great! Obviously another one who'd read his file.

'No, I'm not scoping fruit,' he replied.

'Then why . . .?'

'I'm looking at two guys who aren't farmers stand-ing next to a truck they don't own,' he replied to her unfinished question as he activated his CommLink. '4518 Wilding to Central, requesting a V-check on truck index Sierra – Charlie – Two – Niner – Oscar – Delta – Six.'

'Stand by, 4518,' crackled the reply.

Kaspar waited while Guardian Central entered the truck's ID into their computer. He had his reply within a few seconds.

'Central to 4518. No hits on that one. It hasn't been reported lost or stolen.'

'OK, Central. Thanks.' Kaspar was puzzled. Something was wrong, but . . . '4518 to Central. Give me a threat assessment for' – he looked for the street sign – 'targets in the vicinity of the corner of Radial Fourteen and Wissant Avenue.' Out of the corner of his eye he saw Alun coming back.

'Stand by, 4518.'

Impatience gripped Kaspar, even though mere moments had passed.

'Central to 4518. Be advised that 864 Wissant Avenue is a level three comms node.'

'Crap!' spat Kaspar.

'Is there a problem?' asked Sara.

'Just a big one. That truck is stolen and it's parked right outside a fibre-optic data switching hub.'

Alun got into the car, turning to blatantly listen.

'But it isn't stolen,' said Sara. 'Your people just said so.'

'No, they said there were no reports. If it was hijacked this morning, then it probably won't be missed until tonight.'

'But wouldn't the driver report . . .' Her voice trailed off as Kaspar grimaced. 'Oh, you mean the driver is . . .' Sara blinked rapidly as she realized the full impact of what Kaspar was implying.

'Is it a bomb?' asked Alun.

'I doubt it. They wouldn't be standing around like that if it was. More likely they're waiting for someone.'

'Who?' asked Sara.

Kaspar frowned. How the bloody hell would he know? Voss was always disparaging in his opinion of civilians, and now Kaspar was beginning to understand why. '*At the first sign of trouble, they always want someone else to do their thinking for them.*' That was one of Commander Voss's favourite sayings.

'I don't know who they're waiting for,' Kaspar said. 'But I wouldn't mind a few friends on my side too.' He activated his CommLink. '4518 Wilding to Central. Requesting urgent backup at 864 Wissant Avenue. We may have an attack in progress.'

'Roger that, 4518. Your request has gone up to Tactical, but be advised we are swamped right now. It could be a while.'

Damn it! He couldn't sit around doing nothing. 'Alun, could you take off your clothes?'

'Excuse me?' said the chauffeur.

'I need your clothes,' said Kaspar.

Alun opened his mouth to argue, then changed his mind, thank goodness. Kaspar really wasn't up to a lengthy explanation.

Sara looked scared. Alun just looked irritated about losing his suit.

Kaspar put on Alun's trousers, shoes and jacket. He grabbed Sara's datapad, stepped out of the car and walked slowly towards the two men by the truck.

'Hi, guys.' He kept his voice light and friendly. 'I was wondering if you had any fruit you could sell me? I would kill for one of Old Bob's peaches. I remember having them as a treat when I was younger. Just thinking of them is making me slobber.'

'No, sorry, mate. We just offloaded everything we had,' said the taller man.

'Just my luck,' Kaspar sighed. 'I haven't had one for years. I suppose Old Bob is still running everything personally?'

'Oh yes, he sure is,' replied the black man with a smile. 'He's still very hands-on.'

Kaspar whirled so fast he was a blur. He chopped the edge of his right hand hard into the man's groin and raised his other hand to deliver a follow-up blow, but it wasn't necessary. The guy dropped like a brick from a height and stayed down, unconscious. Part of Kaspar's Guardian training had included human anatomy, just so he and the other cadets could learn the vulnerable parts of the body. Much to the amusement of some of the female cadets, they'd learned that a properly executed blow to a man's groin could knock him out or even kill him.

The taller man charged at him. Kaspar took a half-step to his right in order to get the range correct and thrust his right leg straight into the man's midriff. The guy left the ground, flew backwards before he dropped like a rock and hit his head on the pavement. Neither man moved. Kaspar quickly pressed his fingers against their throats to feel for a pulse. Both men were alive. Out for the count, but alive. Kaspar frisked them for weapons before he flipped them face down into the recovery position and plasti-cuffed them to the wheel of the truck. He ran back to the car.

'Call the Guardians and the medics,' he shouted to Sara. 'I'm going in.'

He stripped off Alun's jacket, grabbed his rifle, thumbed off the safety and headed up the driveway of 864 Wissant Avenue.

From the outside it looked like thousands of other suburban homes, but the permanently closed net curtains concealed a hi-tech secret. This house was part of the Guardians' distributed data network. Instead of concentrating all the data, and all the vulnerability, in one place, the data processing and archival facilities were spread out – a practice the High Councillors themselves followed when it came to their separate locations. Some hubs were in data centres, some in little bungalows like this one. It made it all but impossible to kill the entire network.

The door was open. Kaspar stopped and listened just outside the door. Sounds were coming from somewhere on the left. His grip on his weapon tightened. A deep breath later he entered the house, turning to his left, his stance immediately poised and ready.

For the second time in a week he came face to face with a man in a black costume. A *ninja*, as he had now begun to think of them, though this guy didn't wear a mask. He was in his early twenties, with short-cut dark hair and dark-brown eyes. Kaspar instinctively shouldered his rifle and squeezed the trigger.

Nothing. No bang, no blue flash, no smell of ozone and, worst of all, no neural paralysis of the target.

'Oh, well done!' said a mocking voice inside Kaspar's head. 'You just took on a terrorist armed with nothing more than a child-friendly replica gun.'

Now he was going to die. And he deserved it for his complete stupidity. The ninja was equally surprised by what had happened, but recovered quickly to whisk a familiar-looking black-bladed dagger out of his boot. Kaspar dropped into a combat stance, ready to go hand-to-hand. The sweetish taste of adrenalin filled his mouth. This was it – kill or be killed. His first real experience of up-close-and-personal combat outside of the Academy. Kaspar forced himself to slow his breathing, never for a moment taking his eyes off his adversary. Their eyes locked.

But then the man smiled.

A simple, satisfied smile before he angled his knife and plunged the dagger into his own stomach. One shocked moment later, Kaspar ran over, but there was nothing to be done. The knife was hilt-deep in the man's solar plexus. It must have transected his descending aorta. He was already dying and there was nothing Kaspar could do about it.

And as the man died, he was still smiling.

8

The good news about the afternoon's excitement was that a terrorist attack had obviously been thwarted, but the bad news was starting to stack up fast. Kaspar was sitting in the conference room with Voss and a Justice Directorate liaison officer called Devon Salisbury. And Ms Salisbury was not happy, to say the least.

'It really isn't acceptable, having suspects die like that during deployments.' She said the word 'die' as if it needed handling with tongs. 'On top of which' – she turned narrowed eyes to Kaspar – 'it wasn't even an authorized deployment. Tell me, Guardian Wilding, just how you managed to convert a visit to a primary school into an unprovoked assault on two farmers, an unauthorized entry into a secure communications facility and the avoidable death of a suspect?'

Kaspar's jaw dropped. He wasn't sure which part of that pile of crap he should tackle first. Maybe he should just throw the pen-pushing harpy out of the window.

'Avoidable?' he asked. 'In what way was it avoidable? I walked into the room, he stabbed himself. He didn't ask for my permission.'

'He should have been rendered unconscious by means of your standard issue mark six neuro-paralyser rifle,' she replied in a please-slap-my-face tone of voice.

'Well, I didn't have my mark six neuro-paralyser rifle with me, Ms Salisbury. It was confiscated by the Media Affairs department on the grounds of health and safety.'

Voss shook his head. 'Stow the sarcasm, Wilding. Just tell us how you got involved.'

Kaspar pressed his thumb and index finger together just as hard as he could, a technique he used whenever he needed to take control of himself.

'I recognized the truck, sir. It belongs to Ned Robson from Robson's Farm, near to where I grew up. I've known him all my life. I learned to drive in that truck. Anyway, I know all Ned's workers and I didn't know those two. And Robson's have had an exclusive contract with a supermarket chain for the last two years. No way should they have been making deliveries in a suburban street.'

'The photographs from the scene show the truck was from Old Bob's,' frowned Voss.

'Yeah,' said Kaspar ruefully. 'When I asked them if Old Bob still ran the company, they said yes. That was the clincher.'

'Explain,' prompted Voss.

'The company is run by Ned, always has been. But it isn't named after him. Old Bob was Ned's dog, and that dog has been dead for six years.'

The computer on Voss's desk chirped and he turned to look at the screen. After a few seconds he turned back.

'Well, that's confirmed then. We found the driver out cold and trussed up in the back of the truck. He's going to be fine. Apparently he was hijacked on the way back from collecting a new pump from an engineering depot this morning.'

'And as for unauthorized entry,' Kaspar resumed, 'I don't think that it was my presence there that was the real problem. A better question would be how did the *terrorists* get in? In fact, how did the terrorists even find the place?'

Devon Salisbury's lips pinched together with annoyance.

Yeah, got you there! Kaspar thought with satisfaction.

'Commander Voss, I hope I don't have to remind you of the absolute moral necessity for the Guardians to act non-lethally? The Council is very clear on this. We can't have anyone' – and she glanced sideways at Kaspar as if he were a pool of vomit – 'thinking that one dead terrorist is a "good start". Am I clear?'

Kaspar opened his mouth to say something cutting or sarcastic or obscene or all three, but Voss silenced him with a gesture.

'We all know our duty, Ms Salisbury. Thanks for dropping by.' Voss stood up and opened the conference room door, signalling that the meeting was now over.

Devon Salisbury got to her feet, her lips pursed into a fair approximation of an outraged duck's face. She took the unsubtle hint and departed without saying another word. Voss quietly closed the door before heading back to the high-backed chair at the head of the conference table.

Kaspar stood before him, his hands behind his back, wondering if he was supposed to leave too.

'Sir . . .'

'Guardian Wilding, in spite of my better judgement, I actually like you,' said Voss. 'You have the makings of an excellent Guardian.'

'Thank you, sir,' said Kaspar, surprised.

'But you have a really annoying habit of drawing attention to yourself – and not always in a good way,' Voss continued.

Kaspar knew it was too good to be true. An unqualified compliment from Voss? Yeah, right!

'Now let's have the whole full story and not just the edited highlights you gave to that twig-necked civilian,' ordered Voss.

'That was the whole story, sir. I entered the comms building, forgetting I wasn't properly armed, and before I could get to the Insurgent he turned his knife on himself.'

'What did you do when he dropped?'

'I checked for a pulse, but there wasn't one,' Kaspar replied.

'What was he after? Did you check the data screens?'

Kaspar hesitated; only for a moment, but it was more than long enough for Voss to pounce. 'Spit it out, Guardian. And don't make the mistake of treating me like a civilian.'

'No, sir.' As if! 'I did look at the data screen the terrorist had been using, sir. He'd called up the blueprints of a number of underground tunnels far beyond Capital

City's boundaries. Tunnels that haven't been used in years, sir. And he'd also retrieved info on a number of out-of-the-way places, like Pelham Forest, which is even further away than the Badlands.'

Voss frowned. 'Did he have some kind of recording or transmitting device on him?'

'No, sir. I checked. One of his colleagues I pacified outside the building did, but the guy who killed himself didn't get the chance to pass on the information.'

'Listen, Guardian, this is important.' Voss leaned forward, the look in his dark eyes intense. 'Are you absolutely certain he had no way of passing on any information?'

'Positive, sir.'

'Hmmm. Good work, Guardian Wilding,' Voss said, sitting back. 'Let's keep this between ourselves, OK? He must have failed in his mission if he was only looking at some locations of no importance, so there's no need to mention the blueprints and scenery in your official report. Understand?'

'Yes, sir.' Kaspar didn't understand, but he wasn't about to question his boss's motives.

'Dismissed, Guardian.'

'Thank you, sir.' Kaspar made sure he was out of the room with the door shut firmly behind him before he allowed a smile to take up residence.

Wonder of wonders! His boss liked him!

9

Unarmed combat practice was in full swing in the gym when Kaspar got back from seeing Voss. Everyone was paired up and going through knife-disarming drills. Just as he arrived, Trey, a new transfer, was holding a knife and circling the diminutive Mariska. He feigned leaping towards her but constantly drew back, a supercilious smile plastered across his face. Mariska stood watching him, her body very still. Uh-oh! Trey came loping in to close the distance, swinging the knife down in a lazy overhand before dancing away from Mariska, who still hadn't moved, though her eyes never left Trey's.

Kaspar winced.

He knew what was coming from painful experience. His first week at the Academy, Kaspar had been paired with Mariska for unarmed combat. Being brought up by his uncle to respect 'those of the female persuasion', he had held back. Despite Mariska's repeated demands that he 'get with the programme' and 'get serious', he had soft-pedalled. Finally she had screamed. Not a girlie scream. Actually, not like any scream he'd ever heard. It was more of a psycho mental death howl. She'd launched herself at him, kicked him in the groin, swept his feet out from under him with a calf-high spinning kick, split his lip by smashing his head into the mat and then knelt on his back and put him in a choke hold.

'Don't ever patronize me again, you lanky piece of shit,' she had hissed in his ear. 'You come at me with anything less than one hundred per cent and I will tear your balls off and use your scrotum as a change purse.'

Point made.

Later, as he was applying an ice pack to his lip and a bag of frozen peas to his genitals, Janna had been her characteristically sympathetic self.

'Serves you right, Kas. We're all training to be Guardians, you know. Even us delicate girlies. We all have to handle the same stuff,' she said. 'You don't do anyone any favours by going easy on 'em in training. If someone can't handle the rough stuff, it's better they find out now in the gym, 'cause later on, out there, it'll be too late.'

'Yeah, I hear you,' Kaspar muttered. 'And I'm not lanky, I'm lean.'

'Man, couldn't you apply the ice pack to your tenders and the peas to your lip?' moaned Dillon. 'I'm on catering attachment this month and I was going to use those peas in a shepherd's pie later.'

'You still can,' said Kaspar, peeved. 'It's not like I've taken them out of the packet.'

'Are you off your nut?' Dillon replied, scandalized. 'No way is even one of those going anywhere near my lips.'

'Your loss,' Kaspar replied, unconcerned, readjusting the packet of peas before he got frostbite.

Next session, Kaspar had broken one of Mariska's ribs with an elbow strike. It wasn't intentional; it wasn't pay-back in any way. It was just what happened sometimes when you committed fully.

'That's more like it,' she had grunted, and actually smiled as he had tried to get her to breathe.

As he regarded Trey, who was still dancing around his opponent, Kaspar shook his head pityingly. Should he shout a warning? He'd just opened his mouth when, 'Hey, Kas. I was looking for you,' said Dillon, who had just emerged from the changing rooms.

'I've never seen anyone, male or female, spend so long in the shower,' said Kaspar.

'Those of us not born on farms like to be clean,' Dillon said loftily.

Kaspar shook his head, 'But you take it to a whole new neurotic level.'

There was a blood-curdling scream, and out of the corner of his eye Kaspar saw the unconscious Trey hit the deck like a sackful of hammers.

'Anyway, welcome back to the real world,' said Dillon, ignoring the unconscious heap on the gym mat. 'How come you aren't being exhibited around Capital City today?'

'Oh, that is so over,' replied Kaspar with some delight. 'I guess being involved with a death put a severe dent in my ability to act as a walking advertisement for non-lethal law enforcement. So I am done for good with Media Liaison.'

'I hear you decked a couple of farmhand impersonators.'

'Yep.'

'Nice one, mate. And is it true that terrorist boy stabbed himself?' Dillon asked.

'Yeah, that's right. Why?'

'Oh, you know . . . some of the guys were thinking that maybe . . .'

'Maybe what?'

'Well, maybe you . . . kind of . . . took him out?'

Kaspar looked around. A number of his mates were watching him, their gaze speculative. Kaspar turned back to Dillon.

'No, Dillon, I did not take him out. I stood watching while he took *himself* out.'

'Then you must be one scary bugger,' approved Dillon. 'Like a taller version of Mariska!'

And they both laughed. They were still laughing when Trey was carried past them unconscious on a stretcher to the infirmary.

Later, Kaspar lay in bed staring at the ceiling. Normally he went out like a light after a session in the gym, but tonight sleep was a stranger. He sat up, switched on his light and grabbed his datapad from the bedside table. Maybe the questions buzzing around his head would make more sense written down.

1. Why suicide?
2. Why the massive interest by the Insurgents in totally isolated locations?
3. Why don't they equip themselves with any kind of radio or CommLink?
4. Why didn't they kill the truck driver?
5. **WHAT DO THEY WANT???**

The last question he double underlined, but it didn't help. He was no closer to finding an answer. Swinging his legs out of the bed, he got up, crossed to the desk and turned on the datalink. If I can't sleep, I may as well do some research, he thought.

The back of his neck began to prickle. Maybe he should just leave well enough alone? But he wanted answers.

Funny, then, how the phrase 'curiosity killed the cat' kept dancing about in his head.

10

Kaspar started the research engine on his screen and spent the next half-hour failing to understand a single word. He knew the engine was a brilliant tool for doing research and spotting patterns in data, but you needed a brain the size of a planet just to read the online instruction manual. Sections headed 'Heuristic Contextualization' and 'Para-Linguistic Hybridization Factors' simply bounced off his skull without a hope of penetrating.

He finally admitted defeat, grabbed his jacket and took the short walk to Library Services. Through the door, Kaspar could see the duty librarian seated behind a desk. She wore her purple hair in a choppy hairstyle and the red ID Badge at the end of the lanyard prominently displayed around her neck meant she had the highest security clearance. She was scrutinizing data on a holo-screen to her right, a slight smile on her lips. Kaspar was surprised at how young she looked, not much older than him. And best of all she didn't look too nerdy. He knocked once and went in.

She smiled the moment she saw him. 'Hello. I'm Mackenzie, call me Mac. You're up late. Are you a night owl like me or are you on some kind of punishment detail? Hang on! Aren't you the cadet who's been all over the news recently? Milding? Rilding? Something like that? Sorry, I'm rambling! How can I help?'

Kaspar blinked at the verbal barrage. Wow! And his first impression of her had been correct. She couldn't have been more than a couple of years older than him. She had full lips, the largest almond-shaped brown eyes he'd ever seen and long, dark lashes. Kaspar wondered what had driven her to work at the research centre of the Guardian Academy. And how on earth had she managed to get such a high security clearance at her age? Surely proof positive that she had to be considerably older than she looked?

'Hi,' he replied. 'It's Wilding, actually. Can you help me? I'm trying to use the research engine but I can't understand a word of it.'

Mac gave him a quick assessing glance. 'Sure thing. I spend half my life explaining that manual. Grab a chair and come round.'

Kaspar wheeled over a chair from the nearest table and placed it behind Mac's desk next to hers.

'So what is it you want to know?'

'OK, I get the basics,' Kaspar began. 'You describe what you want, the areas you are interested in, the timespan you want to examine and so forth. Once you've done that, a bunch of semi-intelligent databots are launched off into cyberspace. Right?'

'Right,' replied Mac. 'They interrogate systems, access archives and they negotiate with each other in order to produce a comprehensive response to your query.'

'Well, I get that bit. So far, so good,' said Kaspar. 'But what about the rest? All that contextual . . . linguistic . . . hybrid doodah factor stuff?'

'OK,' laughed Mac. 'Suppose you were to launch a search on . . . let's say – "farm".'

Damnit! Had everyone on the planet read his biography?

'So most of the databots will go haring down what you might call the obvious route. Farm, farmer, farming, agriculture, hydroponics, food production, pesticides and so on. But some of them will find other linkages – like "ant farm", and start researching insects. And some will recognize that "farm" is phonetically similar to "pharm", and that will lead off towards pharmacology, drugs, addiction. Now depending on what you are trying to achieve, that will either be a waste of time and resources, or it'll be a breakthrough into a whole new area of investigation – a light bulb moment. Your various doodah factors control how narrowly focused the search is. You can impose a real straitjacket on the databots, or you can let 'em off the leash and see where they take you. Any clearer?'

'Yes,' said Kaspar. 'Finally!' Human talk, instead of pretentious academic guff. 'Go on.'

Forty-five minutes later, he was all set. Mac had shown him how to use a small but powerful subset of the available features and he was ready to launch the bots. If he could get the bots to figure out the pattern to the Insurgents' attacks and unauthorized computer breaches,

71

then maybe he would be able to work out exactly what they were after and in that way predict where and when the next attacks might come. For once the Guardians would be one jump ahead instead of the other way round.

There was just one question left to answer. Security code.

Kaspar started to type in his personal access code – the one he used for accessing his bank account and personal data. This was private research, after all. But then he stopped. He was trying to understand the terrorist threat better, trying to learn how to defeat the killers in their midst. That sounded like work to him. So he deleted his personal passcode and typed in his Guardian access code instead.

The first data came back almost immediately. Kaspar eagerly leaned forward.

'Best to let it stew for a while,' Mac advised. 'Think of the bots as painting a picture. They start off by drawing a few lines, blocking out the composition, sketching. Then they start filling in a detail over here, reshaping something that isn't working over there. If you look too soon, you'll see construction lines and false starts. Give the picture a while to develop before you start appreciating the art.'

'Oh, OK,' said Kaspar, trying to foster some patience.

They sat in silence for a moment. Mac turned to another data screen to resume what she was doing before Kaspar had interrupted her. Kaspar stole surreptitious glances at Mac. He'd never seen anyone quite like her before. She was about as far away from his old life on his uncle's farm as it was possible to get.

'Is something wrong?' asked Mac, even though she wasn't directly facing him.

'No. Why?' Kaspar's gaze instantly returned to the data on the screen.

'You're staring a hole through me.' Mac swivelled round in her chair to look directly at him, amusement in her voice.

Where had Kaspar heard that phrase before?

'It's my eyes, isn't it?' said Mac. 'People always notice my eyes.'

Kaspar frowned at Mac. Her hair colour and style had caught his attention more than . . . The twinkle in Mac's honey-coloured eyes alerted Kaspar to the fact that he was being wound up.

'Yeah, it was definitely your eyes,' Kaspar agreed with a grin.

They both laughed.

'So, Mac, if you don't mind me asking, how long have you worked here?'

'Three years. Since I was sixteen.'

'*Only* three years?' said Kaspar, astounded. 'Congrats. I thought you had to have one foot in the grave to get red security clearance.'

'Or be the only member of the library staff to be working late at night when an insomniac general can't get the data she requires because she doesn't know how to access it and you don't have the proper clearance,' grinned Mac.

Ah, that explained a lot. 'This general must've been desperate.'

'She was,' said Mac.

'What made you want to work here in the first place?' Kaspar couldn't help asking.

'Knowledge is power. My dad is always telling me that.' Mac looked at Kaspar pointedly when she said that, then laughed as if she'd heard a good joke and changed the subject. Kaspar gave her a sideways look, wondering at her in-joke which left him on the outside. He shrugged inwardly. Mac was kind of weird.

After about half an hour of albeit pleasant small talk, Kaspar could wait no longer. He turned back to the screen and started appreciating. There were maps and charts, timelines and frequency counts, all showing the details of the Insurgents' attacks on the Alliance, stretching back for years. But what was missing was any kind of coherent pattern or wholeness to it all.

'That's strange. Looking at what seems to have been targeted, there seems to be two separate groups working,' Mac mused aloud, peering over his shoulder. 'What did you say the one who stabbed himself looked like? A ninja? Well, let's call them *ninjas* and the others . . . *phantoms*. The ninjas are really good at getting into places they aren't meant to be. They're not particularly violent – the casualty rates resulting from their actions are surprisingly low, even though they sometimes hurl flash grenades around like confetti – like at your graduation ceremony. They love getting access to Alliance computers and their motto is

74

apparently "You'll never take me alive" – judging by the number of attempted suicides that have taken place before you Guardians have been able to make an arrest. I think, for the ninjas, it's all about psychological confusion rather than actual physical damage. That and keeping the Guardians occupied.

'But look at the other kinds of incidents – when there are bombings and lots of casualties. That seems to be a completely different way of operating. That's the work of the vicious ones, the phantoms. And they're never seen – the arrest rate is non-existent, although there've been some deaths reported occasionally, like when they get caught up in their own explosions. They're the ones who plant bombs in public places and really work the terror angle.'

'You can tell all that from this stuff on the screen?' said Kaspar, moving in closer to try and see what Mac was seeing.

'Like all this stuff, it's about knowing what you're look-ing at and how to interpret it,' said Mac. 'Check it out. Look, the intelligence suggests that there are definitely two different *types* of groups where one group doesn't seem to know what the other group is doing. As I said, one lot seem to go for the computers, to attack our communi-cations and technology, while the other lot carry out violent terrorist atrocities on civilians.'

'But look at the rate of the attacks,' said Kaspar. 'The ninja attacks and the phantom bombings ramp up in synch. Doesn't that imply coordination?'

'Or maybe competition between two groups of Insurgents, each with different aims and methods?' suggested Mac. 'Maybe rival political parties among the Crusaders?' Suddenly alert, she drew Kaspar's attention to a flag on the screen. 'Oh, hello! We've got an out-of-tolerance hybridization factor.'

Kaspar looked at her blankly. 'We've got a what?'

'The bots might be off the leash,' she explained.

Leaning in closer, Kaspar saw that a group of bots were researching the suicide angle. 'Suicide, suicide bombings, sanctity of all life, honourable death, atonement for failure, unrequited love, intractable pain, shared near-death experiences, mythical heroes of legend . . .'

The bots were definitely starting to wander a little too far off-topic.

'I'm not really in the market for poems of hopeless love or fairy stories. Can we lace up the straitjacket a little tighter?' asked Kaspar.

'Sure.' Mac sent an advisory to the search engine and the bots raced off in another direction.

'What I'm after is more insight into the terrorists' psychology,' said Kaspar. 'Can we nudge the bots in the direction of the interrogation reports on the Insurgent captives?'

Mac issued the commands and then read through the summary. 'It's all variations on a theme.' She frowned. 'Some long-suffering body from the Justice Directorate spends hours offering the captured Insurgents coffee and biscuits and asking questions. In return, they get nothing but meaningless rants, abuse, vile threats and some hair-raising displays of self-harming. Finally they give up and write an intelligence assessment that seems little better than reading tea leaves.'

'So let me see if I've got this right,' said Kaspar, exasperated. 'The enemy is stupid but quite smart sometimes. They are precise in their targeting – though we don't know what they are looking for in our data archives – except for when they go for some pointless bloody massacre of civilians. Some of them trap themselves when they could escape, some stab themselves when they could shoot you, and others are totally invisible except when they stand right in front of you and smile.'

'I couldn't have put it better myself,' said Mac.

'Yeah, but that gets me precisely nowhere,' Kaspar sighed.

'What can I tell you? The data is the data.'

Kaspar tried to bite back his intense disappointment. But what made him think he could discover more about the Insurgents and their motives in a couple of hours than the High Council had in decades? It was just that no one seemed to be asking questions – the right questions, at any rate. Kaspar couldn't forget the smile on the face of the Insurgent who had killed himself. His expression hadn't been that of someone thwarted or defeated or even defiant to his last breath. No, his smile had been one of satisfaction, of triumph. And there was no hint of insanity in the Insurgent's final expression, at least none that Kaspar's admittedly untrained eye could see. The High

Council didn't seem to care about the Insurgents' deeper motives. As long as the Insurgent threat was being contained, that seemed to be enough for them and most of the Alliance civilians. Why were there never any serious calls for talks to end the war?

What did the Insurgents *want*?

There had to be a rhyme and reason to what they were doing, at least in their heads. So what was it? Why weren't the High Councillors actively seeking answers on that front? The Guardians certainly didn't question the motives behind the Insurgents' actions; that wasn't their job. But Kaspar was troubled. He needed to make sense of his enemy, to convince himself that what he was doing was right.

'Thanks for your help, Mac.' He stood up. 'I really do appreciate it, but I'm no further forward.'

'Give it time. Give yourself a chance to mull over what we've just learned,' Mac replied. 'You can't expect to find all the answers you wanted in one evening.'

But that was the problem, because Kaspar had hoped for some insight, some inkling as to the Insurgents' motives.

'I think I just wasted your time and my evening,' Kaspar sighed.

'So you're going to give up then?' said Mac. 'Already?'

'No. I'm not.' Kaspar's lips set into an obstinate line.

'Good!' smiled Mac. 'Then I'll see you tomorrow, Guardian.'

After the War to End All Wars, the will of the people decreed that twenty-one High Councillors should be elected to serve for all time the needs of the Alliance. Those who would be High Councillors were subjected to rigorous physical and psychological testing. In a process which took not just months but years, finally twenty-one High Councillors were chosen. Consensus decreed that the High Councillors would pass their role on to their children and their children's children, thus there would never be the battles for power we in the Alliance had seen throughout our history.

But how to keep the High Councillors safe from those so-called Crusaders who would seek their destruction?

There was only one solution. The High Councillors must never all be in the same place at the same time. This edict was pronounced, not just to protect the High Councillors, but for the very survival of the Alliance. We in the High Council were – and are – deemed to be the new guiding hand, leading those who follow us to a new beginning, a brighter future and a promise that the interests of the Alliance will always be protected.

Extract taken from 'Towards a New Morality' by Sister Madeleine

11

If Kaspar was depressed at the outcome of his search, things got markedly worse at 0700 hours the next morning. He was just sitting down to breakfast with Dillon and Janna when he got paged on his CommLink.

MY OFFICE. NOW. VOSS.

'Oh, hell!' said Kaspar.

'What's the matter?' asked Janna.

'Why would Voss want to see me?' Kaspar frowned.

Dillon gave Kaspar a speculative look. 'Voss never sees anyone before his fifth cup of morning coffee and he's probably only on his second or third, so whatever the reason I'll bet it's not good.'

'Thanks for that.' Kaspar stood up and glared at his friend. As if he wasn't anxious enough.

'Any time,' Dillon grinned.

Janna shook her head at Kaspar pityingly. 'What've you been up to now?'

'Nothing. Absolutely nothing,' Kaspar replied. 'I'd better go. Voss doesn't like to be kept waiting.'

Minutes later, a quick knock on Voss's door and the

subsequent barked 'Come in' did nothing to quieten Kaspar's sense of unease.

He entered his boss's office, closing the door behind him before coming to attention. A cup of coffee in his hand, Voss glared at him before getting straight to the point.

'Imagine my early morning surprise when I got to my office to be informed by Central Audit that one of my off-duty Guardians launched a priority, broad-spectrum net-trawl from an unsecured terminal in Library Services.'

Kaspar stared. One little search and it'd been reported back to his boss? Bizarre, or what?

'At the peak, you had, let's see' – Voss flicked through a couple of holo-screens to get the figures – 'nearly thirteen billion bots searching everywhere from sewage reclamation pump control to classified Guardian and Justice Directorate archives and using twenty-four per cent of available net resources. You want the exact number of bots?'

'No, sir,' mumbled Kaspar.

Thirteen billion!

'Well?' prompted Voss. 'Explain yourself.'

'I was just curious about something and Mac is cleared to access secure material,' Kaspar offered weakly.

Mistake.

'I don't care if she's got "Top Secret" laser-etched on both earlobes,' ranted Voss. 'She's a librarian, not a Guardian. And you *are* a Guardian, at least for now. Your job is to stun bad guys, not to waste the time of purple-headed librarians. Stay away from her from now

82

on. You hear me? Don't use semi-public datalinks. Don't use your Guardian clearance for freelance fishing expeditions in other people's lakes. Don't clog up the network with loosely constrained searches. And do *not* play intelligence analyst or psychologist or any other amateur twatting about that you aren't trained for. If you pull a stunt like this again, I'll transfer you to a desk job that is so bum-numbingly tedious it'll make you wistful for your stint in Public Relations. Is that clear?'

'Yes, sir.'

'Get out.'

Kaspar left the room and sagged the moment he closed the door behind him. Talk about being verbally flayed to within a centimetre of his life! He certainly didn't much feel like finishing breakfast after that. Instead, he went across to Library Services. He had a horrible feeling that Voss's anger may well have spilled over in Mac's direction. As he entered, she saw him and waved. Damn, but she really was pretty.

'Morning,' she said brightly. 'You don't sleep much. Back for more research?'

'Hi, Mac. Actually, no. I came to apologize for getting you in trouble.'

Mac's eyebrows shot up. 'Am I in trouble?'

'I thought maybe someone would have had a word about last night? Apparently we . . . I . . . used a horrendous amount of computer power.'

'Nobody said a word to me.' Mac frowned. 'You got in trouble?'

'Oh, yeah. Big time. I got told in no uncertain terms that using the entire datanet for pursuing my hobbies is not a great career move.'

'Oh dear. I'm sorry. That's my fault. I assumed you were working on official Guardian business, so I didn't put an activity constraint on the bots. How many got spawned?'

'Close to thirteen billion apparently. I didn't realize I could screw up everybody else by doing what I did. My boss says I was hogging a quarter of all net resources.'

'Not really. Voss was being a bit dramatic.'

'I don't think he's the type to make stuff like that up. He read me the stats.'

'You know what they say – there are lies, damned lies and statistics. Look, we were running overnight. At that time, a lot of computers are not working on serious business, they're doing background tasks, like planning how much geothermal energy usage will increase in the next five years, or searching for radio signals from extra-terrestrials. If our bot usage had really been having a negative impact, we would have got an automatic warning.'

'Voss made it sound like civilization was ending because I'd hijacked most of the bots in the system.' Kaspar heaved a sigh of relief.

'He would!' Mac laughed. 'The system is much more robust and adaptable than that.'

Just then, Kaspar's datalink and Mac's monitor bleeped simultaneously. Kaspar keyed the 'Accept' switch on his link and an automated message began playing through his head-up display or HUD. It was a message directing him to log onto a computer.

'Mac, I just got a—'

'Message to go online? Yeah, I know. I just got the notification too 'cause this is the node that launched the search. Some of your bots are still active from last night.'

Kaspar's heart, not to mention his stomach, plummeted. 'Please tell me you're joking.' He saw his career evaporating like dry ice on a hotplate. 'Stop them. Now. Please. If I use one more processor cycle Voss will murder me.'

'You have to log in and do it as you initiated the search,' said Mac. 'If I use my code to stop them, it'll be automatically reported.'

Kaspar practically shoved Mac to one side in his effort to get to the screen to key in his Guardian passcode. An alert message flashed up but he was too panicked to read it properly.

'What are they doing? No, don't tell me. I don't care what they're doing. Just stop them.'

Mac quickly scanned the report. Her eyes narrowed. 'One of the things you asked about last night was odd patterns of computer usage.'

'Oh, hell! Did we just report ourselves?'

'No, not us. The bots have uncovered an unauthorized computer access.'

'When did it happen?'

'It's happening right now. This is a real-time report. That's what the alert we just got was about.'

'Really? Where's this going down?' frowned Kaspar.

Mac pointed at the screen. 'Terminal one, level one, Sluice Control, Kehone A?'

Kaspar leaned in closer and read the summary. 'It says that place is fully automated and it isn't scheduled to have a regular maintenance inspection for . . . another three weeks.'

'Maybe there was a problem?' offered Mac.

'No, look. Operational effectiveness is at one hundred per cent and no alarms have been flagged since . . . two years ago.' An icy chill crept along Kaspar's back.

'Kehone A? Where have I heard that name before?' said Mac.

Kaspar was already running for the door. If he didn't do something – and fast – there would be a major catastrophe. He shouted back over his shoulder to Mac as he ran, 'Kehone Reservoir is where all our drinking water comes from!'

12

Kaspar ran like he'd never run before.

'4518 Wilding to Central. Send units to level one of Kehone A Sluice Control. We have an unauthorized computer access in progress.'

'Roger that, 4518.'

Kaspar wasn't quite sure how he wanted this to turn out. If he was right, then there was a potentially devastating terrorist attack in progress on a hugely important target. Sabotage of the sluice gates could cause both droughts and flooding to a wide area. Worse than that, if terrorists were to introduce some bio-toxic agent into the water supply, there would be casualties on a massive scale.

On the other hand, if he was wrong . . . What would Voss do to him if he'd sparked a major alert for no reason? Kaspar shook his head. He couldn't worry about that now. How would he feel if something terrible happened because he'd been too cowardly to do anything about it? Besides, he was positive he was right. Almost positive. There *was* unauthorized activity happening at the reservoir, he'd seen that much for himself. So what else could it be but a group of Insurgents, no doubt carrying out some deadly mission?

'Kaspar, you're doing the right thing,' he told himself as Guardians came on the Link, reporting their proximity to Kehone.

'361 Tilkian to Central. Responding to Kehone A. I'm less than five minutes out.' Wow! Guardian Tilkian himself was responding. Now there was a Guardian whose reputation preceded him. Guardian Tilkian was head of the Special Support Group – elite Guardians whose responsibilities included acting as bodyguards to the High Council – what they liked to call 'close personal protection'. Kaspar's heart sank. If he was wrong, then with Tilkian present the High Council would inevitably hear about it. His hands suddenly felt clammy and beads of sweat were breaking out all over his forehead and his armpits.

'3944 Clendenning to Central. ETA to Kehone, seven minutes.'

Five and seven minutes would mean the same as five or seven hours if they got there too late to stop the terrorists from poisoning the water. Uncle Jeff was the only farmer in the whole of the Alliance who had his own water supply, at least that Kaspar knew about. If the terrorists succeeded . . . well, it didn't bear thinking about. Kaspar arrived at the vehicle park at the same time as Dillon.

'Why couldn't you start a major security shitstorm after breakfast?' grumbled Dillon as he headed for a ground vehicle.

'No, not that one,' said Kaspar. 'If we take a hovercar we can cut straight across the lake and save time.'

Both men jumped into a hovercar and Kaspar spun it hard towards the lake. The manual said that transitions from ground to water were meant to be handled smoothly, but Kaspar just slammed open the throttle and slewed sideways off the manicured grass bank so hard that a wave came over the side and splashed across their laps.

'You mad bastard. It's a hovercar, not a bloody submarine,' Dillon shouted above the whine of the fans.

Kaspar gritted his teeth and shot off across the water, heading north. 'Sorry. You can kill me later, if Voss doesn't get me first.'

Dillon glared at him, and then slowly smiled at the prospect of Voss's wrath as he reported their IDs to Central. Behind them, Kaspar could see another hovercar following, but he couldn't make out who was in it until over the link he heard, '4515 Toth and 4517 Weavis approaching Kehone from the South. ETA ten minutes.'

'Mariska and Mikey are on their way too,' said Kaspar.

'Yeah, but they're probably dry,' Dillon retorted. 'Do you want to tell me what all this is about now?'

'There might be a terrorist taking over the sluice controls at the reservoir as we speak.'

'And you're thinking . . . ?'

'Nothing good.'

By the time they had crossed the narrow North Cross Causeway that separated the lake from the reservoir and crossed the last click to Kehone A station, there were forty-six other Guardians already there.

'And with us and Mariska and Mikey, that makes a nice round fifty,' said Dillon as he checked the settings of his stun rifle.

Kaspar felt sick before he even brought the hovercar ashore. The Guardians weren't deploying; they weren't fanning out to surround the station. There was no urgency, no verbal traffic on the link tactical channel. There was just a massive group of Guardians standing around chatting. If it weren't for the weapons, it could have been the Growers' Association annual wine and cheese party.

For everyone else, it was a massive anti-climax. For Kaspar, there was a momentary sense of relief followed by a pit-of-his-stomach feeling of impending doom.

'What gives?' asked Dillon of the nearest dry Guardian as he squelched ashore.

'Absolutely nothing,' came the reply. The dry Guardian, a tall, lean guy with steel-grey eyes and matching coloured buzz-cut hair, raised a quizzical eyebrow in Kaspar's direction once he read his nametag. Kaspar didn't recognize the senior Guardian, but his nametag read TILKIAN. 'We've already cleared the building. No intruders, no bombs, no sabotage – nothing.'

'Then why are we all here?' asked another.

Forty-nine pairs of eyes turned and looked at Kaspar expectantly.

'I . . . I thought . . .'

Suddenly there was a squawk from Kaspar's link that was so loud he had to turn the volume down.

'229 Voss to deployed Guardians. Verification Omega-Two-Epsilon. Code green. Stand down. Repeat, stand down. Voss to 4518 Wilding. Get your arse back here. If you aren't in my office by 0830 hours then don't bother coming back at all.' The line went dead.

'Man, what've you done? You have really stepped in something this time,' added Dillon unnecessarily.

Kaspar turned away. 'Shut up, Dillon,' he snapped as he walked back to the hovercar.

The fiasco with the plastic stun rifle and the dead ninja had been a setback, but survivable. The unauthorized bot-fest with Mac had used up any lingering goodwill that his boss may have felt. And now this . . .

Sick to his stomach, Kaspar knew that his military career, short and eventful as it had been, was probably over.

13

Kaspar would have preferred the ride back to be conducted in silence, but that was never an option with Dillon around.

Dillon on extra-curricular bot-searches: 'You did what? Are you a frickin' idiot?'

Dillon on inter-departmental co-operation: 'You cooked this up with who? You mean the one with the rainbow hair and the nice butt in Library Services? Kas, you gotta start diverting some blood supply back to your head!'

Dillon on crying wolf before breakfast: 'Even after what Voss told you? You *are* a frickin' idiot.'

They arrived back at base just in time to prevent Dillon's death. Another minute and he would have been found floating face down in the lake. Kaspar parked the hovercar and sprinted towards the accommodation wing. He reckoned he had seven minutes or less to change out of his soggy uniform before he had to see Voss.

This is going to be bad enough without me being improperly dressed, he thought.

He was surprised to find the block full of Guardians he

didn't recognize, and even more surprised to be asked for his ID before he was allowed to enter his own room. But the biggest surprise came when he got inside. His room was occupied.

'Good morning, young man.' Brother Simon was standing by Kaspar's bed. 'It's nice to see you again.'

Brother Simon extended his hand and Kaspar immediately accepted the handshake. The councillor was so clean and smooth he might have been polished from marble. Not a silver hair on his head was out of place. His suit was simple but beautifully tailored.

'I'm honoured, sir. Please sit down. What can I do for you? Can I get you something? A drink? I mean, water? I wasn't offering a beer or anything, unless of course you'd like a beer.' Kaspar was hyperventilating – and gibbering. 'Have you been waiting long? I'm sorry, I only just . . .'

'Relax,' smiled Brother Simon. 'I know where you've been. And I know where you're supposed to go next. Don't worry about Commander Voss. I'm sure he'll understand if I keep you a little late.' Brother Simon glanced down at Kaspar's sodden uniform and the puddle forming around his boots. 'Perhaps you'd like to change? I don't mind waiting.'

Kaspar hesitated. Undressing in front of a member of the High Council just didn't seem appropriate – but on the other hand, sitting talking to one while squelching didn't seem too good either. He couldn't exactly ask the High Councillor to leave while he got dressed; that would appear rude. Kaspar compromised by stepping behind his wardrobe door before slipping off his uniform. He felt faintly ridiculous.

'I just came to say that I am impressed with you, Kaspar Wilding. You are very like your mother.'

'You knew my mum?' Kaspar paused from towelling himself.

'Oh yes. She was in the Special Support Group and one of my close protection officers for six months. A very strong, very capable woman.'

Kaspar's mouth fell open. His mum had been a bodyguard to a member of the High Council? That was news to him.

'I've checked your file. Why didn't you put your parents' names on your Guardian application form?' asked Brother Simon.

'Is there any particular reason why I should've, sir?'

'Is there any particular reason why you didn't?' asked the High Councillor.

'I wanted to be judged on my own merits, not those of my mum and dad,' said Kaspar.

'The Special Support Group are always looking for Guardian recruits of the right . . . calibre. You would've been fast-tracked for bigger and better things if you'd used your family history.'

Kaspar was well aware of the kudos attached to belonging to the SSG. They were the elite, given the best jobs, not to mention a salary and perks to match. But everyday Guardians couldn't stand them. Members of the SSG swanned around, noses held high, as if their pee was vintage champagne.

'I'm satisfied with the track I'm currently following, sir,' he said carefully.

Brother Simon leaned forward, considering Kaspar. 'Do you lack ambition, Guardian Wilding?'

'No, sir. But I know I still have a lot to learn and I believe Guardian Voss is best placed to teach me at the moment. I wouldn't want to bring anything but my absolute best to the SSG,' Kaspar replied.

'And you don't feel you're there yet?'

'Not yet, sir. But I will be one day. And sooner rather than later, I hope.'

'Less than your best is still noteworthy, Guardian Wilding,' smiled Brother Simon. 'I, indeed the whole Council, was greatly impressed by your exploits at the graduation ceremony. Kristin would have been so proud.'

'I'm afraid my exploits *since* graduation haven't been quite so impressive, sir. I've been making a lot of mistakes.'

'Which brings me neatly to the point of my visit. We've all been struck by your bravery and your zeal, but those qualities are not exactly rare among Guardians. Certainly not unusual enough to qualify you for a visit from the Council. No, what brings me here today is your desire to learn.' Brother Simon's eyes twinkled as he said that. He had obviously been fully briefed on the bot incident. Kaspar cringed.

'Brother Simon, I was just trying to understand,' said Kaspar. 'All the data seems contradictory. If we understood their motivations better, we could predict the Insurgents' actions, disrupt their plans.'

'And d'you really think you're the first to try and analyse the behaviour of the Insurgents?' said Brother Simon. 'Forgive me, but better minds than yours in the Ministry of Information and Intelligence have tried and failed. They don't have a coherent plan, as you said yourself.'

'Yes, sir, but there is something. A lot of data seems to indicate that they are all wild, unthinking, vicious – almost deranged.'

Brother Simon sat back, his gaze speculative. 'Go on.'

'But I've seen two of them now, close up. They weren't mad. They were calm and collected. I don't know what they were doing, but they were definitely doing something rational, something with a point and a purpose.'

Brother Simon smiled knowingly. 'You are right, up to a point. They aren't entirely devoid of cunning. I must admit we tend to exaggerate their stupidity so as not to scare the populace. But they are still *relatively* unintelligent. Their ancestors may have had an educational system second to none, but that was a long time ago. They are smart enough to realize the importance of our data network, but they are not smart enough to grasp that it is practically invulnerable. They are nihilists.' At Kaspar's blank look, he explained, 'They have no moral principles or beliefs. Their fate was of their own making, and because they believe their lives are meaningless, they feel they have nothing to lose by terrorizing us in the Alliance. Have you read some of the transcripts of their interviews?'

A moment's hesitation, then Kaspar nodded.

'Then you saw for yourself. Savage unreason for the most part. Mindless, ruthless fanaticism, bent on domination and exterminating everyone who is different from them. They are also superstitious, with bizarre, unintelligible belief systems.'

Brother Simon's words sounded rehearsed, like they'd been delivered many, many times before. Kaspar nodded, trying to suppress his doubts.

'Why the suicides, sir?'

Brother Simon raised his immaculately clad shoulders. 'Who knows? Perhaps they really don't care about anything. Maybe they really do prefer death to life within the arms of the Alliance. We believe that all life is sacred, that one death diminishes us all. Read your history, Kaspar. Any time a society has started down the path of expediency, arguing that the end justifies the means, they've inevitably ended up more vicious than the ones they were fighting. It wouldn't surprise me if that was their ultimate goal, to make us animals too. That's why we send you into battle armed only with non-lethal weapons. We have right on our side. That's why the Insurgents – the Crusaders – will not win.'

Kaspar sought to keep his expression neutral and accepting. But each of Brother Simon's words sat like a jagged stone in the pit of his gut. Kaspar's short career had shown him that real life was more complicated than an academic treatise on moral philosophy.

'I want to say something about what you did today,

raising the alarm about the unauthorized access to the Kehone Reservoir—'

'I'm really sorry about that,' interrupted Kaspar. 'I just got hold of the wrong end of the stick. I was convinced that—'

Brother Simon held up his hand to silence Kaspar. 'You didn't get it wrong.'

'Excuse me?'

'You weren't wrong. You were correct. There *was* an unscheduled access.'

'But—'

'I'm afraid I have a confession to make,' said Brother Simon. 'Today you stumbled across . . . well, let's call it what it is, a cover-up. Traditionally, when someone discovers such a thing, they can either be effectively silenced, or included.'

'Silenced, sir?'

'Not what you're thinking, Guardian,' said Brother Simon drily. 'We in the Council have found that a posting to some godforsaken, remote part of the Badlands to guard grains of sand works wonders.'

I just bet it does, thought Kaspar. Was that what they were going to do to him? If so, then he would've preferred Voss's retribution.

'Now we could order you not to pursue it, but you would disobey. We could threaten you with dire consequences, but your mother's stubbornness would prevail,' sighed the Brother. 'No, for a man of your intelligence and drive, the only sensible thing is to enlist your assistance.'

'Sir, I don't understand . . .'

'What I am about to tell you is not to leave this room.' Brother Simon leaned forward, his expression earnest. 'Do you understand?'

'Of course, sir.' Kaspar nodded.

'The attacks in our cities are bad, but they could be much, much worse. The Crusaders have access to deadly weapons – poison gas and a nuclear arsenal. In the hands of their Insurgents, they're capable of causing tens of thousands of deaths.'

Dread, so icy cold it hurt, shot up Kaspar's spine. He was silent for a while, stunned by the enormity of what he was hearing. 'Why have they not used them yet? Wouldn't nihilists just deploy them?' he asked finally.

'We in the Council believe it's only a matter of time before they do – that the Insurgents are conserving what weapons they have until they can locate a significant target or, more likely, they are seeking the knowledge to learn how to use them. That's why we think they are hitting particular data nodes. Unfortunately, there is method to their madness.'

'How did they get hold of nuclear weapons in the first place, sir?'

'During the War to End All Wars, Guardian Wilding. That war decimated our planet's population, but un- fortunately the same cannot be said for our planet's weapons. Up until now, the Insurgents' attacks have been all about retrieving the launch codes for those weapons so they can use them against all of us in the Alliance.'

Shocked, Kaspar stared at the High Councillor. 'But surely those weapons wouldn't work after all this time?'

'Wishful thinking, soldier. Nuclear weapons are like cockroaches, they will outlast all of us,' said Brother Simon. 'That's why we hit the Insurgents hard and fast and we make sure that they never get to a place or a space where they can become a serious threat.'

'I see.' And Kaspar did see.

'I hope you do, Guardian Wilding. If the Insurgents *could* strike decisively at the Alliance government, they would plunge us into chaos and bring about their total victory. That is why we twenty-one Brothers and Sisters of the High Council never meet face to face.'

'So that you can't be simultaneously targeted?'

'Exactly. And because we fear their use of bio-toxic weapons, a special detachment of Guardians adds a cocktail of protective drugs to the water supply every month.'

'So someone did sneak into Kehone today. It was Commander Tilkian, wasn't it?' Kaspar realized.

No wonder the guy had got to the scene so quickly. Kaspar should've smelled something fishy from the time Tilkian announced he was less than five minutes away. No routine patrol would've put such a senior Guardian anywhere near the reservoir.

Brother Simon nodded, obviously impressed that Kaspar had managed to put it together.

'But why a covert Guardian operation? Why not just add the drugs at the same time as the water management teams add all the other chemical treatments to the water? Why the secrecy?'

'Because the more people that know a secret, the more likely it is to leak.'

'But why make it a secret anyway? Why not just tell everyone that you are adding chemicals to the water as a matter of public health?'

'Then we'd have to tell them why. What do you think would happen if people knew that the Insurgents had bio-toxic weapons? They would be paralysed with fear, and fear is corrosive, Kaspar. It falls to some of us to bear the extra burden of knowledge. It is not for all to share.'

Kaspar thought for a moment. 'Why don't the water management teams detect the drugs during their regular checks?'

Brother Simon chuckled. 'They send their samples for analysis. We doctor the results before sending them back.'

'But then, why . . . ?'

Brother Simon stood up. 'Guardian Wilding, I believe I've answered more than enough of your questions. And I'm only here telling you all this out of respect for your mother. I could've just had you transferred to some god-forsaken outpost for the rest of your military career. Remember that.' Brother Simon kept his tone light

'Of course, sir. My apologies.' Kaspar bit back the many other questions ready to spill off his tongue.

Brother Simon scrutinized Kaspar for a few moments. 'We'll be keeping an eye on you, Guardian Wilding. I think your parents would've been very proud. We foresee great things for you, once you have some more experience under your belt. Now that you know there is more to keeping us safe than just patrolling with a stun rifle, I hope you will – how can I put this – temper your zeal?'

'Yes, of course, sir.'

'I shall be personally following your activities with a great deal of interest,' smiled Brother Simon.

'Yes, sir.'

The High Councillor exited the room, his smile the last to leave. Kaspar sat down on the edge of his bed, a frown digging a trench across the bridge of his nose. The idea of Brother Simon keeping tabs on him didn't sit well with him at all.

More importantly, he was still trying to digest everything the High Councillor had told him, but it left a deeply unpleasant aftertaste in his mouth. The Crusaders had to have a festering hatred that ran marrow-deep for them to allow their Insurgents to even contemplate using nuclear and biological weapons against the Alliance. Hadn't they learned anything from their own history? They'd tried to alter the shape of their lands, and as a consequence had rained down destruction on the entire planet. And having turned their homeland into a fiery wasteland, they then waged war against the Alliance to take by force that which didn't belong to them – Alliance homes, Alliance land, Alliance lives. Decades later, they still thought lethal weapons would solve all their problems.

It was truly pathetic.

The Crusaders were beneath contempt and beyond stupid. No wonder Brother Simon kept stating that the Crusaders would never win. But their Insurgents had to know that the Alliance had the means to neutralize their chemical weapons, so why still bother with them?

Kaspar's head was buzzing with questions. The lack of answers was giving him a headache.

Oh, crap! Voss!

'4518 Wilding to 229 Voss.' Kaspar activated his CommLink. 'I'm on my way over to see you now, sir.'

'Belay that, Wilding,' Voss growled. 'I no longer require your presence. Brother Simon has explained everything.'

Hell, but Voss sounded pissed.

'Yes, sir,' Kaspar replied.

Voss disconnected the call without another word. Kaspar could only hope that Brother Simon's intervention hadn't put Voss's nose permanently out of joint. Voss was one guy who could make his existence a living hell.

The surviving narratives of our ancestors tell of the horror, the carnage wrought by those who, in their overriding arrogance, tried to reshape the very continents for their own gain. As a direct consequence of their actions, our planet screamed. The Earth itself fought back. Frequent earthquakes of unparalleled ferocity split the land and sea in both hemispheres. Increased volcanic activity baked the atmosphere. The very air we breathed and the water we drank became charged with chemicals and pollutants.

Thousands upon thousands of lives were lost to nature's wrath. Many more died of famine, fear and panic.

Had mankind brought about its own extinction?

But the human survival instinct cannot be denied. Those who remained began to turn the tide. We, who had decried the acts of the East, worked together to establish a safe haven, a land and a future we could share. Thus the Alliance was born. But there were those amongst the Crusaders who tried to lay the responsibility for nature's fury at our gates.

And having devastated their own lands, they sought refuge amongst us. We welcomed them, until it became clear that peaceful co-existence was not their goal. We had no choice but to remove them to the Badlands, giving them the tools and the equipment required for their survival. Our very existence was at stake. The wall built around our Capital City was for the protection of our people, and it was at this time that the Guardians — an elite fighting squad sworn to protect our citizens with their lives — was formed. The High Council decreed that our people of the Alliance deserved no less.

The Crusaders countered by training their own elite group, known as the Insurgents, to take what they felt should have been theirs. But they will not win. God is on our side. We will prevail.

Extract taken from 'The Origins of the Insurgency' by Brother Telem

14

Kaspar sat with the rest of his watch in the Ready Room, waiting for the day's duty assignments. He wasn't holding his breath for anything good. It was probably only thanks to Brother Simon that he still had a job, but Voss was still punishing him for his expensive evening with Mac in Library Services and the 'false alarm' at the reservoir.

Dillon wasn't happy either. Voss was making him share the pain for venturing an ill-judged opinion on a week of bullshit assignments.

'I swear if I get another crap assignment because you're still on the naughty list, I'm going to strangle you,' Dillon growled.

'What do you want me to do?' Kaspar said. 'Buy him a fruit basket?'

'I wouldn't recommend it,' said Janna brightly. 'He hates brown-nosers almost as much as he hates screwups.'

'Rindt,' shouted Voss.

'Yes, sir,' Janna shot back.

'You're on the Rapid Response team. Check in with Laird for a full briefing.'

'Yes, sir!' Janna's grin was so wide the top of her head was in danger of dropping off.

'Wilding, Greenhill.'

'Yes, sir,' Kaspar and Dillon chorused together.

'Here it comes,' muttered Dillon.

'You two will be spending a couple of days up at Station Rose investigating some suspicious activity. Do you think you can do that without me giving you a typed summary of your job description?'

'Yes, sir.'

Kaspar sighed inwardly while Dillon's glare gave him third-degree burns. Everyone else laughed or groaned sympathetically.

Dillon wasn't happy and Kaspar could hardly blame him. Station Rose was right out on the edge of the volcanic Badlands. It was named after Petra Rose, the famous agricultural scientist, and its 'fragrance' was well known. Its close proximity to endless supplies of geothermal energy at the edge of the Badlands and its great distance from anything else made it the perfect site for a bio-conversion facility – or as Dillon called it, 'a crap farm'. It produced a large amount of high-quality, detoxified, nutrient-rich fertilizer for the Alliance farms, but the hi-tech did nothing to disguise the fact that it was several hectares of settling ponds: literally shallow pools of manure festering in the sun. Add to that the sulphurous fumes wafting off the Badlands, and you had a duty station that every Guardian would chew off their own arms to avoid.

'Don't even speak to me, Kas,' said Dillon as Voss dismissed the shift. 'Janna gets to ride shotgun on a cavalry wagon and we get to investigate a shit farm. Thank you so very much.'

The two had to run a gauntlet of remarks on their way to the transports.

'Glad to see you getting your hands dirty again, Kas.'

'You two gonna sniff out some trouble?'

'Do you think the shit will hit the fan?'

Dillon replied to all with a surly 'Bugger off.' Kaspar sighed and trudged wearily after his seething friend. This was going to be a *long* day.

'It's my turn to drive,' said Kaspar, already making his way to the driver's seat of the hovercar.

Dillon shoved him out of the way and jumped behind the wheel. 'In your dreams, Wilding.' He scowled. 'I'm driving, and don't even think about arguing with me.'

One look at Dillon's expression and Kaspar headed for the passenger's side without saying a word. It wouldn't take much for Dillon to jump out of the car and try to kick his arse, his friend was that annoyed. Kaspar could only hope that the ride to Station Rose would help Dillon to mellow out a bit.

The one good thing about Station Rose – and it was the only thing – was the view on the way there. The spectacular panorama of the high volcanoes in the north, through to the rich farming land in the west and the golden desert to the east, never got old. Instead of skirting the volcanic wilderness by going north and then east,

Kas and Dillon decided to save themselves three hours by 'cutting the corner' and actually entering the Badlands. Travelling by hovercar was really the only way to travel over the Badlands. Everything else either bogged down, sank without trace, melted or caught fire. It was hot in the open cockpit but at least the wind rushing past made it bearable – just. The smell was bad enough to require the use of respirators, though.

By the time they were nearing their destination, Kaspar was grateful that Dillon had finally transferred his wrath away from him and back to Voss, where he felt it belonged.

'That guy is such an arse,' Dillon fumed, his voice distorted by his gas mask. 'Sending us all the way to the crap capital of the north to investigate "suspicious activity". What a load of—'

'What the . . . ?' Kaspar caught sight of a glint in the sunlight.

'What is it?' asked Dillon.

Kaspar shouldered his rifle and squinted through the scope, using it as a telescope.

'Hey, Dillon,' he said. 'I think there's someone over there, about a click thataway.' He pointed to their right.

'Who'd be stupid enough to be out here?' Dillon frowned. 'There's nothing to see and even less to do.'

'Well, I definitely saw something. Let's check it out.'

'Oh, hell.' Dillon shook his head. 'We can't even drive to our next assignment without messing it up. Voss will disembowel us if we call in another false alarm.'

Dillon had said 'we' instead of 'you', for which Kaspar was grateful. Dillon really was a good mate.

'That's why we're going to check it out first without calling it in, and if it turns out to be nothing . . . well, I won't tell if you don't,' Kaspar replied.

'We are here to investigate suspicious activity,' Dillon pointed out with a slow smile. 'And besides, if we do call it in and Voss goes ballistic, it won't have been a wasted journey. We can just apply for permanent jobs as bio-conversion technicians.' He swung the hovercar off to the right and headed in the direction Kaspar had indicated.

Kaspar was still looking through the scope, scanning for signs of life, when he glimpsed a flash of light. Dropping his rifle slightly, he tried to spy what had caught his attention. Kaspar glanced at Dillon, but Dillon's peripheral vision was hampered by his respirator. Something was travelling at speed in their direction.

'Grena—'

Kaspar had no chance to finish his warning. A massive explosion at the right rear of the car slewed it violently to the right, then to the left. A sheet of flame shot forward, and Kaspar felt the heat right through the armoured back of his bucket seat. The car flipped over completely. He was thrown out of the cockpit and flew several metres through the air before tumbling across the ground to land with a series of bone-jarring thuds. He finally came to rest on a bed of broken, jagged rocks.

Kaspar wasn't sure how long he just lay there with his head ringing and every atom of his body hurting. But slowly his brain got back in the game. There was a check-list they had been taught to go through in basic combat training for just such a contingency as this.

'Weapon . . . Cover . . . Injuries . . . Situation . . .'

Or was it: 'Cover . . . Situation . . . Weapon . . . Injuries?'

Kaspar tried to focus on something besides his pound-ing head and the screaming pain radiating from every part of his aching body.

How many attackers?

What weapons? Well, an RPG for a start. The way that thing had scored a direct hit against . . .

Reality arrived like a kick in the teeth.

'Dillon . . .' Kaspar struggled to his knees and looked around. No sign of his mate. Kaspar had his head at the swivel, trying to spot where Dillon had taken cover.

'Where are you?' he muttered. Maybe by that rock outcrop only a few metres away? It would provide great cover. 'DILLON?'

No answer.

Kaspar looked back at the burning hovercar. He dragged himself across the sand, digging his elbows and boots into the scorching earth to pull himself along. He made it to the upturned car and crawled round to the driver's side. Acrid smoke billowed around the hovercar like an angry fog. At first Kaspar didn't see him, but some of the smoke cleared and there was Dillon, slumped back-wards in his seat, his eyes closed. Immediate relief was quickly swamped with intense concern. The hovercar might explode at any second.

'Dillon, hang on, mate. I'll get you out.'

Kaspar reached in, grabbed Dillon's arm and pulled, but he couldn't shift him. Dillon's seat belt was still in place. Kaspar clicked it open and tried again. Dillon still didn't budge. Kaspar needed a better grip. Pulling off his gloves, he reached further and got his arms around Dillon's chest.

'Come on, you bastard. You're not helping.'

Kaspar heaved as best he could. He altered his stance slightly so that he could use his good leg to apply some force against the body of the hovercar, and readjusted his grip on Dillon again. And then Kaspar realized why Dillon wasn't helping, why he wasn't moving.

Dillon had a hole the size of a fist in the back of his skull.

15

Kaspar slumped down next to the hovercar beside Dillon's body. He couldn't move. He just stared at Dillon, too shocked to feel anything but numb. If he stayed very still and closed, then slowly opened, his eyes then maybe, just maybe this would turn out to be nothing more than a nightmare. The very worst nightmare of his life. Kaspar began to cough, spasmodically at first but it rapidly got worse. The smells around him were beginning to permeate – sulphur from the volcanic vents, burned plastic and rubber from the smouldering car . . . and blood. The unmistakable metallic odour of the blood that was now pooling darkly underneath Dillon's ruined head and staining his back. Kaspar was sickly hypnotized by Dillon's head. He could see bone and brain. People shouldn't look like that. Dillon shouldn't look like that. His friend had always been so neat and tidy – he would hate to see himself in this state.

Kaspar rolled away from the car and vomited his guts out.

The puking cleared his mind. It occurred to him that the dead would have to wait. He had more pressing problems to deal with. There were still armed hostiles in the area and he was injured. If he stayed put, he'd be joining Dillon. He forced himself to face his friend.

'Later, mate,' he said softly, and then turned to hunt for his rifle. He spotted it about ten metres away, crawled over to it, grabbed it and rolled into the cover of some rocks. Now to make sure his rifle was still working. He checked the emitter, popped the power pack, wiped the terminals on his dust-covered trousers and slammed the battery back into the gun. The ready light came on and he flicked off the safety. Fishing his auxiliary headset out of his pocket, Kaspar took a quick look around before putting it on. The max charge tone sounded in his ear. Kaspar pressed 'Reset/Align' on the scope and then started scanning for hostiles. Looking left, down the gully – nothing. Spinning to the right – nothing. He was desperate to spy someone, somewhere – for Dillon's sake.

'Where are you, you bastards?'

Something scraped against the rocks above his head. Kaspar looked up just in time to see the soles of two boots descending towards his head. He dived to his left, only just managing to avoid having his skull crushed, and tried to bring his rifle to bear. Too close. The rifle caught on the man's knees. Kaspar fired anyway but the bolt went wide, doing nothing. The man was carrying the launch tube of the rocket launcher, which he swung down like a club, aiming for Kaspar's head. Kaspar rolled again and came up onto his knees. Another swing from his attacker, but this time Kaspar managed to block it with his rifle before launching himself flat out at his assailant's legs. This wasn't the way they taught unarmed combat at the Academy – this was a fight for survival, brutal and desperate. Kaspar clawed his attacker to the ground and managed to land a short punch to his left kidney. The man responded with an elbow to Kaspar's ribs and, with a quick spin, a vicious chop to his left shoulder. Kaspar screamed and fell back. As the man prepared to dive in again, Kaspar kicked out hard with both legs, straight through the man's knees. Now it wasn't Kaspar who was screaming.

Feel it! thought Kaspar as he threw himself on the man. There were a few more punches, but Kaspar hardly felt them. He head-butted the terrorist, breaking his nose, then he kneed him in the groin, forcing his attacker to throw his head back and expose his throat. Kaspar had a flashback to when he was a boy, a memory of two wolves fighting. When one wolf had realized it was losing, it lay down and exposed its throat, a gesture of surrender, an acknowledgement of the other's superiority. The alpha wolf had then symbolically snapped at the exposed throat, but hadn't bitten down. Evolution. Kaspar loved wolves. Wolves were so civilized. Point made, nobody had to die.

'You killed Dillon, you son of a bitch.' And Kaspar chopped his right hand down hard, crushing the man's larynx.

He collapsed down onto his knees next to the dying terrorist, watching as the man tried to breathe with lungs rapidly filling with blood. A blurred movement only just visible out of the corner of his eye caught his attention.

But before he could turn, he was knocked away from the man's body and sent spinning into the dirt. Kaspar had no idea what move his new attacker had used on him, but he had been simultaneously flattened and lost the use of his right arm.

He tried to stand to face the new threat, but had no clue where his new assailant was. He spun round, then felt an agonizing pain shooting down his back and radiating into his legs. Kaspar hit the ground face down. He tried to move, but his body was no longer his to command. He tried to at least raise his head but his neck seemed incapable of supporting its weight. A wave of despair flooded through him. Kaspar had lost fights before. Master Tariq back at the Academy had regularly used him as a demonstration partner, flipping him all over the gym and generally owning him, but even then Kaspar had never felt quite so helpless. He was getting a kicking and he hadn't even seen his assailant yet.

He knew then that he was finished.

The fight against the first guy had been brutal, but it'd been a fight between equals. This was something else entirely. He tried to look up again to at least get a glimpse of his tormentor, but he saw nothing. He tried to flip over, but his arms and legs were frozen. His hair was grabbed and his head was yanked up. He was tossed over onto his back and all the air driven from his lungs as his opponent jumped on his chest with both knees.

Now helpless, winded and paralysed, Kaspar looked up at the slight figure kneeling on his chest. Black-clad.

Another ninja. There was absolutely nothing he could do but pray that his attacker would be reasonably merciful and kill him quickly. The ninja pulled off his right glove before his bare hand moved swiftly to Kaspar's neck and gripped it firmly. Downward pressure on the windpipe and inward pressure on the carotid arteries.

Classic.

Kaspar feebly tried to swing his one semi-functioning limb, his left arm, but the ninja disdainfully paralysed that one too with a two-fingered jab.

Come on, you sadistic git, thought Kaspar. Get it over with. His peripheral vision started to fade and he knew his last moments had come. There was nothing left to do now but wait for death.

16

'Please . . . oh, please . . . I'll be good.'

Kaspar was running — fast. Just as fast as he possibly could. But it wasn't fast enough.

Paws scrabbled on the rocks behind him.

'I promise, I'll never wander off again.'

Fifteen, maybe twenty paces, and then they would be on him. Even a full-grown person couldn't out-run or out-fight a whole pack, and Kaspar was only six. He would never see seven. His life could now be measured in mere seconds. To his left and right, he saw some of his pursuers actually overtaking him and circling back. Overhauling their prey, encircling it, trapping it, tormenting it, howling and snapping at it as they slowly closed in before surging in together and ripping it apart was how they lived. Kaspar didn't even know why he was still running. It was pointless, and yet he had to try. Try to reach the boat. Try to get to his mum. Try to survive. At that moment that was all he knew or wanted to know.

'Mummy!' he screamed as the circle closed and he was forced to stop. Yellow eyes and bared fangs were all around now.

'Mummy . . .'

He could smell their hot fetid breath as they drew ever closer. The huge alpha male in front of him considered his quarry. Kaspar looked into the eyes of death. The alpha male sat back slightly on his haunches, then pounced. Kaspar closed his eyes and screamed. He was bowled over by the momentum and knocked to the ground. A crushing weight landed on his chest, pressing hot and hard against his skin. He couldn't breathe. He opened his mouth but didn't know if it was to scream or to suck air down into his starved lungs. Why hadn't he been bitten yet?

He kicked and elbowed at the fur-covered muscles pinning him down, then forced himself to open his eyes to see what he was hitting. He was making no impression. The weight remained on him. Eventually, he managed to scramble out to the right and the beast rolled off to the left. Kaspar kicked out hard, catching it in the chest, but there was no reaction. He kicked again. Still nothing. Kaspar stared at the huge jaws – but they were still now, the lethal bite aborted in mid-leap. He didn't understand what had happened, but as he whirled to see where the next threat was coming from, he became aware that the air was filled with blue flashes and the howls of animals in pain. All around, the pack were falling, and those that weren't falling were sprinting for cover.

Kaspar looked up straight into the eyes of his saviour.

'Mummy!'

The relief, the love Kaspar felt at that moment overwhelmed him. Tears flowed down his cheeks. He didn't even dare blink in case she vanished the moment his eyes closed, never to return. His mum lowered her rifle and smiled at him.

'Kas, love. Are you OK? Did they get you? Show me where it hurts.'

'Mummy . . .'

The clouds parted and rays of sunshine fell across her face. Kaspar struggled to sit up. His chest hurt where the wolf had landed on him.

'I'm sorry, Mummy. You told me not to wander off. I'm sorry.'

'Never mind that now. Up you get, love.' She held out her arms to him. 'Come on, Kas.'

Kaspar stood up and reached out to her. She was so close he could smell her flowery perfume, the one she always wore because it had been his dad's favourite.

'Come on, Kas.'

He stretched further, but he couldn't quite reach.

'Kaspar, it's OK. You can come to me now.' His mum's arms beckoned and her face was so beautiful in the sunlight, her smile so dazzling – but still he couldn't grasp her. She was just beyond his fingertips. And then she started to move away.

'Wait, Mum, wait for me.'

The light around her grew brighter.

'Kaspar, love, come on.'

His mum was drifting away further and faster now.

'Mummy . . .' The muscles in his arms strained as he reached out towards her, desperate to hold onto her any way he could.

But she was gone.

17

Kaspar was confused. There were hands around his throat, though they weren't exerting any pressure. He wasn't in the forest, he was in a desert. And that figure wasn't his mum, it was . . .

Reality came back in a rush.

Kaspar knew exactly where he was and what was happening. But the coup-de-grâce hadn't come. Instead, the grip on his throat was abruptly released and the ninja got off him, leaving Kaspar gasping on the ground, still unable to move. The ninja walked over to the other terrorist and checked for a pulse. From the look the ninja directed at him, Kaspar knew that the man was dead. As dead as Dillon. The ninja carefully examined the injuries Kaspar had inflicted, particularly the fatal one to the throat, before returning to where the Guardian still lay helpless. The black-clad figure stood over him for a while, as if deciding what to do, and then he took off his mask.

Kaspar's jaw dropped. It was a girl of about his age with short brown hair streaked with blonde highlights. She walked over to the burning car, squatted down and leaned inside the cockpit.

'Get away from him,' Kaspar shouted hoarsely.

Or what? He was in no fit state to even stand, far less anything else.

But she wasn't gone long. She soon came back, carrying the standard Guardian emergency pack from the hovercar. She grabbed Kaspar by the tunic and pulled him up into a sitting position against a nearby rock. Kaspar watched, bewildered, as she opened the emergency pack, took out a bottle of water, popped the cap and leaned over to squirt some water into his mouth. He swallowed with difficulty, never taking his eyes off her. Close up, she was stunning. High cheekbones, luminous, intelligent green eyes, hair short enough to be practical but still feminine. And she wasn't even out of breath. Kaspar couldn't stop staring. This girl was a dangerous terrorist who had just kicked seven shades of crap out of him.

And yet . . .

She didn't look like a terrorist.

The girl scrutinized him, a frown forming on her face and deepening with each passing second. She took out the Search and Rescue beacon, pressed the XMIT button and laid the device beside him before walking off. The Guardians would now receive a distress signal and would be there within the hour. Kaspar was going to survive.

He blinked after her in shocked amazement.

What on earth . . . ?

She had saved him, actually saved his life. Why had she done that?

'What's your name?' he croaked.

She paused for a long time, before turning her head and speaking over her shoulder.

'Rhea.'

And she was gone.

18

Kaspar still lay propped up against his rock, but things were improving. Rhea had put him on the shady side, so he wasn't baking, and the paralysis was wearing off. He still felt like he'd been run over by a truck, but for the first time in a while he felt hopeful. The digital readout on the SaR beacon showed it had been eleven minutes since activation. In a couple of hours, he would be home, messed up but alive.

But Dillon . . .

Kaspar took another look at the SaR beacon, a chill trickling through him. Why had Rhea activated it? Could this be an attempt to draw more Guardians into an ambush? He considered it, but rapidly dismissed the idea.

They'll be expecting that, he thought. They'll survey from the air before they land.

He tried to relax, his eyes turning back to the wrecked car. It was burning fiercely now. An overwhelming sense of loss hit him, deeper than his anger, fiercer than his need to survive. At the end of a day like this, he would normally have shared a drink with Dillon. He'd have explained, very seriously, what had happened, and Dillon would've teased him mercilessly.

'*There's a name for guys who get the hots for girls who beat the crap out of them.*' Kaspar could almost hear Dillon's voice mocking him now.

They'd met on the first day at the Academy – and Dillon had teased him every single day since. Teased him about being a melon farmer, about being too short even though Dillon was only a couple of centimetres taller, and after his secret came out, about his famous parents. There was no facet of Kaspar's life that Dillon hadn't felt free to disparage or turn into a comedy routine. But through it all, Kaspar had never once doubted that Dillon had his back. He'd even had a go at Voss on Kaspar's behalf, hence the reason he'd been stuck with Kaspar on Voss's garbage assignments.

And now he was dead.

And it should've been Kaspar. He was the one who should've been driving. He should've insisted when Dillon had pushed him out the way and taken his place behind the wheel. But what would that have got him? He'd be the one with half his head missing.

Dillon was dead . . .

One day at the Academy, Dillon had shared his opinions of death.

'First, I want it to be quick. Bang. Dead,' he had said. 'Second, no sodding autopsy. Those medics are weirdos. They do all kinds of sexual stuff to you once you're dead that you wouldn't let them do when you're alive. And three, I don't want to become compost, I wanna be cremated.'

127

'Well done, mate,' Kaspar whispered ruefully. 'Three out of three.'

He was replaying yet another one of Dillon's hilarious diatribes in his head when he suddenly became aware of a vibration in the ground. Here we go, he thought. Search and Rescue responding to my beacon.

But then he realized that the frequency was too low and the vibrations too powerful. The ground rumbled deep beneath his body. It couldn't be a vehicle. This was more seismic. Hell! Most of the earthquake activity in the Badlands was centred along the DeVries Fault – about twenty-five clicks east – but quite bad shocks could happen anywhere; occasionally they were even felt in Capital City in spite of the geo-stabilizers deep beneath the ground all around the city walls and beneath the ground of the city itself. Kaspar waited for the shaking to die down, but it didn't. It got worse. The amplitude built and now he could actually see ground waves, the floor of the gully undulating like choppy water.

'Is there anything else that can go wrong today?' he wondered as he tried to force his legs to move.

Rhea had placed him under a rock outcrop for shade, but now he was being peppered with falling stones. He needed to shift before twenty tonnes of rock shook itself loose and turned into an avalanche. Kaspar's arms were working pretty well now, but his legs had all the strength of wet noodles. He crawled about fifteen metres using just his arms, but he was still in the gully. The vibrations were still building, and rocks the size of his head and larger were now crashing down all around him. Kaspar kept crawling but his luck couldn't hold for ever.

It didn't. A rock struck him a glancing blow on the right temple. Everything seemed to go quiet, and for the second time in less than an hour he had tunnel vision. The last thing he saw before he lost consciousness was the rock that had hit him. It looked exactly like a melon. Dillon would have loved that.

Kaspar's first impression of the afterlife was that it was confusing and uncomfortable. He was flying backwards, above a desert, and there wasn't a single part of his body that didn't hurt. He was swooping over sand and mountains, and he could hear the sounds of falling rocks over the roaring of the blood in his ears. From the distance came the voice of an old woman calling him to dinner. Kaspar didn't recognize the voice but he did know that she was calling to him. The pounding in his head was terrible and surely all his ribs were broken? His legs probably were too, but somehow he flew on.

'Grandma,' he heard himself shout. 'I'm coming.'

He hadn't realized it before, but he was famished. He could see the woman in the distance and he waved to her as he raced down the grassy slope towards the little cottage by the bridge. The air was so warm, the sunlight so bright and in the cottage there would be fresh-baked bread and—

Another jolt of agony from his tortured ribs interrupted him and he opened his eyes. The grassy slope, the cottage, the bridge, they had all vanished. Now he saw sand and rocks again. Perplexed, he remembered that all four of his grandparents had died before he was born, and as for the cottage . . . He closed his eyes again, trying to place it.

There it was again. The smell of freshly baked bread. He could actually taste it, and it was so good. It brought back memories of his face buried in Grandma's apron, and she smelled of baking and dried mellisse berries and . . .

Kaspar's mind started to clear. Pain forced its way past his memories and his senses sharpened. The mountains were only rocks and pebbles; he wasn't as high as he thought, only a metre or so above the ground – and he wasn't flying; he was being carried. He was wedged in the beak of a black-backed hawk as it returned to its nest high in the mountains where . . .

No, that wasn't right either.

He could see running feet below him, but not his . . .

He was slung across someone's shoulders and they were running – fast – across the hot sand. Kaspar could smell sulphur and fresh bread, he could see pounding feet and pain ripped through his body and Grandma . . . he could hear his grandma singing to him. The memories of things never said, never done crowded in on him, simultaneously comforted and disturbed him as the pounding feet carried him off the sand and onto solid rock. Up and up, until the sounds of avalanche faded, and the feet stopped moving.

Kaspar was laid gently on a granite shelf – the most comfortable, warmest granite shelf – and his grandma pulled the blankets up to his chin and sang him to sleep.

19

When Kaspar woke up, he was surprised to find he wasn't in the soft feather bed in the cottage by the bridge. He was lying on an outcrop of volcanic rock in the Badlands. From his position about twenty metres above the desert floor, he could see the gully, and there in the distance, the burned wreck of the hovercar where they had crashed and Dillon had—

Kaspar looked around. He was alone. His uniform was shredded and burned, he hurt like hell and he had a field dressing around his head, but he didn't appear to be missing any vital parts. The medical kit, a half-full water bottle and his Search and Rescue beacon lay beside him. Where was the rescue team? Standard protocol for an emergency SaR beacon activation would have been for a Rapid Response unit to secure the area before the medics moved in to attend the wounded and pick up the bodies, but he was alone.

So who had bandaged his head? An unexpected movement caught his attention. About a kilometre away, running fast and skirting the rocks, was a slight, black-clad figure. She looked back briefly before disappearing, just as

Kaspar heard the distinctive sound of help arriving. Two gunships cleared the ridge behind him. One stayed high as top-cover while the other swept low to check out the area around where he was lying.

'Here! I'm up here,' Kaspar shouted pointlessly. His voice was no more than a hoarse croak, and besides, nobody could have heard him over the racket of the gunships. The low scout swung by, and Kaspar saw a Guardian point to him through the open side door, then turn to say something to her colleagues. And even though he knew they'd seen him now, Kaspar still kept trying to shout, 'I'm here. I'm here!'

Ten long, short minutes later, Kas was on his way home.

The speeding gunship was even noisier on the inside, so no one spoke much on the way back, except for the occasional word of sympathy or reassurance. Kaspar had plenty of time to think while his superficial wounds were patched and his broken ribs strapped up. He was missing Dillon already.

And he was confused.

Why had he had such a vivid dream about some elderly woman with silver-grey hair and twinkling green eyes whom he'd never met? And why call her 'Grandma'? But most puzzling of all, why would a ruthless, fanatical terrorist pass up not one, but two chances to kill him, and instead carry him nearly one kilometre to safety?

Much was lost in the War to End All Wars. Perhaps the saddest loss of all was the destruction of our past. So much historical data was destroyed. The books, libraries and computer data we had for so long taken for granted were also casualties of the War. Our enemy realized that our dependence on our computer networks could be used to their advantage. Their tactics included the design and implementation of computer viruses to seek and wipe out any reference to the Alliance. Thus they sought to erase us, not just from the future by depriving us of our present, but from history itself.

The High Councillors were therefore given the task of reconstructing the historical texts from what little data remained, not just of the Alliance's past but also of all the many and varied nations that used to exist on our planet. Even after a significant number of decades the task is not yet complete. Our responsibility may be daunting, but we cannot use that as an excuse for complacency.

The time for grieving about our past is over. It is incumbent upon all of us to learn and grow from the reproduced historical texts. Only by learning from the past can we move forward with confidence into our future.

And we cannot, we must not, allow the Crusaders to hold us back from that goal.

Extract taken from 'The Origins of the Insurgency' by Brother Telem

20

A fortnight later, Kaspar was still in the Clinic – and climbing the walls. He was undergoing his sixth operational fitness assessment and it wasn't going any better than the first five.

'Come on, Doc,' he pleaded. 'I'm fine. My ribs are healing, the pain is very nearly gone and I should be getting back to work. Just sign the release and I'll be out of your way.'

'Not so fast, Guardian Wilding,' Dr Hondo replied. 'There's more to it than the broken bones. We've only just got the infected burns under control and your brain chemistry is still not back to the baseline set at your last pre-accident physical.'

'It wasn't an accident,' said Kaspar quietly.

Everyone in the Clinic referred to what had happened in the Badlands as 'the accident', as if someone had slipped on a bar of soap. Nobody seemed to want to discuss the fact that a Guardian had died in a terrorist attack. Of course there had been a debrief. Some pencil-necked clerk from MII, the Ministry of Information and Intelligence – or, as those at the Academy called it, the Ministry of

135

Insensitive Ignorance – had come round and spoken to him about 'the accident'.

'You have nothing to worry about, Guardian Wilding. The paperwork has all been taken care of,' smiled the unctuous clerk. Kaspar had taken in his dark blue suit and his pristine collarless white shirt and taken an instant dislike to him, something he very rarely did.

'So if you'd just like to sign here.' The clerk waved a data-tablet and an electronic stylus under Kaspar's nostrils. He was moving the tablet so quickly Kaspar could only make out the odd word or two.

Kaspar took hold of the stylus and tablet, much to the clerk's annoyance, and settled down to read what he was signing.

'There's no need to read it,' the clerk announced quickly. 'It's all perfectly in order.'

'Nevertheless, I never sign anything without reading it first, otherwise I might end up agreeing to give you my liver and both of my kidneys while I still have need of them,' said Kaspar.

The clerk wasn't happy. And by the time Kaspar had read the short document on the tablet screen, neither was he. He reread the offending paragraph out loud just in case he'd read it wrong the first time round.

'*A near-miss with a rocket-propelled grenade induced a lateral stabilizer failure on the hovercar, resulting in an uncontrolled grounding and unfortunate injuries and a fatality. This accident may be put down to Insurgent activity and an inappropriate pilot response resulting in inadvertent pilot error.*'

He hadn't read it wrong at all. In fact, it was actually worse on a second reading.

'You must be seriously bat-crap crazy if you think I'm signing this.' Kaspar threw the tablet down on his bed in disgust.

'Guardian Wilding, this text has been authorized by Brother Simon himself,' said the clerk.

'I don't give a damn. First of all, there was no near-miss with an RPG – it was a direct hit. And second, third and fourth, there was no pilot error. It wasn't Dillon's fault, and I'll see you and the whole High Council in hell before I sign anything that says otherwise.'

'We *have* stated that it was *inadvertent* pilot error . . .'

' "Inadvertent" isn't the word I'm having a problem with,' Kaspar replied coldly. 'What's wrong with telling it like it was? A murdering, scumbag Insurgent shot us down and killed my partner.'

'The High Council need to be careful how many . . . deaths are attributed to the Insurgents, and we have already reached this month's quota,' said the clerk.

Kaspar stared. Seriously? The truth was being bent to the point of breaking to make some statistics work?

'I'm not signing that,' he repeated quietly.

'Guardian Wilding, let me remind you that you and your partner deviated from the prescribed route to get to your destination. If you'd followed the established travel protocols all of this might have been avoided.'

Kaspar sat on his hands to stop himself from punching the clerk's face clear through his head. Did this guy think

Kaspar didn't already know that, hadn't agonized over that day in, day out since he'd been rescued?

'As I explained in my debrief,' he said coldly, 'we saw a flash of light east of our position and went to investigate.'

'You should've called it in and waited for backup.'

'Going in to investigate without calling it in first was my decision, not Dillon's. The blame should be laid at my door. The hovercar's data recorder would've told you that.'

'Guardian Wilding, you survived. Dillon didn't. You're already in the public eye as a hero. How would it look if we were to suddenly say that you aren't?'

'I don't care.'

'Well, that kind of attitude is a luxury the High Council can't afford,' said the clerk.

Kaspar shrugged. Not his problem.

The clerk gave Kaspar a calculating look.

'I'm not signing that,' Kaspar stated once more. 'If you think I'm bluffing, try me.'

'Very well. I am authorized to omit the last sentence as that's obviously the one you find so objectionable,' said the clerk.

Kaspar watched as the clerk input a passcode onto the tablet and swiped his finger over the offending sentence to delete it. He handed the tablet back to Kaspar.

'Brother Simon has instructed me not to leave this room without your signature on this document,' said the clerk.

Kaspar read it carefully again to ensure that the line blaming Dillon for what had happened had indeed been deleted. But what was to stop the MII from putting back the sentence once they had his signature? He signed on the indicated line at the bottom of the document, then he signed his name right across the body of the text as well. He handed back the tablet and stylus. It wasn't fool-proof by any means, but it was the best he could come up with in the circumstances.

The clerk frowned down at the tablet in his hand. 'Why did you do that?'

'If you add or delete anything else to that report, my signature won't match up. I just want to make sure that what I sign is what gets delivered back to Brother Simon and the archives,' said Kaspar.

The clerk glared at Kaspar, his expression declaring that he'd like nothing better than to rebreak Kaspar's ribs. 'Thank you for your time, Guardian Wilding,' he said at last.

'You're welcome,' Kaspar replied icily. 'Shut the door on your way out.'

As soon as the door was shut, Kaspar collapsed back down onto his pillows. Minutes passed before he was able to calm down enough to think rationally. The thing that stunned him was the absolute hatred he felt at that moment for Brother Simon and the others in the High Council. It burned like acid eating its way through him. He had never, *ever* felt anything like it before. Their cause was his cause. Their aim was true. So why this sudden feeling of overwhelming loathing?

Dillon . . .

Kaspar was still angry about Dillon's death. It had to be that. Kaspar wouldn't let himself even contemplate the idea that it might be something else.

And as for Kaspar's vivid dreams, Dr Hondo put that down to a combination of concussion, reaction to stress and the effects of inhaling the fumes from burning insulation. His out-of-whack brain chemistry was ascribed to post-traumatic shock and grief for his friend.

And that was that. All neatly explained, wrapped up and filed away.

The day of Dillon's memorial service was fast approaching. Kaspar was still in the Clinic so he had to put in a request to attend the service, something he considered just a formality.

The reply had been swift: WE CANNOT AT THIS TIME SANCTION YOUR REQUEST TO LEAVE THE CLINIC. PERMISSION DENIED.

That was the last straw. Kaspar put in a call to Mac. Her smile was broad and instantaneous the moment she saw him on her data screen.

'Hello, stranger. How're you doing?' Her smile faded. 'I was sorry to hear about your friend Dillon.'

Kaspar shrugged, unsure how to respond. He got straight to the point. 'Mac, could you do me a favour?'

'Sure. Anything,' Mac replied without hesitation.

Kaspar's smile was weak but sincere. It was good to know that someone, somewhere had his back. 'I need to know who I should speak to about attending Dillon's memorial service.'

Mac frowned. 'Surely your commander—'

'Voss passed my request up the food chain and it's been denied. I need to go to the top to argue my case – because I'm going, come hell, high water or Brother Simon himself.'

A moment's pause, then Mac said, 'I'll get back to you.' And with that she signed off.

Ten minutes later and she was as good as her word. Kaspar had a couple of names and their full contact details, plus Mac's advice on how to get what he wanted. He put through a call to Julianna Jeffers, Chief Supervisor at the Guardian Academy's Public Affairs office.

'Guardian Wilding, a pleasure to speak to you.' Ms Jeffers smiled politely at him over the datalink. 'How may I help you?'

'Ms Jeffers, my best friend Dillon Greenhill died recently,' Kaspar began without preamble.

'Yes, I have your file in front of me,' said Ms Jeffers. 'I'm sorry for your loss.'

'I'd like to go to his memorial service.'

'That's not my decision to make, I'm afraid,' frowned Ms Jeffers. 'And I can see that permission has already been denied. I'm afraid I can't help you—'

'Maybe Vivian Sykes at the *Daily Report* would be very interested in a human interest story about a Guardian being denied permission to attend his best friend's funeral,' Kaspar interrupted.

'I couldn't sanction you speaking to any member of the press at this time,' Ms Jeffers said, aghast.

'You misunderstand me,' said Kaspar. 'I'm not asking

for permission – I'm telling you what will happen if I'm not cleared to attend Dillon's memorial service.'

Silence.

'I see.'

'I hope you do,' said Kaspar.

Ms Jeffers gave him a studied look. Kaspar met her gaze without even blinking. He was sick and tired of being jerked around like he was some kind of puppet. Kaspar knew he was probably shooting his military career full of holes but he didn't care.

'One moment.' Ms Jeffers put him on hold.

Kaspar glared at the image of waves gently lapping at a beach shore in some place he knew he'd never be able to afford to go. He hated being put on hold at the best of times and this most certainly wasn't one of those. Ms Jeffers returned less than a minute later. She studied him. If she thought her stare would cause him to back down, she was going to be disappointed. Kaspar regarded her, his expression stony.

'I understand that you recently had an encounter with a clerk from MII,' began Ms Jeffers.

'Yes, that's right,' said Kaspar.

'He filed a complaint against you, Guardian Wilding.'

'Good for him,' said Kaspar evenly.

'For the sake of your long-term career as a Guardian, I recommend you keep complaints against you to a minimum,' said Ms Jeffers.

'I'll bear that in mind. So, am I phoning Vivian Sykes or am I going to Dillon's memorial service?' asked Kaspar.

Ms Jeffers' lips tightened slightly. 'Permission has been granted for you to attend, Guardian.'

'Thank you,' said Kaspar, disconnecting the link.

The day of the service, Kaspar put on his military dress uniform and stepped out of his room at the Clinic, only to find himself confronted by a Guardian he'd never met before. This woman had to be at least twice his age, with short-cut blonde hair and piercing lime-green eyes.

'Hello. I'm Guardian Thompson from the Special Support Group. I'll be accompanying you to Guardian Greenhill's memorial service.'

Kaspar's frown was immediate. 'I don't think so.'

'I've been told you're not fit enough to travel unaccompanied yet,' Guardian Thompson replied.

'Listen, I don't mean to be rude but I don't need a babysitter. Air transport has been booked to take me to the Academy and to bring me back here afterwards, and all I want to do is say goodbye to my best friend. What's the problem?'

'I am not a babysitter,' said Guardian Thompson, her lips a thin, bloodless line, her eyes sending volts of outrage through Kaspar's body. 'I have my orders, Guardian Wilding, just the same as you. Either I go with you or you don't get to go at all – it's your choice.'

'I don't need—'

'Do you really want to waste time arguing about this?' asked Guardian Thompson. 'Because I've been assigned to you for the entire morning. No skin off my nose if we spend it here debating the issue.'

Kaspar glared at her, but the point was taken. With time marching away from him, Kaspar couldn't afford to delay any longer.

They arrived at the Memorial Hall of the Academy just as the ceremony was starting. Kaspar wasn't surprised to see that the hall was practically full. He sat down in a tiny space in the back row, forcing the others in the row to move up. Guardian Thompson would just have to find her own space.

Dillon's dad stood at the front of the hall, facing those in attendance. He was trying to tell an anecdote about the first time Dillon had told his family that he wanted to be a Guardian, but he had to keep coughing to clear his throat in an effort to retain his composure. Kaspar was getting choked up just watching him.

Dillon was a popular guy who would tease you mercilessly, but it was always done without malice and with a twinkle in his eye. Kaspar had never heard anyone say a bad word against him. He looked around again, gratified by the number of people present. He spotted Dillon's mum and younger sister Rachel seated near the front. Sporadically, Dillon's mum would sit up and straighten her shoulders. But almost immediately her head drooped as if it were too heavy for her body. Kaspar didn't need to see her face to know that she was having trouble holding back the tears.

The seats to the right of the hall were occupied by

family and civilian friends. The Guardians and other military dignitaries filled the seats on the left. Kaspar spotted Voss a couple of rows in front, but to his surprise, Mac was seated next to him. How on earth did she get lumbered with that seat? Voss didn't exactly hide his opinion of civilians, even those who worked at the Academy. Mind you, all the seats on the civilian side of the hall were occupied. Obviously Mac had had no choice.

Once the ceremony was over, Kaspar tried to head over to Janna, Mikey and the others from his unit. A hand on his arm held him back.

'Guardian Wilding, I was given strict instructions to take you back to the Clinic the moment the ceremony was over,' said Guardian Thompson, her hand still on his arm.

'I can't even say hello to my friends?' Kaspar frowned.

'No, Cadet.' Guardian Thompson moved to stand in front of him. 'I have my orders.'

Kaspar tried to walk round her but she stepped in front of him again. There was no way for him to proceed without making a scene, and this was neither the time nor the place. People were on their feet and milling about now. Voss had moved to talk to Janna and the others and Mac seemed to have disappeared. With a sigh, Kaspar gave in and left the hall. The air transport was waiting directly outside.

So much for escaping from the Clinic for a few hours to be with his friends.

★ ★ ★

145

The day after the service, he tried to discharge himself, but he found two of the Clinic's security staff outside his door.

One of them was taller than him. The other was the same height and wore a gormless expression like it was the latest fashion. Both were stockier and outweighed him by several pounds.

'Sorry, Guardian Wilding, but we can't allow you to leave.'

'Are you going to stop me?' he asked pointedly.

'If we have to,' the stupid-looking one replied.

Kaspar was more than ready to work off some pent-up frustration with a bit of mindless arse-kicking when the more intelligent security guard intervened.

'Guardian Wilding, there isn't any point,' he said. 'By the time you got back to the Academy, Commander Voss would just have you carried back here bodily. He isn't about to overrule the doctors if they haven't passed you fit for duty, now, is he?'

Kaspar had just glared at both of them and gone back into his room.

At least they allowed him visitors, otherwise he would've been climbing the walls even higher and faster than he already was. Janna had come to see him a number of times, once with nine others from Kaspar's graduating class, and they had smuggled in enough alcohol to give the medics a fit and give Dillon the kind of informal, raucous send-off he would have loved. On one of Janna's solo visits, Kaspar had tentatively shared some of what he knew about the diversionary tactics of the Insurgents and their use of an accompanying ninja to achieve their objectives. Yes, he'd discussed the pros and cons of the idea with Mac, but she wasn't military: she was a civilian, a book-head. Kaspar wanted the opinion of another soldier, someone who would listen to his theories and not give him static about his extra-curricular activities. Janna had listened intently but she wasn't convinced – to say the least.

Mainly, however, Kaspar took his medication, sat alone and thought. And read. The best times were when Mac came to see him. The first time she visited, Kaspar couldn't stop grinning.

'Hey, Mac. Thanks for coming to see me,' he said.

'No problem. What are friends for?'

OK, so they were officially friends. While Kaspar was very happy about that, another part of him which he didn't like to analyse too deeply was disappointed. But he had no right to expect more. She was a brainbox and older than him, though not by much. He was a grunt, nothing less but certainly nothing more.

'I thought I saw you at Dillon's memorial service,' he said after a moment.

'Did you?' Mac replied brightly.

'Yeah, sitting next to Voss?'

'He's kind of cantankerous, isn't he?' smiled Mac.

'That's one word for him,' Kaspar agreed.

Mac took a quick look around. 'I blagged my way into your room at the Academy so I could bring your data-tablet, in case you wanted to do more research.'

'Thanks.' Kaspar grinned. Now at last he could focus his

attention on something besides the window and the four walls.

Mac had stayed for another thirty minutes and Kaspar was grateful for every second of them. She had a quirky sense of humour and her observations about the others in his unit, and about Voss himself, had him doubled over with laughter.

After her visit, Kaspar had taken the opportunity to learn how to properly control a net-search. On her third or fourth visit, he caught Mac regarding him speculatively.

'What?' He frowned.

'Kaspar, what really happened out in the Badlands?' asked Mac.

'What d'you mean? We were attacked and my best friend died.' Kaspar's frown deepened.

'How did you get from the gully floor to the plateau so far off the ground?'

'Why d'you ask?'

Mac's gaze fell away from his, but only momentarily. 'I read your report. You said that when your hovercar went down you were thrown clear, then when the ground started to shake, you crawled to safety.'

Kaspar's heart began to beat just that little bit faster. His mouth became just a little bit drier. 'Yeah. So?'

'You had three broken ribs, burns to your hands and arms and your legs were all cut and bloodied,' said Mac.

'What's your point?'

'I saw the film taken by the rescue team of the area. You had an SaR beacon and water beside you and your head

148

was bandaged. With your injuries, there's no way you could've got up to that plateau carrying the beacon and water. And I closely examined the film and photos of the rocks leading up to the plateau. There was blood on the gully floor but there were only sporadic blood drops on the rocks. And they were *drops*, not smears. Your legs were bleeding copiously but you managed to avoid getting blood on all but a couple of rocks climbing up? And with the damage to your hands, there's certainly no way you could've bandaged your own head so neatly. So the only conclusion is that someone else was there.'

Kaspar regarded Mac. He knew she was geeky smart but now he saw why she'd been trusted with so much responsibility at such a young age. She'd managed to piece together a whole lot more than anyone else.

'Her name is Rhea,' admitted Kaspar.

Mac frowned.

'She's an Insurgent. I killed the guy who killed Dillon and then she got the jump on me. She could've killed me easily, but instead she carried me to safety and bandaged me up.'

'And she told you her name?' Mac asked, aghast.

'Yeah, when I asked,' Kaspar admitted.

'Had you ever seen her before?'

'Nope. Never. And I'm still trying to figure out why she did it.'

'Did she plant some kind of device on you?'

'No. That's the first thing I checked when they put me in here,' said Kaspar. 'No tracking devices, no listening devices, no data-blocking or sabotage devices. Nothing.'

'So not only did she spare your life but she saved your life?'

'Yeah,' Kaspar replied.

'I see,' said Mac.

'Do you? Explain it to me then, 'cause I don't,' said Kaspar.

Mac contemplated Kaspar for a moment. 'I take it back. I don't see.'

'Good. That makes me feel a little less stupid. I don't want to talk about Rhea any more. I've had an idea and I need your help,' said Kaspar.

'All you have to do is ask,' smiled Mac.

A couple of hours later, Kaspar felt like a proper cyber-troll as he scoured every source he could think of for information. He'd learned his lesson, though, and was now using his personal access code, not his Guardian one. Nothing significant popped up on the Insurgency that Kaspar didn't already know. In fact, thanks to Brother Simon, he actually knew more. But he couldn't escape the feeling in his gut that he was missing something; they all were. Since Dillon's death it was almost as if there was something pushing at him, compelling him to discover more about the Insurgents and their motives. It was now close to becoming an obsession. Kaspar supposed it was because once he found their vulnerabilities, then they could be stopped for good.

After the umpteenth session of trawling fruitlessly

through cyberspace for information, Mac came up with a new suggestion. 'Maybe we're concentrating too much on facts.'

'You think we should try researching fiction? That doesn't sound very scientific,' said Kaspar.

'No,' she smiled. 'Not fiction exactly. I was thinking about your dream, or whatever you call it. The images you saw when the girl was carrying you in the desert.'

'That was just me hallucinating,' Kaspar dismissed. He was beginning to wish he'd never told Mac about Rhea. 'I'd been blown up, kicked in the head and breathed in a load of burning chemicals.'

'Maybe not. Maybe the visions really are something? Maybe you saw something and your addled brain reinterpreted it?'

'Reinterpreted?'

'Yeah. Like what if she was wearing earrings that were hawk-shaped, and you remember that as being carried in the beak of a hawk.'

That actually sounded plausible. 'So you think we should treat all my "visions" as possible facts?'

'Well, yes!'

So now Kaspar input every detail he could remember: Rhea, her description, the cottage and the bridge, the hawk, the weather, the smell of mellisse berries, everything.

Once the bots were off and running, Mac stood up. 'I need to get back to the Academy,' she said with reluctance.

Kaspar couldn't figure out why he suddenly felt

strangely disappointed. Of course Mac had to get back home. It wasn't like she could stay with him in the Clinic.

'Thanks for coming to see me, Mac.' He smiled. 'And for all your help. I really appreciate it.'

'Any time, soldier. And you don't need to be quite so formal. We're friends, OK?'

Kaspar nodded, though he couldn't help wondering what it would be like to be more than Mac's friend. In fact . . . 'Mac, I don't suppose—' He ground to an abrupt halt, his face burning.

'You don't suppose – what?' Mac prompted.

'Never mind. It doesn't matter.' Kaspar shook his head.

Mac opened her mouth to speak, only to close it again without saying a word, for which Kaspar was grateful. He was all kinds of a coward for not asking her out, but what was the point? She was older than him and smarter than him. She was bound to say no.

'You're not going to tell me what's on your mind?' Mac urged gently.

Kaspar shook his head.

'You do know you can ask me anything, right? Any time, day or night. And you've got all my contact details.'

'Yeah, thanks,' said Kaspar.

The silence between them began to stretch into something uncomfortable.

'I'd better get back to my library,' said Mac.

'OK. Thanks again.'

'See you soon,' smiled Mac.

Kaspar nodded, and then she was gone. He lay back to

try and get some sleep, but he couldn't relax. His thoughts kept jumping about like demented fleas. The more he thought about it, the more he thought Mac might be on to something. His visions made no sense as mere dreams. They were too vivid – and too ordinary. He didn't buy the 'inhaling fumes' explanation any more. He knew five people back on the farm who had got a good lungful of burning poly-trimethyl-xanthine insulation. They had all hallucinated all right, but every one of them had had surreal, nightmarish hallucinations. Like Old Man Kyle, who saw an invading horde of thirty-metre-high chickens armed with laser cannons.

That was one hell of a lot different to seeing a sweet old granny who baked delicious bread.

Kaspar closed his eyes and he could almost taste it again. No, he *could* taste it. It was here, in the room with him, fresh-baked bread with mellisse berries. And he could hear the sounds of a family at dinner, laughing and chatting. The air was filled with the unmistakable odour of volcanic sulphur and the temperature in the room was much warmer than comfortable, but in spite of all that he felt warm and enveloped, a part of it.

He opened his eyes and sat up sharply. Now he didn't even have to be asleep for his senses to take him to some place he'd never been before. He felt like his body was being hijacked. No way could he share what he was going through with anyone, not even Mac. If the doctors at the Clinic got the slightest hint of what was going on in his head, he'd never get back to the Academy.

21

The view was like nothing Kaspar had ever seen before – and yet it was strangely familiar. How was that even possible? As Kaspar stood on the crest of the hill drinking in the scene around him, he felt at peace, at home. Gorse and heather provided a soft, springy carpet beneath his feet. The recent rains had left the air smelling fresh and sweet enough to eat. He took breath after deep breath, trying to fill not just his lungs but his entire body with this good feeling. He looked around. Blue sky with top-lit clouds called him upwards. Distant valleys and hills pulled him onwards. The cottage at the foot of the hill in the valley behind him beckoned him home. How could there be anywhere else on the planet as perfect as this? After the concrete and steel and cold blue and yellow lights of Capital City, this place was like an oasis for his eyes, not to mention his soul. Kaspar felt like he could stay there for ever. This scene, this peace, was something worth fighting for. Here was a place worth dying for.

Someone was calling him. Kaspar turned his head. Grandma stood at the bottom of the hill, one hand on her hip, the other waving frantically. She'd obviously been calling him for a while.

'Coming, Grandma,' Kaspar called down to her.

He started to race down the hill, loving that almost out-of-control feeling of acceleration he got every time he did this. He laughed excitedly every time he almost pitched forward, managing at the last moment to regain his balance – but only just.

'Rhea, be careful,' Grandma called out urgently.

Rhea?

My name is Kaspar, he thought.

And the thought made him lose his footing. Kaspar tried to lean back, to regain his centre of gravity, but it was too late. He pitched forwards and hit the ground with a thud. Then he began to tumble, tumble. The ground was no longer soft. Each part of his body made painful contact with the ground as he tumbled downwards. An elbow here, the side of his face, a knee, his back. Pain punched through his body till he must surely pass out.

Kaspar sat bolt upright, his breathing heavy.

What the hell . . . ?

Oh, great! Now he was dreaming about the terrorist. Maybe the Clinic really was the best place for him. He took a deep breath to try and steady his nerves, only to halt abruptly. He could still smell it, the aroma of grass and gorse and heather and the sweet, fresh smell of the air after the rains.

Since when were dreams so vivid that even the scent of them lingered when awake?

He buried his head in his hands. For the life of him, he couldn't understand why he kept having these dreams. Was he cracking up? Is that why they were keeping him in the Clinic? Was he losing it and the officials were just waiting for the right time to tell him?

Or was the explanation much simpler than that?

22

After three and a half weeks in the Clinic, Kaspar was finally allowed to return to the Academy. His wounds had all healed and he was pronounced fit for duty. His brain chemistry still wasn't quite back to normal, but it was stable enough and none of the psych tests had indicated responses outside established parameters. Kaspar made sure to restrict his answers to what he felt they wanted to hear rather than the truth as he saw it – and he certainly kept his continued visions of 'Grandma' to himself. Now he was seated in the briefing room waiting for Voss to arrive with the day's assignments.

'What are you hoping for?' Janna asked him.

'After weeks of medical jail, I'll take anything,' he replied.

'What? Even school visits toting a plastic gun?'

'Even that.'

Voss walked in and strode briskly to the podium. 'Good morning, everyone,' he said. 'And welcome back to Guardian Wilding, who has finally returned from his three-week vacation at a health spa. From what I hear – and I heard a lot – they were glad to see the back of you.'

Kaspar's face burned. There was a good-natured chorus of insults and abuse before Voss restored order, but from the piercing look Voss gave him Kaspar knew his boss had been kept informed of all he'd said and done while at the Clinic.

'OK, to business. As *most* of you are aware' – Voss looked pointedly at Kaspar – 'the Insurgents have stepped up their mass attacks lately, and quite frankly we aren't handling them as efficiently as we should. We are taking too long to respond, we are taking too many casualties and the bastards are getting away with too much. So, today we are going on a little outing to the Garrom Forest exercise area where we will spend all day on section strength, live-fire training. And nobody gets to go home until you all get perfect scores. Let's go.'

'Oh, man,' Janna grumbled. And she wasn't the only one. 'I thought this intensive training crap would be finished once we graduated.'

'At least you lot are in shape,' Kaspar pointed out. 'After three weeks in the medical centre, I'm probably going to embarrass myself.'

Ten minutes later, the section was loaded into the transport and heading towards the Radial 14 interchange.

Kaspar studied the scenery out of the transport window as the others chatted around him, the buzz of their voices turning into so much background noise.

'Hey, Kas, you looking forward to a day playing kiss-chase in the woods?' asked Janna, nudging him.

'That's not going to happen,' replied Kaspar.

'Are you implying I won't catch you?' said Janna indignantly.

'Well, unless the driver is lost and the satnav is malfunctioning, we're going the wrong way.'

'Give that boy a cookie,' said Voss from the front of the transport. 'He's right – we're not going to the range.'

Now Kaspar wasn't the only one checking out the scenery. The Guardians exchanged puzzled looks.

'We've had a good tip from Intelligence,' continued Voss. 'And we think the Insurgency are going to hit a network sub-node in the Thirteenth District, so we're going to set a trap for them.'

'Then why say we're going to the range?' asked Janna.

'Because we think that there's a leak somewhere at the Academy or in our Governmental Liaison department. We always seem to be one step behind, and we think that someone is playing for the wrong team, tipping off the Insurgents before we can really hurt them. So this time we're not informing anyone of what we're doing until after we've done it.'

'Do we suspect who the spy might be?' Kaspar asked, appalled. He could hardly believe it. Someone at their base was a *traitor*?

'No.' Voss's expression was grim.

'Are we sure the Insurgents are going to hit District Thirteen today?' asked Mariska.

'No, but apparently there's a good chance. Look, there's no point asking me a bunch of questions about stuff that's way above my pay-grade. Just concentrate on your job.

The transport is going to drop us one click south of the sub-node. Here.' Voss activated the mission planner and a 3D image of the area appeared on all their HUDs. A small wood shielded the south and west of the building. To the north of the sub-node there was less shelter, a few trees but mostly just neat lawns and shaped shrubs. 'We infiltrate on foot and take up positions around the station. Then we wait.'

The mood on the transport was sombre now. All the Guardians rechecked their equipment and then cross-checked each other. By the time they arrived at the drop-off point close to the sub-node, they were ready. The transport pulled off the road and parked under the branches of a large tree. The Guardians bailed out like it was on fire and stood tense and alert at the edge of the road, peering into the trees, trying to see something un-toward. After a quick check, Voss led them into the undergrowth and they fanned out tactically through the trees. In just a few minutes, they had surrounded the sub-node and had blended into the terrain so skilfully as to be virtually invisible.

An hour went by and nothing happened. Everyone stayed perfectly hidden around the perimeter. Kaspar was on the treeline to the east of the sub-node. He lay in a shallow ditch hidden by a tamayada bush. He knew Janna was off to his left, but he couldn't see her – she was too good for that. Over to his right, however, he could see another tamayada twitching suspiciously. He keyed his throat mike.

'Hey, Hytner, stop fidgeting. That bush looks like it's about to take off.'

'Hell, Kas, I really need to pee,' replied the anguished Hytner.

'Hytner, you micro-bladdered twat,' hissed Voss. 'If you screw up this mission I will have you court-martialled, I kid you not. So either hold it or do it, but *nobody* moves until I say so.'

'But, sir—'

'And everybody stay off this channel unless you have something *tactical* to say.'

Kaspar looked on sympathetically as he saw the bush stop waving. He hadn't meant to drop Hytner in it but they couldn't afford to make even one mistake. Another forty minutes went by before anyone spoke again on the CommLink.

'Maintenance van just did a second slow drive-by on Purple One. Multiples on board, possibly three or more.' That was from Gina on the main road to the north.

'Roger that,' replied Voss.

A long-standing joke at the Academy was that the only reason for having numeracy and colour-blindness tests during the selection process was to allow for the use of the tactical mapping schema. Any selected area could be overlaid with a 'target' – a red bull's-eye in the middle, surrounded by an amber ring, then yellow, green, blue, grey and purple – with the numbers one through twelve arranged around the edge like on a clock face, with twelve always pointing true north. They practised with it constantly and not just on training exercises.

'Hey, check out the hot brunette at Green Three.' 'Hunk alert, Amber Twelve,' and similar lines were not uncommon.

'We've got four . . . correction, five unknowns entering Grey Six on foot – the same way we came. All armed,' Janna whispered from her position at Blue Six.

'Roger that. Weapons hot, people, but let them through,' ordered Voss. 'I want them right in the middle of it before we open up on them.'

Kaspar switched his rifle from standby to active and tried to spot them. He couldn't see the area code-named Grey Six from his position – it was shielded by a clump of trees and he was at Blue Five – but if Janna could see them then they were only metres away.

'The van has parked up on Purple Two. We have three more Insurgents deploying on foot.' Gina kept her voice low. 'And they're moving at a fair pace across the lawn towards the north of the building.'

'Stand by,' steadied Voss.

Moments later, the five Insurgents Janna had reported came into view. They were dressed in everyday clothes and didn't look around. They had the confident, single-minded gait of people who thought they had no need to worry.

Man, are they in for a shock, thought Kas. It was going to be like shooting fish in a fish tank.

The five stopped, looked around, then separated. Three split off to the left and headed towards the south-west corner of the building – no immediate threat there – but the other two were headed straight for Janna's position. Using his scope, Kaspar sighted midway between them, but kept the other eye open so he could see all five. This was Janna's call now.

They kept advancing.

Five metres . . .

Four . . .

Three . . .

Two . . .

Kas tightened his grip on his weapon and wondered if Janna planned to let them stand on her before firing. Just then, there was a sharp crack and a blue flash. It seemed to come almost vertically out of the ground and hit the guy on the left. Kaspar immediately shifted his aim onto the other guy and zapped him too while simultaneously shouting into his mike, 'Contact Blue Six, contact Blue Six. Two bogies down.'

He was already swinging his rifle around to the left to track the other three, but they had disappeared behind some trees. Janna was on her feet now and gave him a quick thumbs-up before running off to give chase. The comms loop was alive with reports.

'Contact in Green Two. Three bogies down,' came a smug report. Sounded like Mikey. 'All the guys from the van are out for the count!'

Oh, congratulations, thought Kaspar sarcastically. It couldn't have been exactly hard to shoot three unsuspecting guys moving across a manicured lawn with no cover.

Mikey needed to come play in the woods and try that.

'Green Seven Contact. One bogie down.'

Kaspar could visualize the area and could tell where the bad guys had been hit and where there was still a worrying silence. He dropped to one knee to consider his options.

If I head back to Purple Six, I can cut off any attempt to double back to the road, Kaspar thought.

He ran through the undergrowth, staying low, and headed towards where he thought someone might pop out. Sure enough, he emerged just in time to see two of the Insurgents running like rabbits towards the road. Kaspar fired at the guy in the lead, and he went down. Almost simultaneously, Hytner burst out of the trees and actually tripped over the second guy. Both their weapons went flying, so they would have been reduced to brawling on the ground – that's if Mariska hadn't arrived on the scene. A stun-shot would have zapped Hytner too, so she simply reversed her rifle and broke it over the Insurgent's face.

'Purple Six. Two bogies down,' reported Kaspar.

'Roger that. That's all of them then,' acknowledged Voss. 'Bring them all round to Amber One ready for transport.'

There was a general breakdown in strict loop procedure at that point, with a certain degree of whooping and congratulations. For once, Voss let it pass.

Kaspar looked down at a face that resembled a hamburger. 'Ouch. Do you think the Clinic throws in free facial reconstructive surgery?' he asked no one in particular.

Mariska beamed like a lighthouse as she helped Hytner carry the guy away. Kaspar knew better than to offer to help.

He slung his rifle and collected an armful of dropped weapons. He was just about to rejoin the rest on the front lawn when he heard a faint noise behind him. He didn't know exactly what it was, but he knew it wasn't good. Letting one of the captured weapons fall to the ground, he swore theatrically, then bent to pick it up again. As his fingers reached for it, he suddenly dropped all the weapons, shot out his legs to propel him sideways out of the line of any incoming fire and rolled onto his stomach to face the oncoming threat. As he swung his rifle round into a firing position, he half expected to be confronted by a startled squirrel, but instead he saw a masked ninja crouching right in front of him. No weapon, not even the deadly dagger, and a dozen metres or so from cover. This was a shot he couldn't miss. No ninja was fast enough to evade him now. As his gun came level and Kaspar's finger closed on the trigger, his target looked directly at him – and removed the mask.

It was Rhea.

Kaspar had his gun pointed directly at her – and yet he hesitated. He brought the gun up to his shoulder and sighted directly, making him even less likely to miss, but still he held back. He watched her through the magnifying scope and she stared back at him. How long did the look last? It couldn't have been as long as he thought. His finger was still motionless on the trigger as she quickly turned and slipped away into the trees bordering the road.

'Wilding? Are you going to honour us with your presence, or do you have a problem there?' asked Voss over the comms.

'No, sir,' replied Kaspar. 'No problem, I'll be right there.'

He'd let her go. She was a Crusader, worse still a ninja terrorist, and he'd let her escape. Kaspar could only hope that his decision wouldn't turn round and bite a chunk out of him.

But what else could he do? Rhea had saved his life.

'Now we're even,' he whispered.

Next time would be different.

And there would be a next time.

23

The ride back to base was a party.

'I swear we didn't really have to shoot the ones on the front lawn. They just dropped from sheer surprise when we opened up,' said Gina.

'Just as well considering how accurately you and Mikey shoot,' jibed Janna.

'Oh, that's cold,' Mikey said in mock outrage.

'Hey, Mariska, it was nice to see you hurt someone who wasn't one of us for a change. Exactly when did they teach us the break-a-gun-in-his-face technique? I must have been away that day.' Hytner had been exiled to the back of the wagon on account of his rank pee smell, but was obviously still high enough on adrenalin to be daring.

'Same day they taught us the don't-trip-over-a-terrorist technique,' she shot back.

Hytner smiled in good grace at the hoots of laughter that followed.

'That was fun!' said Mikey. 'Hey, Hytner, is it true you were so scared you wet yourself?'

'Nah,' said Gina. 'Hytner wasn't scared of the terrorists. It was Voss who made him water his legs.'

'Now now, ladies. I really don't know what you mean,' added Voss, beaming from ear to ear. 'For instance, I haven't even dismembered anyone for opening fire before I gave the order.' He looked pointedly at Janna.

'C'mon, boss. I waited as long as I could,' said Janna. 'The guy was so close I practically had to shoot up his nose.'

'That's OK, Rindt. In combat you sometimes have to improvise. So long as we get the results, that's fine.'

The only ones not joining in the general jollity were Russell – who had a badly twisted knee and a dislocated shoulder caused by putting his size twelves in a rabbit hole, losing his footing and falling shoulder first against a tree – and Kaspar.

'Has anyone got any painkillers?' Russell begged. 'I'm dying here.'

Four or five bottles of painkillers were hurled in his direction.

'Thanks, guys,' Russell said drily. 'Like I'm not hurting enough already.' Flicking open the top of the one bottle he'd caught, he shook a couple into his mouth and downed them in one.

'Want me to pop your shoulder back, Russell?' asked Mariska.

'Hell, no!' Russell replied immediately. 'You touch me, I'll shoot you!'

Everyone in the transport laughed.

'Did you get any of the Insurgents, Kas?' asked Gina.

'Yeah, I got a couple,' Kaspar replied.

'Then why the long face? We did good.'

'I'm just . . . Nothing. I've just got some stuff on my mind.'

'Like what?' asked Janna.

'Like the ninja,' said Mariska. 'Right, Kaspar?'

'What?' said Kaspar, whipping his head round in her direction. Oh, hell! How did she know? Had she seen what he'd done?

'The ninja,' Mariska continued. 'Isn't that what you call them? Janna said you described them as little acrobatic bastards dressed in black who skulk around in the shadows. She told me that you reckon these attacks usually feature one or two of them, but today there wasn't one.'

Why on earth had Janna told Mariska what he'd said at the Clinic? OK, he hadn't told Janna that his theory was confidential, but damn it, he hadn't expected her to blab it all over the barracks. Kaspar cast a glance in Janna's direction, who blushed and lowered her gaze to busy herself with checking her rifle.

'Kinda disproves your theory, doesn't it?' Mariska pointed out.

'Yeah,' nodded Kaspar. 'I guess it does.' Only too aware that Voss was watching him, he added, 'From now on I'll stick to soldiering and I'll leave the theorizing to others.'

'Makes a change for you to get something wrong,' smiled Mariska.

Kaspar shrugged. Waves of relief washed through him, but they weren't powerful enough to sweep away the guilt. He couldn't help feeling he'd just made the worst mistake of his life.

'Ninja,' he heard Voss say with a chuckle. 'Good name, Wilding! Good name.'

24

Back at base, everyone had to write up their 'After Action reports' describing everything they'd seen or done. Kaspar didn't want to lie, but how could he admit in writing that he'd had one of the Insurgents in his sights and had let her escape? To keep quiet or not to keep quiet, that was the dilemma. He was still agonizing over what to do when Voss stuck his head round the door.

'Wilding, the medic says that Russell's leg might be pretty badly messed up and he should have a full scan. Since you don't seem to be in a party mood, you can take him over to the Clinic and wait with him 'til he gets seen.'

'Yes, sir.'

Kaspar was only too glad to get out of his room and away from the din of what sounded like the others having one hell of a time. A trip off base was just what he needed to clear his head.

A few minutes later, he helped Russell to hop across to a ground car and secured him inside. Then he drove them the five clicks to the Clinic. Neither spoke much. Russell was slightly out of it thanks to a couple of painkillers, and Kaspar was too busy thinking he had committed treason by not shooting Rhea when he had the chance.

In just a few days, all the fixed points in his life seemed to have disappeared. First Dillon, and now his unshakeable views about 'us against them'. The Insurgents were savage, evil. The historical texts all said so. Their actions screamed their true nature. Having ruined their own lands, they were intent on dominating those belonging to the Alliance. Over the decades, overt hostilities had evolved into covert terrorist acts. The Insurgents weren't interested in peace. Their cause was nothing less than the total sub-jugation of the Alliance. They were heartless, ruthless murderers – and Rhea was one of them. So why hadn't he fired on Rhea when he had the chance? What did that say about him?

At last they reached the Clinic, which stood in the midst of huge, beautifully maintained grounds. Entry was via not one, but two rings of security fencing and Kaspar was frequently challenged to explain his presence. He had to show his ID so often it would've been quicker to glue it to his forehead. The last time he'd entered the Clinic had been as an escorted patient, so he hadn't been subjected to all this hassle, but from the little he could remember, the procedures hadn't been anywhere near as rigorous.

'I wonder why all the security?' asked Kaspar.

'They've had a lot of thermometer thefts,' replied Russell, still blissfully out of it.

'No, seriously. Why so tight?'

'You don't know anything,' said Russell with glee. 'I shall tell you – for Dillon's sake.'

'Thank you,' said Kaspar drily, wondering just how many painkillers Russell had taken. One thing was certain: it was more than the two he'd taken in the transport – and probably swallowed down with the help of a beer or five.

'There are a lot of worthwhile targets here, my uninformed friend. It's full of damaged Guardians like me. Plus Insurgents get treated and held in the detention cells here until they can be shipped off to maximum security. Plus it's a major bio-medical research facility. Plus this is where they bring sick Council members. Remember last month when Sister Kepple had a suspected heart attack? Treated right here, she was, in the new cardio unit. Plus . . . plus—'

'Yeah, thanks, I get it,' Kaspar interrupted now that Russell was finally running out of steam.

'They also step up the security when there's a High Councillor in residence, so that must be the case. Am I right, or am I right?' asked Russell. 'Or am I right?'

Kaspar sighed. When they came to a halt, he helped Russell onto the travelator that led to the main entrance, then went to Reception to book him in.

The receptionist scanned their IDs yet again. 'Sorry,' she said. 'Normally you could go straight in, but today we've had three major incidents so we've got lots of casualties to process. I'm afraid there might be quite a delay before we get to you, Guardian Russell.'

'That's OK,' shrugged Russell. 'I'm good, as long as I don't have to walk or stand for too long. Plus' – Russell leaned in further towards the receptionist and lowered his

173

voice to that of a stage whisper – 'plus, don't tell anyone but I can't walk or stand for too long.'

At the receptionist's bemused look, Kaspar explained. 'Painkillers.'

As they headed back to their seats, Russell said, 'Kas, you may as well go.'

'It's all right. I'll stay until you're done. Besides, you'll probably need help getting back to base,' replied Kas. 'But I wouldn't mind taking a look around. I didn't get to see much when I was a patient here.'

'OK. I'll comm you when I get seen by a doctor.'

Kas didn't need to be told twice. 'See you later then.'

The new part of the Clinic was ultramodern with a Major Trauma centre, a High-Dependency unit, a state-of-the-art Nuclear Medicine department with Imaging Laboratory, and a whole host of other specialist departments with names that Kaspar had never heard of – like LaserBaro Therapy. He wandered around for a while, reading the user-friendly info screens at the entrance to each section that described what they did, and a lot of it was truly amazing cutting-edge stuff.

Eventually, he reached a door marked NORTH WING – ANNEXE. Kaspar could see through the window that it led to the old, disused building that used to house the Clinic before the new building had been built. The door was chained shut and a sign across it read: NO ENTRY. DANGER OF DEATH. A smaller notice underneath explained that a combination of dilapidation, hazardous building materials and low-level nuclear contamination from antique medical equipment made the old building unsafe, and that no one should enter without protective clothing and the permission of the Clinic's Administrator.

Kaspar turned right, strolled past the immaculate dining room, on through the kitchen and out into the gardens. They were beautifully kept, and the smell of the wild melon plants reminded him strongly of the farm. He tried to identify the species. It was definitely a wild type, but the variegated leaf looked like it belonged on the genetically engineered varieties that only grew in the vast hydroponic towers on farms. His inner farmer wondered how they had made that work, so he stepped off the path, ducked under the lowest branches and cleared away some bark chips and topsoil to reveal the graft point. As he stooped down to examine the roots more closely, he could see through to the old building beyond – the North Wing.

That was odd . . . One of the side doors was open and two men were moving in and out. But what was weird was that they weren't construction workers or clean-up guys. They weren't wearing protective overalls, respirators, masks, hard hats or even gloves. They were doctors. And the open door didn't reveal the dingy, unlit interior of a derelict building but the bright clean interior of a functioning unit.

What was going on? Why would anyone be working there?

Maybe the warning notices were out of date? Or maybe they never related to the whole North Wing building?

But as a Guardian, Kaspar always had to consider less innocent explanations. Criminals using the building as a hideout? Or a drugs lab? Or terrorists scavenging nuclear waste in order to build a dirty bomb? Hell! What if there was something bad going on over there, this close to Council members?

Kaspar needed to get closer, to get a good look inside before he informed anyone else. He really didn't need the embarrassment of calling for another full Guardian raid only to discover two amorous doctors enjoying a private moment. He scraped out some more soil from around the roots of the melon plant, then lay down and wriggled his way through the plants until he cleared them and was on the other side. The two doctors had gone but they had left the door open. It wouldn't stay that way for long. Kaspar sprinted over to the old building, covering one hundred metres in less than twelve seconds. He caught the heavy door just before it swung shut, pausing for a moment to catch his breath. Until he found out what was going on, he couldn't afford to be seen. Strange. He noticed that although the door was old, the digital keypad on it was fairly new. Sliding past it into the building, he immediately felt and heard the industrial air conditioning.

So much for the North Wing being abandoned.

Senses on high alert, Kaspar peered through the glass panel in the first door on the left. The vast room was empty of both people and standard hospital furniture. Instead, it had a whole wall filled floor to ceiling with large drawers, each of which looked big enough to store a body.

A morgue.

Kaspar shuddered. He'd never liked morgues, and after getting Dillon's take on post-mortem romance, he liked them even less. The door had a datapad beside it, set into the wall. Kaspar swiped his fingers across it, only to be confronted by a series of numbers and names that meant nothing to him. He made his way to the second room. He peered through the glass panel again but had to duck down quickly. The two doctors were in there. Fortunately they were too busy to spot him, but this room seemed to be the same as the first. One of the drawers was open and the two were peering in. Kaspar ducked beneath the glass panel in the door and headed down the corridor. The third room was the same, as was the fourth, and the fifth. Each room was full of body cabinets, some against the walls while the majority were placed back to back in columns throughout the room. Each door had a datapad beside it, filled with virtual page after page of numbers and names or – more often than not – the word 'Unknown'.

How many bodies do they have here? thought Kaspar.

This old building wasn't derelict at all. It was air-conditioned, spotlessly clean and full to the rafters with neatly filed corpses. So why all the secrecy? He flicked through the datapad outside the room at the end of the long corridor. The numbers . . . were they dates? Yes, they had to be. All the dates on this datapad were recent, within the last three months. He needed to get a closer look . . .

Only just suppressing his natural instinct to avoid dead bodies, Kaspar slipped into the room, carefully shutting the door behind him. Apart from a faint but constant buzzing noise, it was quiet inside. And at least it didn't smell like a morgue. Just a standard hospital smell. He approached the wall of drawers and peered at the closest one. Near the handle there were a cluster of LEDs, presumably to show the status of the refrigeration. Under them was a digital label with a long central filing index reference. Kaspar pulled tentatively at the handle and the drawer slid out smoothly to its full extent with barely a sound.

He was right. There was a body inside.

But it wasn't dead.

25

The occupant of the drawer wasn't a corpse but a patient. This one was a man, naked and fully plumbed in with tubes, catheters, drips and electrodes attached to various parts of his body. He was motionless apart from the slow rise and fall of his chest, but his eyes were open and his eyeballs were scanning rapidly back and forth – like someone in a dream. But there was something strange about his eyes. Kaspar bent down for a closer look, only to recoil, shocked. The man's eyes were open and would remain so, permanently. He had no eyelids.

Looking down the body, there were numerous fresh scars where there had obviously been major surgery. Kaspar was about to close the drawer again when something made him walk down to the man's feet and look at him the right way up.

A shock of recognition made Kaspar gasp. This was the black guy he'd encountered outside the level three comms node in Wissant Avenue. What had happened to him? Why was he in such a state?

During the attack, Kaspar had knocked the guy out cold. But he would have sworn that the man was completely uninjured when the medics picked him up. Now he had scars everywhere.

And what the hell had happened to his eyelids?

Kaspar slid the drawer closed and looked at the long number. Now it made some sense. The first bit of the number consisted of a date and a time – about an hour after his encounter with the Insurgent. And the rest of the number? Kaspar had a hunch. He activated his CommLink, switched it to data mode and said, '864 Wissant Avenue.'

The screen of his HUD immediately displayed the quickest route for getting there and also displayed its exact coordinates. The coordinates matched the rest of the digits on the drawer.

Kaspar checked the labels on the front of the other drawers surrounding him. One had almost the same numbers on it. Kaspar opened the drawer. It was the second guy from Wissant Avenue that he'd knocked out but he was the same state. Tubes everywhere, scars all over his body and no eyelids. Kaspar checked some of the other drawers. A number had earlier dates. Quite a few were from the date of the Academy's graduation ceremony. These drawers contained the Insurgents from the attack on the Academy. But why were they all in medical stasis? Why hadn't they been shipped off to the maximum security holding facility?

Curious, he pulled open another drawer. A woman this time, but apart from the gender it was exactly the same story. Tubes, multiple scars, rapid eye movements and no eyelids.

What is it with the eyelids? Kas wondered. Could it be some kind of secret side effect of being zapped?

Kaspar thought back to the attack. Gina and Mikey had caught a guy who had tried to escape by jumping in the lake, and rather than risk him drowning when they zapped him they had jumped in after him and wrestled him out of the water next to the statue of Virtue Triumphant.

Kaspar used the zoom facility on his CommLink to locate the statue, and its coordinates appeared. He scanned the room for a drawer with the appropriate date, time and location.

'Eureka!' He found the drawer he wanted and pulled it open. But his elation turned to confusion as he looked at the man. Kaspar shut the drawer slowly. He knew from his friends that not only had this man been uninjured when he was picked up, but he'd been conscious too.

So how the hell did he end up here, scarred, on life support, and with no eyelids?

On his way out, Kaspar looked into a couple of the other rooms. They were all the same. Insurgents neatly stacked from floor to ceiling. Some of them had dates going back thirty years, and not one eyelid between them.

26

Kaspar was sitting on bone-dry grass. He stared off into the distance. He loved it up here so much — it provided the best view in the whole world. A stream meandered past the back of the cottage. To the far north lay more glens and hills, but a turn of his head and beyond the horizon . . .

That was where *they* resided.

He made no attempt to dampen down the burning hatred gnawing away at him.

It shouldn't've been this easy to feel like this about people he didn't know, but with each passing moment the feeling grew rather than lessened. They didn't understand peace and they certainly didn't understand compromise. Theirs was an 'if you're not one of us, to hell with you' philosophy. Children, women, newborn babes, it made no difference.

Kaspar deliberately turned away to try and drink in the serenity of the cottage and the surrounding greenery. But his eyes were constantly drawn back towards the horizon. And like a fire being stoked, his hatred flared and grew. Moments passed before he realized what he was doing, clutching at the grass beneath his hands and pulling it out of the ground in clumps.

His hands . . .

Those weren't his hands.

The hands he was looking down at were smaller, more feminine and considerably paler than his own brown skin. But Kaspar barely had time to notice and wonder before a tremor shook the ground beneath him. This one was bad, worse than any of the others that had gone before.

And it was getting worse.

Kaspar leaped up. He had to get off this hill. Get away. But to where?

He raced down towards the cottage. Nowhere was safe once they started running their experiments. Sometimes, if they were lucky, the ground only shook for a few hours. But sometimes, and more often than not of late, the after-shocks lasted for days. Crops, dwellings, people had all disappeared once the fissures in the earth opened wide to roar in protest. And the strength of the last few tremors had shaken the cottage to its foundations, causing plaster and chunks of the wall to fall. The thatch of the roof had split in places and no longer sat true on the cottage walls. The numerous cracks and gaps in the walls and roof meant the wind howled around the cottage like a banshee, and when it rained they had precious little protection.

Lost homes, lost lives, lost souls – all thanks to *them*.

One day . . . one day, he would make them pay . . .

27

Kaspar had never been one for dreaming. While his schoolmates had enjoyed or endured vivid dreams of surreal intensity, he had never been able to remember anything in the morning. Once or twice he had had the standard naked-in-public nightmare when a big exam or something stressful was coming up, but for the most part, nothing. All that had changed with Dillon's death. Every night now, he had vivid dreams that employed every one of his senses. Intense, three-dimensional, surround-sound dreams. And the dreams weren't just about Grandma and the cottage.

He never saw the rocket being fired, but he saw it fly towards the hovercar – and he saw and felt the exact moment it exploded. Every sight and sound was seared on his brain. He might have expected to relive the death of his best friend, but it didn't end there. Now the floodgates had opened, he dreamed of places he'd never been and people he'd never met and things he had never done – the peace of the idyllic cottage, the sense of freedom experienced while exploring the Donadara Forest, enduring with many others the cramped, unbearably hot living conditions in the Badlands, raids by Guardians Kaspar didn't recognize who used battering rams to break down doors that were already flimsy and rotting. The images were relentless.

Nor was it confined to sleep. He had what could only be described as mini-hallucinations all the time now. He would have suspected a brain tumour but his medical scans would have picked up on that. In particular, the smell of Grandma's bread was so intense that he had taken to wandering the market district in his off-duty hours, trying each family bakery he came to in the hope of recapturing the taste. None were exactly right.

On his next day off, Kaspar was strolling along a little side street just north of the Semler Bridge munching a mellisse croissant that came closer than most to the remembered smell and taste when he came across a small dance studio and gymnasium. The gym was mostly glass-fronted, revealing a foyer dominated by a large reception desk, behind which sat a woman in her twenties wearing a black T-shirt with the name of the gym written upon it in large white letters – LURIE'S SPA AND GYM. Kaspar stared at the place, knowing for certain that he'd never seen it before. Yet it was so strangely familiar, he felt compelled to go in. What was that about? Moments later he stood in front of the receptionist with a three-quarters eaten pastry in his hand and no idea what to do next.

'Hello,' said the receptionist, eyeing the croissant with something between suspicion and lust. 'May I help you?'

'Hi,' replied Kaspar, shoving the last morsel into his

mouth to give himself time to think. His eyes found a price list on the wall behind her, and he chose the first thing on the list. 'Massage, please.'

A wave of panic swept over him as he realized that the word massage could cover a multitude of things. But the menu also mentioned martial arts classes and aerobics – so it was probably legit. The receptionist took his money and gave him a towel before showing him through a door behind her.

'Room number three,' she said cheerily and left him to it.

Kaspar ambled down the brightly lit corridor. Holographic posters extolling the benefits of a healthy diet and lots of exercise lined the walls, their images changing every few seconds, the messages variations on a theme. He entered room three, which was halfway along the corridor. Thank goodness it wasn't as brightly lit as the corridor, which was almost blinding in its intensity. Inside the room, there were posters of the musculo-skeletal system on the wall and a smell of liniment that the air freshener couldn't quite mask. Kaspar got undressed before wrapping the towel around his waist and lying face down on a professional treatment table with the appropriate face-shaped gap at one end.

'What the hell am I doing here?' he asked himself again as he positioned his face over the hole which gave him a fine view of the dark wood floor.

Less than a minute later, his masseur arrived, or rather his masseuse. All he could see was a pair of sensible tennis shoes, two rather shapely legs and the hem of a crisp, white, knee-length overall.

'Is there anything in particular you'd like me to concentrate on?' she asked.

'Er, my left shoulder blade area?' Kaspar said tentatively.

Here we go. The moment of truth.

All he could do was hope this place was strictly above board. The slightest hint of impropriety and Voss would be down on him like a Badlands avalanche. A firm, warm hand came to rest gently on the point of his left shoulder and traced the outline of his shoulder blade, exploring the muscles. Kaspar began to relax. This was the real thing; this girl knew her joints.

'What's your name?' she asked as her other hand joined in the ballet of rubbing and pressing that was starting to spread warmth throughout his shoulder.

'Kaspar,' he replied lazily. She was good, and he was already starting to drift off. The nagging ache that he'd had ever since his fight in the desert was receding and he was back at the cottage by the stream.

'You have a lot of minor injuries,' she said as she continued, expanding across the spine to his other shoulder. 'Are you an athlete?'

'No, I'm a Guardian,' he replied.

The hands paused momentarily. 'A Guardian? Then why come here? I thought you had extensive gymnasium and medical facilities at your barracks?'

'Oh, we do, but I just like to get out of there from time to time and explore the town. Besides, you have softer hands than Carlo. He could strangle a wildebeest.'

The hands resumed their ballet, working the muscle groups in his neck. Her thumbs pressed expertly alongside his cervical spine while her fingers inched up by his larynx.

'Why did you pick this place, may I ask?'

'I dunno really. I was just passing and eating a mellisse croissant when I saw the sign.' He was really sleepy now. The faint sound of Grandma singing him a lullaby filled his mind.

'Mellisse croissant? They can be very bad for you if the mellisse berries aren't picked at the right time.' Her voice was calm, her hands worked deeper.

'Uh-huh,' he mumbled, more than half asleep. 'But all of a sudden I love 'em. Can't get enough of them. What's your name?'

The hands stopped again.

'Rhea,' she said softly.

A moment's pause as his brain processed the name, then the room suddenly clicked into focus. But too late. While the mental fog was clearing, Rhea leaped onto the table and straddled him, using the weight of her hips to pin down his waist. Her arms slipped around his neck into a full choke hold, cutting off the flow of blood to his brain. Her upper body pressed down on his back while her legs wrapped around the supports of the table, reducing his ability to wriggle free.

An expert could strangle you unconscious in less than five seconds – and Kaspar already knew she was an expert. He couldn't bring his arms into play. He was face down so he couldn't kick, and her legs wrapped around the table meant he couldn't slide off the table onto the floor. Instead, the world grew faint, and the lights around him dimmed. He was seconds away from passing out, or worse . . . After the initial panic, it didn't feel so bad, though. He felt relieved, unburdened, like he wasn't actually playing the game any more, but watching from the stands and able to enjoy the spectacle.

He was past and present, everyone and no one.

He was both Guardian and Insurgent.

He saw Brother Simon in conversation with his mum.

And there before him, standing stock still as they faced him, were thousands of people dressed in white, and all staring at him with lidless eyes in unsmiling faces. Kaspar was desperate to look away, but he couldn't. The eyes pulsed with an intense, white, blinding light, which grew brighter and brighter until the light was all he could see, and then . . . nothing.

Except an enormous frackin' headache.

Kaspar's eyes hurt. There was a roaring in his ears and the worst pain in his skull that he had ever known. He blinked a couple of times against the light. He was sitting on the floor? Where? Oh yes. The massage place . . .

Shit! Where was she? He swung round.

Rhea was also sitting on the floor, on the opposite side of the room. Her breasts were heaving from exertion under her overall, and she was watching him intently, warily. Her face was flushed and her hair dishevelled. Kaspar couldn't just see her fear, he could *feel* it.

He tried to get to his feet, but he moved too fast, got light-headed and wobbled. In any event, she moved faster, springing to her feet before he was up. She stood for a moment, poised like the fighter she was, ready to move in any direction, attack or defence.

'Do you know your enemy?' Rhea asked unexpectedly. 'Because it isn't me.'

He tried to speak, but all that came from his battered larynx was a croak. What was she up to? Surely she wasn't trying to recruit him to her side?

'Kaspar, why are all of you so accepting? Is it because it's easier to let others do your thinking for you?'

Kaspar had no idea what Rhea was on about.

They watched each other silently for a few moments, but when he tried to take a step towards her, she ran from the room. One moment she was there, the next she was gone, and there was nothing he could do about it.

28

Two painkillers had taken care of Kaspar's headache, but had done nothing to dispel his much larger problem. That he had failed to mention Rhea's help in the desert was bad enough. He didn't even know why he hadn't mentioned her. Everyone – except Mac – had just assumed that he had escaped from the hovercar crash on his own and he hadn't corrected them. Was he suffering from survivor guilt? Or a fear that he would be suspected of something if it were known that he had been helped by the enemy?

But then he had let her go at the Thirteenth District network sub-node ambush. He justified that one to himself as a quid pro quo, a case of 'now we're even'. But he had seen her so often now he could have painted her portrait from memory. He should at least release her description. And for all he knew, the gym was a hotbed of Insurgent activity. Certainly some of the locals would know who worked there. They might've seen things, useful things. He should call it in, organize a full-scale raid, interrogate everyone.

So why was he sitting in a café and agonizing? Why

was he protecting an Insurgent who had probably been involved in any number of outrages?

It came down to one question.

Why hadn't Rhea killed him?

Everything he'd been taught throughout his life told him that she was a vicious terrorist, utterly amoral, who would stop at nothing.

Except killing him.

Why did they keep meeting?

How had he found her again? Coincidence? Hardly.

He pushed his treasonous behaviour to one side for a moment and thought about the other stuff – the dreams, the hallucinations. He did a datanet search on near-death experiences and found that some of what he had seen was pretty classic. A bright light, the edited highlights of his life flashing by, figures dressed in white, feelings of detachment. The medics said they were symptoms of hypoxia, a lack of oxygen to his brain, and the mystics said they were evidence of an afterlife. But what about the rest? The cottage in a valley by the stream and Grandma weren't from his memory. And yet they seemed so real.

Up until very recently, Kaspar had been absolutely clear about what he was doing and why he was doing it. He and the other Guardians were on the side of the angels, and terrorists were pure evil. It was as simple as that. So why the creeping doubts, the sudden capacity for nuance? Why did the Insurgency seem more benign in dreams? Obviously he was grateful to Rhea for saving him, so was this a case of misplaced gratitude? Which led on to the question of why the Insurgents were in long-term medical stasis at the Clinic instead of in prison somewhere? And what the hell was the eyelid thing about?

Question after question battered at him relentlessly, giving him no peace. Kaspar's head was spinning. If only Dillon was here to talk to. Even Dillon laughing at his worries would've given him some much-needed perspective.

But Dillon was gone.

And Kaspar had never before felt so alone.

29

When Kaspar returned to barracks the recreation room was deserted and there was nobody on the accommodation floor. He had to go down to the Comms Centre to find anyone. Janna was working a shift on the Liaison desk. Kas wandered over.

'Where is everyone?' he asked.

'There was a major incident while you were out,' she replied sombrely. 'The chemical plant on Radial Four got hit at 1100 hours. They got clean away with a tank of luxothane gas.'

'Was anyone at the factory hurt?'

'No. They sneaked in, grabbed the gas and were gone before we could respond.' Janna spoke in a low monotone.

'Well, at least they can't do much damage with that.' Janna's deep frown told Kaspar he was missing something. 'Luxothane is the stuff we use for crowd control and hostage situations, right?'

Janna nodded.

'So what's the problem? The stuff is non-lethal and non-toxic, and you can't even use it unless you have an ultrasonic dispersal unit. It's useless to them.'

''Fraid not, genius,' she replied. 'The non-lethal stuff we use is luxothane-G. You get that by diluting pure luxothane a million times and adding the ultrasonic inhibitor.'

Now it was Kaspar's turn to frown. 'So that means . . . ?'

'If you have a tank of the raw, concentrated form, it's *absolutely* lethal, and it only takes a few minutes to weaponize it.'

'Oh my God . . . so they have a serious weapon.'

'It's more than serious, Kas. We're talking about a weapon of mass destruction.'

'Yes, but how the hell—'

The comms board made a muted bleep. Janna held up one hand for quiet while using the other to press her headset to her ear. As she listened, the colour drained from her face.

'What is it?' Kaspar asked.

She didn't reply. She just sat looking stunned.

'Janna? What is it? What did the report say?' That pricking sensation that Kaspar knew so well and dreaded so much was back.

Janna turned, her movements halting and jerky, like those of a puppet. 'The tank of gas . . . they don't have it any more.' She was on the verge of tears.

'What's happened?'

'They've already used it.'

'Shit. Where?'

'A school. Loring Primary School. Ten minutes ago. Oh, Kas, the bastards have killed over two hundred children and teachers.'

30

Kaspar was so angry. Even angrier than when Dillon died. He was furious at the Insurgents and at Rhea for making him question what was right, and most of all furious with himself for letting some ridiculous notion of chivalry and respect between enemies turn him into an idiot and, worse than that, a traitor.

He went straight to his room, logged onto the datanet and dictated a full After-Action report on his latest encounter with Rhea. He was thorough, even including the exact time and the address where he bought the mellisse croissant. The massage he explained as allowing him to observe his suspect surreptitiously. Kaspar read through what he'd just written. The truth in certain places had been bent, but not to the point of breaking.

Massage as covert surveillance? Was anyone going to believe that?

Kaspar needed to write about when Rhea had carried him to safety, but now was not the time. A message came through general comms that all unassigned Guardians were to report to ground zero. He was needed on the front line. But he vowed to submit a full report including his first encounter with Rhea the moment he got back – and to take whatever punishment Voss threw at him. He deserved whatever was coming to him, and worse. The only thing Kaspar regretted was that his parents' reputations could possibly be tarnished along with his. But Kaspar's personal reputation and his exposure to contempt and mockery weren't exactly the highest priority right now.

He tapped 'SAVE' on his half-completed report and headed out to join his colleagues at Loring School. There would be nothing to do except help put little bodies in body bags and run crowd control on grieving parents. But at least he would be doing something. Loring School was one of the schools that Kaspar had visited on his public relations stint. He remembered the five-year-old girl he'd met.

'My name is Gnea – with a G. It's pronounced Ni-ah! Everybody always gets that wrong.'

He still remembered her smile and the way she'd hugged him and thanked him for protecting her.

Protecting her . . .

Kaspar felt heartsick. He'd let an Insurgent go free when he had the chance to stop her in her tracks. Kaspar wondered in despair if Gnea-with-a-G was still alive.

'Stop it, Kas,' he berated himself. 'If you dwell on their faces, you're going to lose it.'

He forced himself to think of the terrorists instead. What kind of soulless evil would target a primary school? It was highly unlikely he'd ever see Rhea again – the last couple of times had been coincidences. But if he *did* see her again, he would zap her evil terrorist arse without hesitation, and take pleasure in doing it. And if the people at the Clinic mistreated her a bit, then so be it. Nobody could say that she didn't deserve it.

Gnea-with-a-G and her friends had got a lot worse.

Kaspar made it to the school, and the horrors painted in his mind by his imagination throughout the journey there were as nothing compared to the real horrors that lacerated his eyes and seared his mind on arrival. Kaspar knew that even if he lived to be one hundred and fifty, the images he saw that day would never leave him. Never in a million years could his imagination have conjured up anything like this.

Reality was more cruel.

It took every gram of control he had, and more he didn't even know he possessed, to keep it together. He and the other Guardians moved like automatons, gathering bodies and placing them in body bags. No one spoke. What words would be adequate?

Kaspar would wait till he was alone to shed tears for the fallen.

And the bitterest tears would fall for Gnea-with-a-G.

31

It was over a week since the attack on the school and Kaspar was still having trouble sleeping. The carnage at Loring School was something he didn't even need to close his eyes to see. Row upon row of tiny bodies laid out on the lawn. Grim-faced Guardians and medics bringing out more and more to join the ranks. It was the unreality of it that got him most, the eerie silence broken only by the sobs of the medics and the gasps of the Guardians who struggled to keep it together. Because it was gas and not a bomb, there was no damage. The victims had all just stopped and dropped. The décor of the classrooms was still bright and cheerful, and the contrast between the effects of the attack and its setting somehow made it that much worse. Some of the children had died painting pictures of their pets. Some had been eating break-time snacks. Some had been playing musical games or reading. The school looked like a playroom after a birthday party, full of books and toys and assorted bric-a-brac.

And dolls.

Discarded dolls lying crumpled on the floor, slouched over the tables, lying back in the chairs.

He had thought the tears would arrive the moment he was alone and able to take in the enormity of just what had happened, but he hadn't managed a shed a single tear. It was as if his mind was frozen. Thinking about the school, not thinking about the school; it made no difference. He'd had to submit to a compulsory psych evaluation along with all the other Guardians the day after the atrocity, but the answers required to pass weren't hard to figure out. It was merely a question of telling the psych evaluator what he or she wanted to hear. He'd passed with flying colours.

Faked it. Aced it.

But he couldn't get any respite from what had happened.

He felt each and every death as if it was one of his own. He eyed his stun rifle with distaste each time he had to clean it and check it. He longed for something more powerful, not to mention more permanent, to tackle the Insurgents. They didn't deserve the humanity the High Council still insisted they be shown. Kaspar's hatred of the Insurgents was nurtured and grew tall and strong with each remembered child's face.

And yet he couldn't cry.

After submitting his report about his run-in with Rhea, the gym had been raided of course, but to no avail. The receptionist was exactly what she claimed to be. No weapons, literature, plans, or secrets were found. Apparently Rhea had provided good references as a qualified masseuse and physiotherapist, using the name of Leah Mettiána, and had worked there for about six months. Of course she hadn't been seen since Kaspar's visit. And as for the delay in submitting his report . . . Kaspar still winced as he remembered how Voss had ripped into him.

'I don't care if she tied your windpipe into a pretzel. If you have any contact with a terrorist suspect, you call it in *immediately*. You do not go to a café for a sodding milk-shake before strolling back to report.'

Kaspar's report had also contained a severely edited version of his encounter with Rhea in the desert. He had put down his reticence to report their meeting to his shock over Dillon's death and the fact that he kept drifting in and out of consciousness and so wasn't sure if the meeting had been real or just a figment of his imagination.

The full story would have to wait. It wasn't that Kaspar was a coward, it wasn't that. But he was desperate not to be bounced out of the Academy before he could make amends for what he'd done. He needed to confront Rhea again, and this time there'd be no more mistakes. He'd make sure she paid – her and every other Insurgent who crossed his path.

Kaspar replumped his pillow for the umpteenth time and tried to get to sleep. His gaze fell on the empty bed that had once been Dillon's. Not for the first time, he wished his friend was still around. He turned to check the clock. Two-ten in the morning.

'Kaspar, go to sleep,' he told himself.

He closed his eyes, determined not to open them again

until morning, even if it meant viewing the back of his eyelids all night.

Kaspar awoke slowly again after less than half an hour, but it wasn't from a nightmare or a hallucination this time. He opened his eyes and was instantly awake, his mind alert. Why was he so cold? Freezing, in fact. The environmental controls had obviously packed up. Hang on . . . that smell . . . that wasn't air conditioning. That was night-time air. He rolled over to look towards the window. The curtains were billowing slightly.

I don't remember opening—

That was all he had time to think before the muzzle of a gun was pressed firmly under his chin. He froze.

'Don't move and don't speak.' The voice was calm – and female.

Looking at the side of his bed, he could see nothing but a shadow seated on his bed and an arm holding the gun, but he recognized the voice.

'Rhea?' he whispered.

'Turn on the light,' she ordered. 'Slowly.'

Kaspar groped behind him for the switch and did as he was told. 'How did you get in here?'

'I can get in anywhere at any time. You should know that by now,' said Rhea.

'I want to know how you got past the Academy's security.'

'I turned into a bird and flew over the electrified fence,' Rhea replied. 'Then I used my invisibility shield to sneak past the guards.'

Kaspar glared at her. Did she think she was funny?

'You people of the Alliance love to tell all kinds of ridiculous tales about us Crusaders,' said Rhea. 'D'you think we haven't read some of the stories you record about us on your datanet? They're laughable, and yet you all choose to believe them.'

'*Our* datanet? The Crusaders have computers and access to the datanet too,' said Kaspar. 'It's not exclusively ours.'

'We may have computers, but your High Council makes damned sure that the data we can access out in the Badlands is strictly limited,' said Rhea.

Was she telling the truth? It would certainly explain why the Insurgents were so hot on accessing data nodes from within Capital City.

'Are you saying the records about your lot aren't accurate?' said Kaspar.

Rhea's lips thinned. 'I'm saying we were left to rot in the Badlands and had no choice but to develop new skills to survive. And for that we are hated. But I guess I'm just wasting my breath trying to get you to see things from our side.'

Kaspar shook his head. He couldn't believe what he was hearing. Was she really seeking to justify what she and the other Insurgents did? 'You must be crazy to break in here.'

'Be quiet.' She glided to her feet like a dancer, but the gun didn't waver. Rhea took a step back as he sat up, putting a safe distance between them so he couldn't grab for the gun, and fished a small packet out of her black form-fitting outfit. He tore his eyes away from hers for long enough to look at the packet that she was now ripping open with her teeth. For one ludicrous second, he thought it was a condom, but it was a transdermal patch – a measured dose of some pharmaceutical on a flexible, adhesive plastic backing. A neat way of delivering all sorts of drugs into the bloodstream.

'Put it on,' she ordered, placing the thing face up on the bed.

It could be any number of toxins, but why would she bother? The silenced pistol would do the trick just as quietly and much more quickly. Unless, of course, she wanted to pass off his death as natural causes?

'What's the drug?' Kaspar asked.

'That's not important.'

'It is to me.'

Their eyes locked. He waited for her to thrust the gun at him dramatically and utter an 'or else', but she did nothing.

'Your gas attack on the school was despicable,' he said into the silence. It needed to be said.

Her eyes flashed. 'Not my attack.'

'Friends of yours, though.'

'No friend of mine carried out that assault.'

'So you don't know every Insurgent,' Kaspar dismissed with impatience. 'That doesn't make you any less guilty.'

'I do know each and every . . . patriot. None of them carried out that assault,' said Rhea. 'That is *not* the kind of thing *we* do.'

'You killed my friend Dillon. That was you.'

204

Rhea sighed. 'I regret that. Your car was getting too close and we couldn't afford to be discovered and have our position reported. My colleague was only trying to take out your car's engine.'

'Then he couldn't aim worth a damn,' said Kaspar scathingly.

'We try not to take life unnecessarily,' said Rhea quietly.

Kaspar stared. Was she serious? 'Yeah, right. Next you'll be telling me you didn't carry out the attack at the Academy during the Guardian Inauguration Ceremony either,' he said.

'No, we were responsible for that one,' Rhea admitted without hesitation. 'But there should have been no casualties . . . Were there many? Apart from my friends, of course.'

Kaspar frowned. One middle-aged woman had had a heart attack, he remembered. Most if not all of the Insurgents had been zapped – and he knew where at least some of *them* were now . . . 'Only one serious casualty during the Academy attack – but that was more luck than judgement on your part,' he said with contempt.

'We never leave such things to luck,' Rhea replied. 'Now put on the patch.'

'Why?'

'I need to know something, and I need to know that it's the truth,' she said quietly.

Kaspar looked at the patch. It really could be anything. He picked it up. 'I put this on or you kill me?'

'If you really believe I could kill innocent children, then killing you wouldn't even make me blink.'

Kaspar scowled, making no attempt to disguise his loathing. Rhea met his glare with composure, though for just a second Kaspar thought he saw a shimmer in her eyes. He was obviously imagining it. Kas wasn't sure if it was because he thought she would kill him anyway or if he just wanted to know why she was there, but he defiantly stuck the patch on his neck.

Within a couple of seconds, his limbs started to get heavy and his head started to swim. It was like being drunk. Very drunk. He collapsed back down onto the bed. She stepped closer and checked his eyes. He felt his brain start to fog over. He struggled desperately to hold onto his senses, though his body didn't move, couldn't move.

'My arms . . .' OK, his voice was still working at least. But his brain felt like it was folding in on itself. 'My arms feel palarysed . . . pa-ra-lysed. Did you poison me? I'm . . . you've . . . you have great eyes . . . they're really green . . . no . . . not green . . . they're turquoise-blue . . . With the lights down low, they look violent. No . . . *You're* violent . . . your eyes are vi-o-let. With the lights down. Low.'

Rhea took his pulse and then sat on the edge of the bed. 'Shh! And I haven't poisoned you,' she assured him, 'It's just a muscle relaxant combined with a strong hypnotic.'

Kaspar nodded slowly.

'How did you find me?' she asked.

'Find you? You found me. I live here.'

'No, before. How did you find me at the gym?'

'Gym? I know someone called Jim. He's really tall.'

'The gymnasium, where I gave you the massage – how did you find it?'

'Oh yeah . . . the massage. You have great hands, apart from the strangling thing. That was bad. But you have great hands – and boobs too. I like your boobs. I like them a lot.'

'Concentrate. Why did you go to that *particular* gymnasium?'

''Cause of the croissant and the cottage by the stream. She smells of mellisse berries, you know.'

'The cottage? What about the cottage?' Rhea's faraway voice suddenly became sharper in tone. 'Where is it? Tell me about it.'

'Oh, you'd like it. It's nice, near a stream that runs into a river. The wind talks to you if you listen carefully. It's such a lovely cottage. There are mellisse bushes out back, and in early autumn they fill the whole cottage with their smell. Wolves don't like mellisse berries. Did you know that? The bushes keep the wolves away. The berries keep the wolves at bay. Hey, I'm a poet! I should turn that into a song.' Kaspar began to hum tunelessly to himself.

Rhea leaned back and studied him hard. After a few moments, she took off her gloves, leaned forward again and placed both palms on his temples.

Kaspar started sweating. The tiny part of his brain that could still operate rationally wondered if she had poisoned him after all, or if he was having an allergic reaction to the drugs. His mind was a whirl of images and memories, some his own, most not. His parents in their uniforms, Grandma at the cottage, working on his uncle's farm, Insurgent attacks, screens with screeds of data flashing past too fast to read, the face of his mother . . .

'What're you doing?' Kaspar whispered.

'Some of us Crusaders have a heightened sense of empathy. We can share emotions and sometimes even memories. Seems you have it too,' said Rhea.

'Did you give it to me? 'Cause if you did, you can have it b-back. It sucks.' Kaspar nodded his head vehemently. His head was swimming and he felt totally blitzed. What the hell had she given him?

'Yeah, it's a bitch, isn't it? Maybe that's what the Alliance needs. More people sharing the pain of others whether they want to or not,' said Rhea.

Kaspar couldn't imagine anything worse. Rhea stood up abruptly and walked to the window. She was going. He was going to be alone again . . .

'Don't leave . . .' he whispered.

'Why not?' Rhea turned to ask.

Kaspar had no idea why he was so desperate for her to stay. She was evil, a stone-cold killer, but after all the recent events Kaspar didn't want to be alone.

'You're having nightmares?' Rhea questioned.

Kaspar nodded.

'So am I. Every night,' said Rhea. 'Every time I fall asleep I see images of death and mutilation and the images don't stop until I'm awake. And sometimes not even then.'

Kaspar wondered at the accusatory tone to her voice. If

she was having bad dreams about her past, how was that his fault?

'I'm sharing the nightmares of all my fallen friends, captured and locked away by the Alliance,' said Rhea. 'Your people are cruel beyond words.'

'I don't understand,' said Kaspar, but at that moment unbidden images from the North Wing of the Clinic crowded into his mind.

'Yes, you do. But you don't want to. That's your trouble,' said Rhea.

They regarded each other. Kaspar couldn't shake the feeling that Rhea was trying to tell him something. 'Talk to me. I need to understand why . . .'

'I should go,' said Rhea. And yet she hesitated.

'Please don't leave me alone.'

After a moment she returned to the bed. She stood looking down at him, as if still trying to make up her mind what to do. Then she sighed softly and slipped under the sheet next to Kaspar. Now face to face, Rhea put her arm round his waist, and closed her eyes. Her face was mere millimetres away. Kaspar could feel her breath, warm and moist, mingling with his own.

Joining the Guardians, meeting Dillon for the first time, hitting on Janna at the Sci-Fair only to realize afterwards that Janna had eyes for no one but Mariska, graduation, Brother Simon . . .

Images tumbled through Kaspar's mind uncontrollably.

The Clinic, Loring School, Gnea-with-a-G . . .

'Oh, my God . . . all those children. All those poor

children. How could you do it? Why? Why? I don't understand . . .' Kaspar started to cry, awkward, racking sobs that he couldn't control.

Lying beside him, holding his head in her hands, tears streamed from Rhea's eyes too.

'Why?' Kaspar whispered.

He was now incapable of saying anything else. He was just desperate to know the reason. But Rhea didn't reply, she just cried with him, holding him tight. Kaspar clung to Rhea as if she were his life raft in an emotional storm, but Rhea didn't attempt to push him away or let him go. And the sorrow in her eyes was a mirror to his own.

Close to four in the morning, Kaspar finally fell into a deep, dreamless sleep.

Lying on her side, Rhea studied Kaspar. He made no sound, though the movement of his chest was easy and regular. It had taken him a long time to stop shaking. The slightest of smiles and a kiss on the lips later, Rhea got up and slipped out of the window before disappearing into the pre-dawn shadows.

32

It took a long time for Kaspar to realize that the incessant buzzing he could hear was real and not just the sound of his brain spinning. His head still buried under the pillow, he fumbled around on his bedside table for the alarm. Finally grasping it, he flung it across the room with as much force as he could manage. The buzzing inside his head still continued.

Kaspar couldn't figure why he felt so wrung out. Normally, he sprang out of bed as soon his eyes opened. Dillon used to hate that. The alarm went off, Kaspar sprang out of bed, had a shower, got dressed and tried to get his comatose roommate to class while Dillon snored, swore, threatened and snored again. But today Kaspar's tongue was stuck to the roof of his mouth and he just wanted to sleep for a week. Everything in the room was a swaying blur, his stomach an erupting volcano of acid, and every muscle in his body felt like Mariska had spent the night using him as a punch bag.

Great! All of the hangover with none of the drinking. Kas wobbled precariously as he struggled to his feet.

'Flu,' he sighed. 'That's all I need.'

He headed for the shower, setting the controls for the lowest temperature and maximum power – what Dillon used to call the masochist setting – and stood there until his head cleared. Once he had shocked himself awake, he showered properly, but there was a sticky area on the right side of his neck that was really difficult to shift. It was also slightly sore. Shower over, Kaspar looked in the bathroom mirror to examine his neck. The area was slightly reddened, but he had no idea what had caused it.

Once dressed, as he was leaving to go down to mess, he realized something. It was the first night in a week that he hadn't had a nightmare.

33

Kaspar's 'hangover' turned out to be the high point of his day.

'Kaspar mate, you look rough,' Janna informed him as they waited in the queue for breakfast.

'However bad I look, I feel worse,' said Kaspar. If only his head would stop hammering, just for five minutes. 'Can't this queue move any faster?' he grumbled. 'I need coffee now!'

The shriek of the siren made Janna jump and shot through Kaspar's head, doing him no favours.

'Damn it.' Janna frowned. 'My tongue was hanging out for bacon, eggs, sausages and toast.'

'I just wanted some coffee,' sighed Kaspar.

But it wasn't to be for either of them. They raced out of the building along with everyone else.

'What is it this time?' Janna called out to Gina.

'An attack on a government building,' Gina yelled.

'Damn. The terrorists are really ramping up.' Janna shook her head.

She and Kaspar jumped into a small transport and eight others also piled in. Janna fired up the motor while Kaspar

213

checked that the computer had correctly auto-logged who was on board. They left the barracks and hit the road as part of a convoy heading downtown.

The traffic on the network was relentless. Reports of terrorist attacks were springing up like weeds.

They'd been driving for less than ten minutes when Voss's voice came over the CommLink: 'Attention, all Guardians. 229 Voss to vehicles three, seven and eight. New target. Power distribution node in the fourteen-hundred block of Radial Eight.'

Kaspar and his group were in car seven, so Janna immediately pulled them out of the convoy and led the group of three vehicles towards the power node to the west of the city.

'This is big, Kas,' said Janna. 'The Insurgents are really going for it today.'

For a couple of hours they raced around from incident to incident. Sometimes they arrived in time to do some good – and sometimes they didn't. At around 1300 hours, a support assistant turned up carrying rucksacks of supplies. One contained field rations, the other spare battery packs for their stun rifles.

Whilst Kaspar was halfway through gulping down a hot black coffee, a major report came through over the net.

'Seismology indicates a large explosion – strength four – in the area of Radial Six and Rowan Avenue. Acoustic profiling confirms. All non-engaged units respond.'

The geology department at the University had

originally set up the network of seismographs to monitor earthquake and volcanic activity, but the instruments were so sensitive that they could also detect explosions. Within seconds of a bomb going off, the Guardians got a location that was good to within twenty metres.

Janna started up the transport and spun the car around to accelerate hard onto the elevated section of Radial Seven heading downtown. Kaspar scanned through his telescopic sight. There was quite a deep valley that separated the road they were on from Radial Six where the explosion had been reported. He tried to get an early glimpse of where they were going.

'Hold on, Janna,' he said.

'No, buddy, *you'd* better hold on,' she replied as she swerved round a civilian who was strolling across the road like he hadn't a care in the world.

'Something's wrong here,' Kaspar persisted.

'No kidding, genius.' Janna took her eyes off the road just long enough to give him an incredulous look. 'Just when in the last five hours of mayhem did you get your first clue?'

'Listen, Janna, that report is wrong. We're being spoofed.'

'Come again?'

'Radial Six and Rowan? Don't you recognize the address?'

'Yeah, of course I do. It's the Museum of Light. Very big, very pretty, and I should imagine, an irresistible target for terrorists.'

215

'Stop! Stop the wagon. Janna, please, I've gotta show you something.'

Janna looked doubtful, but slewed the car to a halt anyway.

A chorus of protests broke out from the back.

'What the hell?'

'Why have we stopped?'

'C'mon, Janna! We're wasting time.'

'This is no time for sightseeing!'

'Look there.' Kaspar was aiming his rifle. 'Bearing twenty degrees.'

Janna picked up her weapon and followed his lead. 'This had better be good. What am I looking for?'

'The Museum of Light.'

Janna lifted her aim slightly, out of the valley, and swept a couple of degrees to the left. 'Well?' she asked.

'You see the Museum Tower?'

'Yeah.'

'Do you see any broken windows?'

Janna's brow furrowed. 'No,' she said quietly.

'Are you telling me that someone detonated a strength-four explosion, and that a hundred-metre-tall glass tower didn't get a single broken window?'

'Maybe the blast was underground?' She didn't sound convinced.

'No, the acoustic profiling microphone network confirmed it. So it was above surface. Someone's messing with us.'

'Don't talk wet, Kas. Who would . . . ?'

'I'm telling you, we're being spoofed. Maybe they've hacked the system. You know these guys have a real thing for computers. Maybe they're running the warning systems?'

'Call it in for instructions,' ordered Janna. 'I'm not getting court-martialled over this.'

Kaspar got on the comms net and spoke to Central.

'4518 Wilding to Central. The seismic alert at Radial Six and Rowan is not confirmed. I repeat – not confirmed. Run an authenticity trace on all the intel.'

'Negative, 4518. You are not authorized to request that trace,' came the reply. It sounded like that snot-rag, jobsworth Nirven.

'Listen, someone is sending in false reports. Either we're being pulled into an ambush, or it's a diversion. You've got to—'

'229 Voss to Central,' the radio crackled. 'Run Wilding's authenticity trace. Do it now.'

'Roger that. Tracing.' The office-bound git didn't sound quite so officious now.

Kaspar glanced down at the hovercar's tactical display. It was lit up with incident reports all over the city. A moment later, it went blank. For ten seconds there was nothing except the rapid blinking of the SECURE light as the Guardian network resynched its protocols and all the computers exchanged authentication codes. Then the map of the city came back.

'Oh, crap!' exclaimed Janna.

Three-quarters of the incident reports were gone. All

over town, Guardian IDs could be seen converging on nothing and setting up perimeters around non-events.

'We've been had,' said Kaspar. 'And I don't think they did it for jollies.'

Attacks continued sporadically for another thirty minutes. Then, around three in the afternoon, a massive tanker bomb exploded at an industrial park on Radial Nine. That one wasn't a fake. Everybody in the city felt it and saw the smoke plume so high that it obscured the sun.

By nine o'clock that night Kaspar and the others had returned to barracks. They had been to every corner of the city, chasing a mixture of ghosts, shadows and real incidents, and Kaspar wasn't the only one who was dead on his feet.

Others started to drift in and tell their stories. A lot of false alarms and some genuine attacks, a few serious and some just nuisance value.

'You should see the office block on R-Nine. Looks like it got carpet-bombed. Lucky for them and us that most of the workers were away at a staff conference.'

'I spent the whole day chasing wild geese,' complained Sykes.

'And they hit a shedload more computer nodes.'

'Waste of time! We can reroute quicker than they can blow 'em up.'

Kaspar sprawled on a sofa, listening intently as his friends recounted their experiences. He would have no trouble falling asleep tonight, that was for sure. Now if only he could guarantee it would be a dreamless sleep . . . The back of his neck began to tingle. Kaspar turned. From further along the sofa, Janna was watching him.

'What?' Kaspar frowned.

'What do you think the point of today was?' asked Janna carefully.

'How on earth would I know?' The room had gone strangely quiet. Kaspar looked around. All eyes were on him. 'Am I missing something?'

'It's just . . .' Janna picked at the words. 'You have a habit of being in the middle of whatever is happening. Either that or you're always one step ahead of the rest of us.'

A chill crept up Kaspar's spine. Eyes filled with varying degrees of suspicion awaited his reply. Kaspar stood up slowly, pressing the thumb and index finger of each hand together until his bones must surely shatter.

'Just what are you implying?' he asked quietly. 'And speak up so we can all hear you.'

'Calm down, Kas,' Janna soothed.

Pressing his fingers together wasn't working. 'Calm down? I want to know what the hell you mean!'

'I don't mean anything,' Janna denied.

'You think I'm the mole Voss was talking about, don't you?' Kaspar challenged.

'No one thinks that, Kas. You're over-reacting,' said Janna. 'I guess you're just more observant than the rest of us, that's all.'

Kaspar looked around again. The moment he caught anyone's eye they looked away or found something else to do, but the very air in the break room was tainted with suspicion. Even Mariska couldn't quite meet his gaze.

He strode out of the room without a backward glance.

34

Kaspar grabbed a snack from one of the vending machines and headed to his room. He knew everyone was frustrated and looking for answers but he had none to give. And he very much resented the way that his so-called friends thought otherwise. The mole in their midst still hadn't been caught, but why suspect him? His best friend Dillon had been killed, for God's sake. Or maybe that was part of the reason why he was under suspicion?

But Kaspar's frustrations ran deeper. Something about this whole last series of attacks was off, at a profound level. Kas retrieved the research he had previously done with Mac. He wanted to add in what he'd learned today, plus he needed some help.

'Hi, Mac, it's me – Kaspar. Are you busy?' he Comm-Linked her.

Her image appeared almost at once. 'Hello, stranger.' Mac smiled. 'Social call?'

'Not exactly. Can you come over to my room? I need you.'

'Oh, really?' There was a throaty chuckle. 'Don't I get a say in the matter? Or even a bunch of flowers?'

'What? No. Sorry. I didn't mean . . . I mean, I'd never ask you to do that.'

'Never?' Mac looked crushed.

Kas took a deep breath. 'Mackenzie, stop torturing me! I was wondering if you'd help me out with some more computer research?'

Mac burst out laughing. 'So you only want me for my mind? Ah well!'

'Mac, please . . .'

'Course I can help.'

Finally!

Mac chuckled again. 'OK, I'll be there as soon as I can.'

Kaspar had time to finish his snack and tidy up a bit before Mac knocked on his door.

'Come in,' he said, holding the door open.

'So what's up?'

'I was just fiddling about and I thought of you.'

Mac smiled as Kaspar groaned inwardly, but luckily she took pity on him and let his comment slide. 'Fine. What searches are you running?'

Kaspar relaxed. 'OK, I'm adding in today's attacks. We have the same two-way split between ninjas hacking the computer network and the phantoms just being hell-spawn. But today we had a new twist. Phoney attacks. Computer ghosts. Can we see them graphically?'

'No problem. If I just do this . . . and that . . .' Her fingers flew through the data screens with elegant efficiency.

And suddenly Kaspar was looking at a map with all the

confirmed attack locations in red, and all the spoof locations in blue.

'Just as I expected,' said Kaspar. 'There's no overlap or obvious pattern between the reality and the fiction. Pull the Guardians away on some fool's errand before actually creeping in somewhere else.'

'If you say so,' shrugged Mac. 'Tactical military stuff is your area of expertise, not mine.'

'Let's try something else. Can you categorize the attacks by death toll?'

'What thresholds do you want?'

'Oh, I dunno. Mindless phantom atrocities with civilian casualties at one end of the scale, down to bloodless ninja stuff at the other?'

'OK, let's try this . . .' The screen cleared, then a new, more colourful display appeared. 'I've plotted more than five civilian casualties in red, diversionary attacks where only Guardians got hurt in yellow and bloodless ninja jobs in blue.'

This time, the spread wasn't so neat. Yellow markers were scarce. Some of the red markers were pretty close to blue. A couple in particular caught his eye.

'There.' Kaspar stabbed his finger at the screen. 'Can you pull up the details for these two?'

'Er . . . they're actually from today. A tanker bomb detonated at an industrial park at the corner of Radial Nine and Kreil at 1417 hours, killing eight workers, and the other was . . . an unauthorized computer access from a node at 7675 Kreil at 1400 hours.'

'How far apart are those two addresses?'

Mac did some more technical magic.

'Two hundred and seventy-two metres.'

Kaspar paused. 'What kind of moron sets off a diversionary attack less than half a click from their target and does it seventeen minutes *after* they achieved their objective?'

'We already thought that the ninjas and the phantoms might be different groups. Maybe they didn't coordinate and this was just a coincidence?'

'No. Today was a big deal. The Insurgents made a concerted effort.'

'A concerted effort to do what?' asked Mac.

'I wish I knew,' sighed Kaspar. 'Look at the blue markers. They hit data archive nodes, electrical nodes, database nodes. That feels to me like there's a method, a plan behind all this. Now look at the red markers. They're more random, an office block here, a car bomb there, and where those attacks happen near blue markers, they're always *after* the event – not before. Believe me, the ninjas wouldn't allow that kind of screw-up.'

'Could it be stupidity on their part? My dad is always saying that they're not too bright.'

Kaspar shook his head. 'I don't believe that any more.'

Mac regarded him. 'A coincidence?'

'I don't believe in coincidences. Can you bring up a list of all high-casualty attacks over the past three years?'

Mac did as requested, and Kaspar peered at the results.

'Anything?' she asked.

'Hmmm. These attacks were all spectacular and deadly, but . . .' Kaspar was worried where his thoughts were leading. 'They didn't kill anyone who was . . . shall we say . . . significant. They didn't do real damage to the infrastructure either. They were all soft targets in residential and industrial areas.'

'What's your point?'

'The terrorists avoid government agencies, they don't directly target Guardians, and they seem to target people who don't count.' Kaspar immediately felt guilty for expressing it that way. 'Sorry, I didn't mean to sound like an elitist twat. It's just that they target—'

'People who aren't vital to the state,' Mac finished for him. Her fingers were a blur as she summoned up more detailed data. 'School children, suburbanites, factory workers.'

'So my suspicion was right,' Kaspar said grimly.

'I don't understand.' Mac's frown deepened. 'Are you saying that there is another group at play here who have nothing to do with the Insurgents?'

'Think about it. The cylinder of gas that got used at Loring Primary School weighed less than twenty kilos and these ninjas are super-fit. I know; I've had personal experience. And they could steal the sugar from your coffee.'

'So?'

'So why waste such a potent, transportable weapon on a primary school? Why not sneak it into somewhere . . . strategic? They could have killed hundreds of Guardians –

or wiped out a government ministry. Why go for children?'

'Maybe there was something else about the school?' offered Mac. 'Apart from the kids?'

Kaspar pulled up the report on the attack and Mac leaned forward for a closer look, her expression sombre.

'Nope,' she said. 'Seems to be a fairly normal school with fairly normal pupils.'

Kaspar stared at the screen. That couldn't be right . . . 'Mendel?'

'Who?' asked Mac.

'Mendel.' He pointed at the screen. 'The Guardian in charge of the Loring School investigation is Lawrence Mendel.'

'You know him?'

'Yes, from the Academy. He's an instructor and a total moron. He has an encyclopaedic knowledge of Civic Code violations, but no common sense and *zero* forensic skills.'

'And he's in charge?' Mac asked, appalled.

'Exactly. Why entrust the investigation of a major terrorist attack involving weapons of mass destruction to a man who couldn't find his own butt with both hands and a satnav?'

Kaspar and Mac stared at one another.

Mac whispered, 'This is starting to look uncomfortably like . . .'

'A conspiracy.'

35

Kaspar had an idea now. The schizophrenic nature of the Insurgency was starting to make sense. On the one hand there were the *non-violent subversives* – precise in their attacks, sneaking into strategic locations and military installations, using just enough muscle to achieve entry. This group avoided civilian casualties wherever possible while doing who-knew-what with the Alliance data networks.

And on the other hand there were the *phantoms* – the maniacs – killing and maiming indiscriminately, keeping everyone in a state of terror. At first glance – and viewed in isolation – the phantoms' attacks seemed random, designed to create chaos and carnage and very little else. But studying the pattern behind them, the indiscriminate attacks hadn't hit one single target of *strategic* importance. Not one. Only soft targets: schools, shopping centres, the odd travel hub. With all the intel they must've gathered over the years, what were the odds of the Insurgents not taking on and taking out one single vital node or hub that would bring the Alliance to its knees, even if only temporarily?

Kaspar suddenly felt sick. What he was thinking was horrible. The idea that school children could be sacrificed like pawns on a chess board in order to achieve some end was totally obscene.

But what else was there?

'So let me get this straight,' said Mac. 'The Insurgency never make any demands. They steal weapons from secure weapons facilities and knowledge from our datanet without being detected. They pass up the opportunity to kill VIPs and Guardians, and yet they go for harmless children. Then someone from our side assigns an incompetent to investigate the affair. And some of the spectacular attacks we've had recently come within a hair of screwing up other Insurgency operations.'

'It doesn't make sense, does it?' said Kaspar. 'The only explanation that fits is that it really is two completely separate groups responsible for all this. And we all buy the line that it's one and the same group responsible for the lot.'

'And one group is deliberately causing mass destruction just to muddy the waters for the Crusaders?' said Mac sceptically. 'Or is it the Crusaders trying to muddy the waters for someone else?'

'It doesn't make sense that way round,' Kaspar pointed out. 'The Crusaders are already viewed as the evil scum of the planet for all the atrocities and the mindless violence their Insurgents carry out. But what if someone – some other group – is trying to make sure this war never comes to an end? That we in the Alliance never negotiate with the Crusaders because of the evil acts of their Insurgents. Except the evil acts aren't theirs . . .'

'But why?' said Mac. 'Why on earth would anyone in their right mind seek to prolong this war?'

Kaspar remembered one of his mum's favourite sayings. 'Mum used to say that there are only two reasons for continuing with any war – power or profit. I was too young to understand what she meant at the time. I'm beginning to get it now.'

Mac and Kaspar both paused to consider what they were saying; it seemed preposterous, outrageous, and yet it smelled strongly of something at least approaching the truth.

'Brother Simon paid me a visit and said, "We are united in our opposition to these people. As long as we stand together, they cannot win." Well, what if the phantoms are a tool to create unity within the Alliance so we all turn against the Crusaders?' said Kaspar softly. 'What if the phantoms are the Bogeyman, the monster under the bed, created to focus our hatred in the wrong place?'

The more he thought about it, the more sense it made. Whatever the Insurgency did, it was augmented with some greater violence – like at Loring School. Anytime there was a danger of a swell of public opinion crying out, 'Let's put an end to the violence and sit around a table to negotiate a peaceful outcome,' there would be a bloody outrage and everyone would rally around the cause of fighting a monstrous enemy.

It was horrible, but it felt like more than mere theory.

Kaspar hated the idea, but it fit the facts. He risked a glance at Mac. Her expression was sombre but no longer sceptical.

'You think I'm right, don't you?' he said quietly.

Mac looked directly at Kaspar. 'I'm desperately trying to come up with another theory that works, but I can't.'

They regarded each other, the full import of what they'd discovered hitting both of them hard.

'OK, we need to figure out how to prove or disprove all this,' said Kaspar. 'Firstly, we need to find out who had access to the gas. The thieves had been and gone before anyone knew anything about it.'

Mac sat back in her chair. Kaspar was grateful that she didn't challenge his use of the word 'we'.

'We also need to know who could get access to the school without raising suspicion,' he added.

'Hmmm . . . maybe we could also follow up the forensics on the explosives in the truck that went off today,' said Mac. 'And determine where the truck came from.'

'The one thing that convinces me more than anything else that I'm right is that someone had to have enough clout to influence the assignment of Mendel to the investigation of the Loring School gas attack. An attack like that should have our best people on the job, not our worst,' said Kaspar.

There was another long pause. Kaspar's mind was racing.

'I could run a correlation study of terrorist events against Guardian trackers,' Mac said at last.

'You're talking "geek" again,' Kaspar sighed.

'Take the truck bombing as an example,' said Mac. 'We know the truck was stolen from behind a supermarket at 0800 hours this morning, parked at the target at 1330 and exploded at 1417. Well, the bots can find which Guardians were near the shop between 0750 and 0805. Then they can determine who was near the target between 1320 and 1340 hours. We can also ask them to determine the nearest Guardians to each outrage and ask them to tell us which Guardians were on shift when the crimes were committed.'

'Or off shift but within the vicinity maybe? If you're driving a huge bomb across the city, you probably don't want to be interrupted by a call to rescue a cat from a tree.'

'Good point. We'll run it both ways. If it works, and we get lucky, then we'll get some statistics telling us which Guardian or Guardians were within a kilometre of all the bombings.'

'Great. Of course, all this is academic,' Kaspar noted sourly. 'If I'm right and there really are high-level Guardians involved, then they're going to notice what we're doing. We already know that they monitor bot-searches.'

'There are ways round that.' Mac winked. 'We make our enquiries in the form of bot-parasites. We infect some bots, ask them some simple questions like where to buy pizza – and initiate the search. Our bots will tell us where to get pizza – and the parasites will tell us what we really want.'

'Yeah, but surely *they*'ll find them too when they run their activity trace or whatever?'

Mac was offended. 'I know what I'm doing, thank you. A routine activity trace consists of trapping a bunch of bots and asking them what they're doing, who they're doing it for and how many other bots they are chatting with. Our bots will simply say they're hunting for pizzas.'

'But your parasites are *not* innocently looking for pizza.'

'Nope. But when the bots are trapped, the security protocols strip out all viruses and parasites automatically.'

'So they can't detect what we're doing?'

'Well, er, under normal circumstances, no . . .' said Mac.

Uh–oh! 'What aren't you telling me?' asked Kaspar.

'I just described a *routine* activity trace. A full trace is much more thorough. If they do a full trace, then we're screwed.'

'When and why would they do a full trace?'

'If they suspect we're up to something.'

Kaspar considered for a moment. 'You realize that if we are right and they catch us . . . ?'

'I know.'

'I don't just mean you lose your security clearance. We could end up . . .'

'I *know*.'

Kaspar looked at Mac's face. Scared, but determined. She really was quite beautiful – and a better friend than he deserved if she was prepared to go through all this with him. He couldn't help wondering why she was doing it, but he wasn't about to question her motives. She was genuine, he'd bet his life on it.

'OK, let's do it,' he said finally. 'But we'll have to come up with a better cover than pizza. And the other thing I need to do is find a way to get back into the Clinic.'

After a full-on week of yet more skirmishes with groups of Insurgents, Kaspar sat against a wall, getting his breath back, next to the bodies of two stunned, unconscious terrorists. This latest attack had involved a prolonged ground car chase through some pretty suburban back-streets and had ended with Mariska immobilizing the terrorist's vehicle by sending an override command to its engine management computer. The four terrorists had bailed out and scattered into the Botanical Gardens, and it had taken twenty minutes of chasing them round the shrubbery before they were tagged.

Kaspar was excited, and it wasn't just the adrenalin from the chase. He had known for some time now that he needed to get back inside the Clinic, and today at last a golden opportunity had presented itself.

It was time to find out what was really going on.

Mariska had zapped the other two, and he knew that she was on her way to him, so he only had a few moments. After a quick check to ensure he wasn't being watched or monitored, Kaspar took out his utility knife and slit a hole in the leg of his trousers. Here goes, he thought, steeling himself. Taking a deep breath, he stuck the knife through the tear and into the fleshy part of his thigh.

For a moment he felt nothing, then red-hot, screaming pain ripped through his body. Kaspar bit down hard on his bottom lip. He looked down at the damage he'd inflicted to his leg. It was bleeding a little too copiously. God, he hadn't hit an artery, had he?

Stop panicking, Kaspar. He'd been careful to aim for a non-lethal part of his thigh. But it still hurt like hell and was bleeding like a water feature.

By the time the transports arrived, Mariska had already stuck a field dressing on the wound. After treating the terrorists, a medic found time for the good guys.

Kaspar gave him a rueful smile. 'One of them got me with a knife,' he explained. 'It looked a bit rusty but it'll be fine, yeah?'

The medic peered at Kaspar's leg. 'It's superficial, but it's safer to come with us and get it checked,' came the reply. 'It might need a couple of stitches. You can't be too careful with open wounds. The last thing you need is for it to become infected. Here, stick this over it for now.' The medic handed Kas a fresh field dressing.

Fifteen minutes later, Kaspar was at the Clinic. He was directed to wait outside Treatment Room B, where he would be seen as soon as the more urgent cases had been dealt with.

'Could you at least do something to stop the bleeding?' Kaspar read the nametag that was part of the uniform of the nurse before him. Nurse Drayton had a sour face and lips that were permanently turned down. It probably took a High Council directive to get her to smile. 'I've got blood dripping down my leg and it hurts like a bastard.'

'I could cauterize the wound and staple it closed, but a doctor has to administer the local anaesthetic,' Nurse Drayton told Kaspar in no uncertain terms.

'And how long before a doctor is available?'

'At least an hour,' said the nurse.

Kas took a deep breath. 'I really can't wait that long. Could you just staple me back together so I can get back to the Academy?'

Nurse Drayton's eyebrows shot up. 'Are you sure? It'll be quite painful if you don't have the local anaesthetic.'

'I'll grin and bear it,' said Kaspar.

The nurse shrugged. 'It's your leg. Just sign the waiver form and I can get right to it.'

A couple of minutes later, Kaspar was seated on a gurney, his leg stretched out in front of him. Nurse Drayton had escorted him into the treatment room and was laying out the necessary medical-ware to fix his leg.

'Last chance to back out,' said the nurse.

Kaspar shook his head, and gritted his teeth. He had to be insane to go through with this but he really couldn't go exploring with blood pouring down his leg and leaving a trail behind him.

But this was going to hurt. A lot.

Kaspar hadn't been wrong. His leg was throbbing, his heart was pounding, and all he wanted to do was put Nurse Drayton in a choke hold. But at last his wound was clean and stapled. The nurse covered it with a fresh dressing, securing it with a bandage.

'You're very brave,' said the nurse, a touch of admiration sneaking into her voice.

Kaspar wiped the beads of sweat off his forehead. 'Not brave. Just stupid,' he corrected.

'Would you like me to call the Academy for a transport to take you back?' asked the nurse.

Kaspar shook his head. 'No, I've got that covered. But thanks anyway.'

'Take some painkillers and keep your weight off it for at least twenty-four hours. OK?'

'OK,' said Kaspar, knowing full well that it wasn't going to happen.

He hopped off the gurney and tentatively tried putting weight on his bad leg. It was manageable. Acutely painful, but manageable. Kaspar thanked the nurse one last time before he headed out of the Minor Trauma department, made his way down to the kitchen, slipped out through the exit into the garden and limped across to the melon patch where he knew he could get to the North Wing.

By the time he'd taken up his position beneath the melon plants, his leg was throbbing worse than ever. Kaspar would've given his left arm for some strong painkillers at that moment; if he didn't take the weight off his leg soon, the wound would open up and the dressing would be saturated with blood. He had to hurry.

He kept his eyes on the entrance to the North Wing.

This time, there was no one there and the side door was shut, but Kaspar reckoned he wouldn't have long to wait. With a large number of captives to process, he figured that medical reinforcements would soon be on their way. Kaspar settled down, hidden among the roots of the plants, and pointed his rifle at the door. Through the telescopic sight, he could clearly see the keypad. Now he just needed someone to arrive. About ten minutes later, two doctors turned up. They obviously didn't think they could be seen, so they weren't at all careful about shielding the keypad. Kaspar watched the movements of the shorter doctor's hand over the keys.

Left side, right side, middle, right side.

Perfect.

Once they had gone in, Kaspar sprinted across to the door and examined the keypad. There was a fine layer of dirt on it – except on the two, four, five and nine.

'No wonder people get burgled.' Kaspar shook his

head. Anyone could see that the clean keys had to be the active ones. And since the code pattern was left – right – middle – right, the code had to be 5 – 9 – 2 – 4. Kaspar keyed in the numbers, satisfied with his logic.

The door remained disappointingly sealed.

How about 5 – 4 – 2 – 9?

Kaspar held his breath as he keyed in the alternative code. There was a satisfying click and the door swung open.

'Yes!'

He followed the now-familiar route down the corridor, peering carefully into each room, but they were all empty. At the end of the corridor, he took the stairs up one flight and walked back along the length of the building, still checking. Nothing. The second floor up was also un-occupied, but when he reached the third floor, he immediately heard noises.

Kaspar tracked the sound to 'Operating Room One' and peeked through the door. He couldn't see everything that was going on, but he could see that there were glass panels just beneath the ceiling, through which medical students above could watch operations. He followed a sign that said VIEWING GALLERY up a flight of stairs. Carefully opening and closing the door so as not to attract the attention of those below, Kaspar began to observe.

The room contained medical staff and a couple of Guardians from the Special Support Group, none of whom were wearing surgical masks. However, they were in the minority. The room was filled to capacity with gurneys, each occupied with strapped-down terrorists. Most were unconscious, no doubt zapped by Guardians' stun rifles, but a few were awake but restrained, alert and looking around, or struggling to get free. Regardless of whether or not they were awake, all of them were immediately stunned by one of the medics. Not anaesthetized, but given a high-power, direct contact blast.

Kaspar winced at each shot. A while ago, back at the Academy during a close-quarter battle drill, a real oaf of a trainee called Micheson had accidentally fired his weapon point-blank into Mikey's thigh during a wall climb. Even after Mikey had woken up with a boatload of painkillers swirling through his system, he was still in agony.

'It felt like the nerves in my leg were being shredded,' he told them afterwards. 'All the way from my lower spine to my toes. My leg felt like it was on fire and the pain just wouldn't let up. If they hadn't sedated me through the worst of it, I'd have thought seriously about killing Micheson and then myself.' And he hadn't been joking.

Micheson had been kicked out and Mikey had come damn close to quitting too.

So to hit someone with a contact shot was not a humane or pleasant thing to do. And after the patients were all unconscious, there was something else. The way they were treated was more reminiscent of a slaughter-house than a hospital. Their bodies were stripped and tossed about like carcasses. They were being slammed, dropped and slung across the room. Occasionally they landed face down on the floor and sustained facial injuries.

This wasn't nursing; it was torture.

Kaspar spotted a intercom by the viewing window and pressed the button to hear what was going on.

'How much longer is this going to take?' asked one of the SSGs, a short woman with fringed, dark brown hair.

'You can see for yourself,' said one of the doctors, indicating the gurneys pushed against both sides of the room.

The medical procedures weren't gentle nor professional. Kaspar crossed his legs involuntarily as catheters were rammed in like drinking straws being stuck into a milkshake. Then each patient was flipped onto their stomach, and their head was allowed to dangle over the edge of the trolley. One of the medics then inserted a large-bore needle into the back of the neck at the base of the skull, and pumped in about ten millilitres of some brown liquid. Kaspar didn't know what that was for, but he shuddered again. Finally the patients were flipped over again and a thermal cauterizing scalpel was used to slice off their eyelids.

'I don't see why we have to be here in the first place,' complained the female SSG. 'Once you jack 'em up with that brown shit, it's not like they're ever going to wake up again, is it?'

'You know the rules,' her SSG colleague told her. 'Two SSGs to be in this room at all times to protect the medical staff.'

'My sanity is what needs protecting. This assignment sucks.'

'You'll get no argument from me on that one,' said her colleague.

'Did anyone see the handball game last night on the TV?' called out one of the doctors.

The previous night's handball final immediately became the topic of conversation. Kaspar had heard enough. He turned off the intercom.

It was like an assembly line. Insurgent after Insurgent being incapacitated and tortured. And throughout it all, the medics laughed and joked with each other as if they were having a picnic.

Kaspar watched until his eyes and his stomach begged him to leave. Heartsick, he crept back down the stairs. He'd seen enough. All he wanted now was to escape this place.

If this was Alliance humanitarianism, then he wanted no part of it.

Truth is an absolute. While there may be many versions or variations of lies, how can this apply to the truth? Our enemy, the Crusaders, believe that truth is on their side. They mistake truth for their own warped perspective. We in the Alliance have tried in vain to bring them around to our way of thinking but they stubbornly persist in their belief that their world view is the only one which is valid.

We in the High Council had hoped that allowing some of the Crusaders to labour and live amongst us would work to the benefit of all of us. But progress has been slow.

Some have criticized the introduction of special ID cards and documents for the Crusaders living amongst us, but even Alliance citizens must carry at least one form of identification at all times. We have asked no more of them than we have of ourselves.

The High Council have a duty of care to all our peoples. We don't doubt that there may be Crusaders who deplore violence and who wish to live amongst us in peace, but they fail to denounce in the strongest possible terms the Insurgents who live amongst them.

We cannot and will not rest until the very last Insurgent is in our custody and subject to Alliance justice. The price of peace is eternal caution. We will never cease in our efforts to form one cohesive society, open and accessible to all, but the Crusaders need to understand that they too must play their part. It is their duty to turn their backs on those amongst them who would seek to maintain the divisions between us.

If they are not for us, then they are against us. On this issue, there is no middle way.

Extract taken from 'The High Council Manifesto' by Brother Simon

37

The problem Kaspar had was lack of info about the Insurgents. Hard facts on their religious beliefs? None. Good intel on their personal lives? Zero. He recalled some data that Mac had helped him retrieve. In all the interrogations that had ever been conducted over goodness only knew how many years, nobody had ever logged anything interesting about captured Insurgents.

There was nothing.

Kas checked out what Mac had previously said – 'Nothing but meaningless rants, abuse, vile threats and some hair-raising displays of self-harm.'

But in less than a month he had met a few of them, and while most had tried to rip his head off, he just knew they weren't mindless thugs. Rhea had walked into an earthquake and risked capture to save his life. He had looked into her eyes. Anything further from an unreasoning animal he couldn't imagine. She and the rest like her were stone-cold killers but they weren't without method. So why had none of the interrogators ever seen anything like that? Rhea couldn't be an anomaly.

Kaspar constructed a quick query, encapsulated it as a

parasite and then launched it on the back of a trivial bot-search. The request he made was very specific in terms of personnel, timespan and content, so the response came very quickly. Kaspar stared at the results.

'Damn!'

He read them again.

'Damn, damn, damn!'

He checked his search parameters, the data identifiers, the authenticators. All the data was complete and unabridged, all logs were certified authentic by Central Records and carried the electronic signature of the informant. Everything was in perfect order, except for one thing. He read his screen one more time, hoping that what he saw would make sense.

Intruder at Computer Core of Guardian Academy . . . disabled by Guardians 0229 Voss and 4518 Wilding . . . while attempting to detonate a thermobaric device . . .
Signed
0229 Voss / 4518 Wilding

Intruder at level three communications node located at 864 Wissant Avenue . . . killed accidentally during hand-to-hand combat with Guardian 4518 Wilding (incorrectly applied choke hold) . . . Recommendation for remedial unarmed combat training for 4518 Wilding.
Signed
4518 Wilding

Kaspar couldn't believe it. These reports were fiction. There hadn't been any thermobaric device in the computer core and he most certainly had not choked anyone to death, accidentally or otherwise. Central Records had rewritten his After Action reports and then falsely authenticated them. Why? And if they had done it with Kaspar and Voss, what about other Guardians?

Why were they so desperate to hide the suicides? Everything else was pretty accurate. The unauthorized accesses, the stunning, the death, the personnel involved. What the intruders were actually doing, however, had been falsified.

If he couldn't trust his own reports on the system, what could he trust? The official records showed no discernible rationale for what the Insurgency was doing, but the official records weren't just useless, they were lies. The sacred, encyclopaedic, tamper-proof computerized archive was being deliberately skewed to reflect someone's agenda. But whose?

As soon as I learn how to use the computers, I find out all the computers are lying to me. What else isn't true? he wondered. Anything coming out of Central Records is now suspect. Kaspar punched the table in frustration. He needed help and a fresh perspective.

He headed across to Library Services.

'Oh my,' said Mac, when he had explained what he'd found.

'You can say that again.'

'Oh my . . .'

'OK. It would be more helpful if you said something else, though,' sighed Kaspar.

'Sorry. It's just that—'

'You've spent your life trusting computers?'

'Well . . . yes.'

'What can we do? I'm out of ideas. I don't know how to proceed if all the data in the computer has been fiddled with.'

'Not all of it,' she said quietly.

'Come again?'

'It hasn't all been tampered with.'

'How do you know?' he asked suspiciously.

'Because there's far too much of it.' She looked a bit happier now, a glimmer of faith in her computers returning. 'Look, at the last count, there were about seven hundred yottabytes of data in the Central Archives.'

'Seven hundred whatabytes?'

'Yottabytes. It's one thousand to the eighth power.'

'Is that a lot?'

'Oh, for the love of—' she spluttered, before reining in her geek umbrage. 'Yes, it's an awful lot. You know what a gigabyte is? A billion bytes of data? Enough to store about ten minutes of HiDef recording?'

'Yes, I can record a whole game of handball on a ten-gig data chip.'

'Well, seven hundred yottabytes is, near as damnit, a billion billion gigabytes. That's one hundred million billion games of handball. Except of course it isn't just sports, it's the history of the world, the results of every scientific experiment ever conducted, astronomical photographs, films, TV programmes, medical records and biographical data on everyone dating back to when we were all pond scum.'

'OK, that is a lot!'

'Point is, nobody, not even with bot-assistance, can read that much data, far less alter it.'

'But I just told you . . .'

'Oh, I believe you.' Mac raised a placating hand. 'But to do what you say you don't have to change everything. Just the tasty bits. All they have to do is alter the circumstances surrounding the suicides. They don't have to change the atomic weight of sodium, or my middle name, or the postal address of the Guardian Academy.'

'Yeah, but it's the tasty bits that we need to see,' Kaspar protested. 'They can change enough to make it impossible to find the truth.'

'Maybe not. Not only is it impossible to change everything, but you wouldn't want to.'

'You wouldn't?'

'Well, if you did change the address of the Guardian Academy, people would notice. There must be dozens of requests a day for that piece of information, like from your numerous female fans, for instance?'

Kaspar blushed.

'So if you change something too obvious, too well-known or too interesting, you'll get rumbled,' said Mac.

'So they'd keep the changes to a minimum?'

'Sure. Which means that there will be back doors to get the information you want.'

'Back doors?'

'Yeah. Queries that don't ask direct questions, but more subtle ones.'

'Like what?'

'I don't know. Queries that uncover inconsistencies between different narratives. For example, if I look for your birthdate, then that's a single, obvious, hard piece of data.'

'Go on.'

'But there are loads of other queries that aren't so obvious, but which *imply* your birthdate. Like when did you first eat solid food, when did you go to school, what was the date of your application to the Academy.'

'Got it. So although it's easy to change my age to make me ten years old, there would be clues left unless you also changed all my other dates.'

'Exactly. And the more anyone searches, the harder it gets to cover up. Your mother's medical records would also have to be altered, and the dates your father took paternity leave, not to mention the diaries and work schedules of all the medical staff. The effects ripple outwards, like a pebble in a pond. You can't tamper with everything – you have to rely on nobody bothering to look too closely.'

'But finding out if someone lied about my birthday is a whole lot simpler than uncovering falsified Guardian After Action reports,' said Kaspar.

'True, but the principle is the same. I guess it's time

you used your imagination and let the bots off the leash.'

'You mean I should relax the tolerance on the bot-hybridization factor?' Kaspar teased.

'Spoken like a true geek.' Mac laughed. 'Welcome to the club.'

38

Kaspar's initial attempts to find the back door were failures. There was either too little control, giving him ridiculously non-specific reports on a wide range of subjects; or too much control, giving him the fictionalized data he already had and didn't want. But gradually he found ways to tweak the queries, interacting with the bots almost the way a musician would play an instrument.

From time to time, the bots would throw up something weird or amusing. He learned that there was a plant that was lethal in humans but to which sand voles were completely immune. He unearthed a ballet created by a composer of atonal music, choreographed by a dancer who'd never performed in public and featuring a troubled prince whose entire court committed suicide when he died and who then lived on as ghosts, sharing every emotion in the afterlife. It had closed after one performance.

Hard to believe that one didn't run and run, he thought.

He was rapidly becoming a walking encyclopaedia of obscure facts – mostly about death. Sometimes, he could discern no reason at all why the bots had suggested a topic, but every time he tried to suppress the really weird stuff, it stifled their creativity and they went back to feeding him the standard lies. He had already deleted a thread relating to some postgraduate student's thesis in the Department of Literature at Capital City University entitled 'Prospecting for Truth: Fable and Legend as Representations of History' before he had really thought about it. Then some instinct made him retrieve the document to read, but he couldn't understand a word of it.

Pretentiously written academic twaddle, he thought, but still he persevered through it.

Kaspar requested a translation of the twaddle and the bots finally obliged with something he could understand. The idea was that myths, legends and fairy stories were sometimes built around a kernel of truth. It made sense, he supposed. Erupting volcanoes became fiery dragons that lived under a mountain; tsunamis were caused by giants fighting in the sea. When people were oppressed by a tyrant, they might be too scared to protest, but they'd tell stories of a plague or some kind of demon that had to be overcome.

Kaspar was excited. If this guy was right, then this could be a way in. This could be what Mac had been talking about. A vast amount of data that was too big to mess with. Data that nobody would bother to alter because it was irrelevant, just 'fairy stories for kids'. He launched a new bot-search.

As soon as the bots were off and running, Kaspar had to

run to be on time for roll call. He pelted down to the Ready Room, slammed on the brakes just outside the door and sauntered in with the nonchalant air of a man in no hurry. After grabbing an energy drink from the vending machine, he slipped into the seat next to Janna.

'Hey, genius, we don't see you around much these days. What'cha up to?' she said.

'Er, not much. Sleeping . . . catching up on stuff I missed when I was in the Clinic.' Kaspar took a sip of his drink.

'Hmmm! Catching up on your research, Kas?'

'Sorry?' Kaspar nearly choked.

'You seem to spend a lot of time in Library Services,' observed Mariska over his shoulder.

'Er . . . erm . . .'

'Closeted with the perky purple-headed librarian,' added Janna.

'Oh, I've seen her. She's cute!' said Mariska.

'Down, girl!' said Janna.

'Woof! Woof!' Mariska barked at the top of her voice, causing more than a few heads to turn in their direction. Kaspar's cheeks grew uncomfortably warm.

'More than cute, she is adorable,' said Janna. 'I hope she's not overtiring you, Kas?'

Kaspar's entire face was now burning. He'd seen this Janna and Mariska double act before. Their bantering was nearly as terrifying as their combat. He leaned forward and tried desperately to bury himself in a briefing memo about standards of cleanliness in communal vehicles. But at least if everyone thought that his relationship with Mac was romantic, that was a whole lot safer than them knowing the truth.

That evening, Mac came round to his room again and they started examining what the bots had found.

'There seem to be several recurring themes,' said Mac. 'One of the more obvious candidates are these legends of men who could fly, become invisible and walk through walls. Doesn't that sound like ninjas to you?'

'If you believe in that kind of thing.' Kaspar flagged that one as a possible, though not very likely, link to follow up. 'It's certainly a better lead than these guys who can run fast enough to outrun lightning.'

'Or men who can melt the armies of their enemies by the friction of their hands, or father storms by mating with animals,' said Mac.

'Oh, I dunno. Have you met Tomas Hytner? That last tale might be at least half true,' said Kas.

'Euww!' said Mac. 'Moving swiftly on, a lot of these stories have a telepathy component. Fairies who can talk without mouths, mind thieves who can steal your thoughts by kissing you, and twinned souls where two minds share a single body.'

Kaspar leaned back thoughtfully in his chair. He remembered the stories his Uncle Jeff had told about the Insurgents and the way he'd dismissed them.

'Sometimes my dreams are like that,' he admitted. 'Like I'm sharing someone else's head filled with thoughts and emotions that aren't my own.'

His head had started acting funny right after Dillon's

death. A certain amount of post-traumatic stress disorder was understandable – nightmares and flashbacks – but what about the other stuff? Why would the death of his friend have given him memories of a grandma he didn't have and a cottage he'd never been in and mellisse bread that he'd never before tasted? Unless . . . Kaspar hesitated. Having hallucinations about grannies and bread was bad enough, but using kids' stories retold from centuries ago to try to explain them was *seriously* nuts.

Except . . . 'Oh. My. God.' A moment of blinding clarity made Kaspar's eyes open wide and his jaw drop.

'Kas, what's the matter?' asked Mac.

'What makes you think . . .?'

Mac raised an eyebrow. Kas decided not to insult her intelligence by insisting he was OK. Besides, he really needed to confide in someone.

'When Rhea saved me from the earthquake, she touched me, skin against skin,' he admitted. 'First when she throttled me, and afterwards when she carried me to safety. My uniform was hanging off in rags by then and she wasn't wearing gloves. What if close contact between us in the Alliance and Crusaders is strictly forbidden by the High Council because they know that the Insurgents pass on some kind of virus or drug through skin-to-skin contact?'

'If you're right, then why would she work as a masseuse?' said Mac. 'That's the last job she'd choose. She'd be busted inside a week.'

Mac had a point. If Rhea and others like her really did

pass on some kind of virus or drug through skin-to-skin contact, then a good proportion of the Alliance population would've been infected by now. So that theory had just been blown out of the water.

'I'm racking my brains for a reasonable explanation and getting nowhere fast,' he admitted.

Mac chewed at one corner of her bottom lip, her gaze dancing away from Kaspar's.

'What?' Kaspar's eyes narrowed. 'What are you not telling me?'

'Kas, maybe she's a touch-telepath,' said Mac slowly.

'A what? Telepathy? Are you kidding? You don't really believe in all that stuff, do you?' Kaspar frowned.

Mac leaned forward and lowered her voice so it was barely above a whisper. 'Kas, this is between you and me or you'll drop me right in it from a great height, but I'm going to trust you.'

Kaspar nodded. 'I won't let you down.'

Mac took a deep breath. 'With my security clearance, I get to see a lot of things that you and even my . . . Commander Voss don't have access to. Now I can't tell you exactly what for obvious reasons, but believe me, my suggestion is more feasible than yours. The High Council believes that some of the Insurgents are capable of something not a million kilometres away from touch-telepathy. They think it's a latent tendency that only kicks in during puberty, and those who have it can choose when and if to activate it. That's why the High Council try to make sure that the terrorists can't . . . contaminate any of us in the Alliance.'

'How?'

'Our water.' Mac lowered her voice even further. 'They add things to our water to keep us safe, to stop the Insurgents from being able to control us.'

'Yeah, I already knew about our water. Brother Simon told me. But touch-telepathy? Come on! That's something entirely different.'

'Don't you believe in the possibility?' asked Mac.

If Mac had asked him that a few weeks ago, his answer would've been immediate. But that was a few weeks ago. 'I'm not sure,' Kaspar admitted.

'But doesn't it fit?' asked Mac. 'And it would certainly explain why the High Council are so hot on no close contact with Insurgents and unapproved Crusaders who still live in the Badlands. Even the ones who apply to live in Capital City are kept segregated for several months in special camps before they're allowed to live among us.'

'But telepathy that's initiated with a mere touch is the stuff of science fiction, not fact,' Kaspar argued.

'Well, certain kinds of telepathy amongst other species are a fact,' said Mac. 'Why not amongst some of the Crusaders?'

'But how? And if that's the case, how come they have it and we in the Alliance don't?'

'I have no idea. Something to do with the War to End All Wars? The biological fallout from that might have caused some genetic mutations. Who knows what decades of exposure to the pollutants in the soil, or in the air or in the water – or all three out in the Badlands – has done to them.'

'So you think what I'm seeing is Rhea's grandmother, and that Rhea is the one who's nostalgic for home baking?' asked Kaspar at last.

'We should at least consider the possibility.'

Kaspar was having real problems wrapping his head around the idea, but he had to admit it would explain so much – the memories that weren't his own as well as his familiarity with things that he should know nothing about. 'Could that be why I can't get enough of mellisse bread? Why I was drawn to the gym where Rhea worked?'

For the first time, he deliberately focused on Rhea, on her thoughts, her memories, her emotions. He concentrated on her face, her body, on seeing her. Almost immediately, images flooded into his head again and he felt faint. He was hallucinating again. He knew it was a hallucination and yet it seemed so real. He wobbled and Mac grabbed him to stop him from falling off the chair.

'I'm in bed . . . and Rhea's with me . . .'

Mac let go of him like he'd suddenly burned red-hot and sat back, shocked.

'We're lying there, cuddling. No . . . not cuddling . . . she's just holding me . . . but I'm not holding her.' Kaspar struggled to remember. 'I'm lying still, while she . . .' The room began to spin and he was sinking, sinking like falling through water. 'She's in my head. Rhea is running through my mind . . . exploring.'

And suddenly Kaspar knew with total certainty that

this wasn't a dream and it wasn't a hallucination either. This was a real memory. Rhea had been here, in his room, in his bed. She had come here and . . .

'Oh, Jeez! I woke up a few days after the Loring School massacre and the right side of my neck was sticky. I remember now. She made me put on a transdermal patch! That little ninja bitch drugged me! Mac, she broke in here and she drugged me and then she did some kind of telepathic voodoo shit to my head.'

'Are you sure?' frowned Mac.

Kaspar nodded vigorously, appalled at the notion that not even his thoughts were his own.

'OK, what could she have found out?' asked Mac grimly.

'Huh?'

'Kas, think. If Rhea did establish some kind of neural link with you, maybe she can read your mind. Maybe she can see through your eyes, learn secrets. What could she have found out?'

Kaspar's eyes widened with horror as the full implications of what Mac was saying hit him hard. Wave upon wave of sheer panic rose up to smother him. He took several deep breaths, trying to get himself together.

'No. No, it's OK,' he said, calming down. 'There's nothing to know. I'm the lowest grade of Guardian there is. I don't attend high-level briefings, don't meet with important people.'

'What about your computer access, your passwords?'

'Nothing classified. She can't learn anything from me

because I don't know anything. The ninjas knew the security code for the Academy's computer core and I certainly didn't. They know the locations of camouflaged network nodes and I don't.' Kaspar finally got his breathing under control.

'Are you sure? What about your meeting with Brother Simon?'

Kaspar thought for a moment. 'I'm sure they didn't learn anything that they didn't already know,' he said at last. 'Even if there is some mental thing between Rhea and me, it can't be doing them any good. It's probably just some freakish accident caused by direct contact.'

'Then why did she come here? She took a hell of a risk breaking into the Guardian Academy. I mean you're cute, but not that cute. Would Rhea really risk life in a maximum security detention centre just so that she could press herself against your manly body?' Mac looked sceptical, to say the least.

Kaspar's face flamed. The glint in Mac's eye told him she was well aware of the effect her words had had. He walked over to the sink in the corner of the room to splash his face. One thing was for certain: with Mac in his life he'd never get too full of himself. She'd see to that. As he was towelling himself dry, there was a knock at the door. Kas wasn't expecting company. Mac stood up.

'It's OK, I'll get it.' Kas crossed the room to open the door as Mac sat back down. It was Janna, Mariska and Mikey, though he could hear others in the hallway.

'We wondered if you wanted to come for a game of

handball?' asked Mariska as she peered past him to where Mac sat on the bed. 'But I can see you already have your hands full.'

At that, half a dozen heads appeared round the door-frame, jockeying for a view of his guest. Kaspar was mortified. The knowing looks had his face burning again.

'Hey, Mac.' Janna gave a brief wave.

'Hi, Janna.' Mac struggled to suppress her amusement. She gave Kaspar a knowing look that raised the temperature of his face by several degrees.

'Thanks for the invitation. Maybe some other time,' Kaspar told Mariska.

'Don't do anything we wouldn't do.' Mariska winked at Kaspar.

'There isn't anything you wouldn't do,' Kaspar retorted.

'Exactly!' laughed Mariska with another wink, this time at Mac.

'You can all bugger off now,' said Kaspar, exasperated.

There were a couple more comments, but surprisingly they weren't too ribald, and Kaspar's door was finally closed.

'Sorry about that,' Kaspar muttered as he sat down next to Mac.

'Don't worry about it.' Mac smiled, though it quickly faded. 'Besides, Rhea is the one in your thoughts, not me.'

'Not from choice,' Kaspar protested.

'Are you sure about that?' asked Mac softly.

Kaspar opened his mouth to deny it, but his reply died

on his lips. He regarded Mac and thought of Rhea and felt like his head was about to explode.

'Let's get back to it,' said Mac with a sigh.

They resumed the research, but the bots' findings were getting less and less likely. After reading about a monster that, whenever it was slain, came back to life with its knowledge increased until it finally learned all the secrets of the universe and became a god, they decided to call it a night.

Kaspar escorted her to his door. Mac turned to him.

'Thanks for an evening that was . . . different!' she said wryly.

'You're welcome. Fancy doing it all again tomorrow?'

'Any time you want,' said Mac.

They stood in silence watching each other, a strange tension springing up between them. Kaspar was struck by an intense desire to kiss her. He leaned forward slightly. Mac didn't back away. In fact, if anything she leaned forward herself. Or was Kaspar just imagining things? He hesitated, just a tad too long.

Mac drew back.

'I'll see you tomorrow,' she said. And she slipped away.

Kaspar closed his door, then banged his head against it. Repeatedly. He flung himself on top of his bed and sighed. Between Rhea and Mac, his life now seemed excessively complicated. He really liked Mac, and he owed her so much. She was the one person in his life with whom he could share any of his thoughts and ideas, and she'd listen without mocking or judging him.

If only . . .

God! His thoughts were racing away with him. Time to reign them in.

With Mac's help he had learned so much, and yet what he'd discovered made precious little sense. More than ever, though, he felt that the myths the bots had reported held the key. It was as if pieces of the puzzle were starting to slot into place, but he was too far away – or maybe too close – to see the full picture.

But it was there and Kaspar wasn't going to rest until he knew what was going on and could do something about it.

Much has been made of the closed-circuit cameras, the monitors, the audio alert alarms we in the High Council have decreed should be placed throughout Capital City. Like all current and future technology, phones, datalinks, the datanet and other communication routes may be used for good or ill. It is the duty of the High Council to protect the people of the Alliance, even from themselves. Surely this is the foundation of benign governance.

This does not mean that every conversation and every message will be scrutinized and interpreted, but they will be recorded and our Guardians and Security officials will be afforded the opportunity to analyse that data as and when necessary.

Those with nothing to hide have nothing to fear.

At times, when we have reliable intelligence regarding increased Insurgent activity, it will be necessary to impose a curfew from midnight to six a.m. This will be for the good of our populace and to make it easier for the Guardians who patrol our streets to serve and protect us all. The curfew will not be broken by the civilian population without strict authorization from the High Council.

Long live the Alliance.

Extract taken from 'Benign Governance' by Sister Elena

30

'Do you have a minute, sir?'

'One minute, only,' replied Voss, motioning for Kaspar to sit.

'Sir, how well do you know Commander Tilkian?'

'I've met him a few times at dress uniform affairs, but we've never worked together. He runs his own little group of hand-picked Guardians – the Special Support Group, which provides the bodyguards for the High Council. Only the best for Tilkian – Guardians with table manners. I'm surprised they didn't ask you to join. Good-looking Honour Cadet like you.'

Kaspar chewed his lip.

'Well? C'mon, Wilding, out with it. Why are you interested in Tilkian?'

'I was thinking . . .'

'Oh, hell. Here it comes. We both know what happened the last time you thought something.'

'I think that Tilkian is a terrorist. I think he's our traitor.'

'What?' Voss was round from behind his desk and closing his office door before Kaspar had finished speaking. 'Are you off your head, Wilding? Tilkian may be a self-important butt-kisser, but he's a Guardian and has been one since before you were born.'

'I know, sir, but—'

'Oh, wait. Have you been doing more "research" with Mackenzie in Library Services?' Voss's expression was stony. 'What did I tell you about unauthorized data-mining? What part of "you are not an analyst" didn't penetrate your skull? Well? Is that it? Have you and Ms Know-It-All had a billion bots running riot?'

'I . . . well . . . yes, but—'

'Then I hope you remember your way around a hydroponics tank 'cause you're going to be a melon farmer again by lunch time.' Voss was spitting nails by now. Kaspar had never seen him so angry.

'Sir, I—'

'What the hell possessed you? And what makes you think you can waltz in here and accuse a Senior Commander and personal aide to the High Council of being a damned terrorist? What—'

'This did, sir,' Kas dropped the data key he was holding onto the desk. 'I know what you warned me against un-authorized bot-searches, but I was sure I was on to something. I refined my queries and Tilkian's name came up too many times for it to be a mere coincidence. So I asked the bots to analyse Tilkian's activities and move-ments and I'm now convinced that he's the mole, sir.'

Voss stared at the little chunk of plastic as if it was an angry sand scorpion. He looked back up at Kaspar and his expression might've been carved from granite. 'Do you really think you know something this time?'

'Just take a look, sir. If I'm wrong, then I'm wrong and you can send me back to the farm. But if I'm even partly right . . . You have to look at this, sir.'

'Damnit!' Voss reopened his office door and stuck his head out. 'Laird, contact the SAP group and push this morning's meeting back to 1400 hours, and hold all my calls until further notice.' He walked back round behind his desk, picked up the data key and threw it back to Kaspar. 'OK, you've got my attention. Talk me through it – and you'd better be convincing.'

Kaspar placed the data key in the reader and called up his first presentation.

'This is a time-lapse display showing the locator trackers of Tilkian and all his people around the times of significant attacks on Capital City. You can follow the whereabouts of all the Special Support Group as little black squares.'

Voss watched as the little squares scuttled around the city, leaving fading snail-trails behind them. 'And the flashing red circles?'

'Terrorist attacks. But only the really nasty ones.'

Voss watched in silence for about a minute, then he turned incredulously to Kaspar.

'There's nothing. Absolutely no correlation at all. When the red flashes go off, there are no SSG units anywhere near. This is your evidence? A display proving conclusively that the SSG came nowhere near the incidents?'

'No, sir, not that. Take a look at the number in the top left of the screen. It shows the total number of SSG personnel that the system is tracking at any time.'

'So?'

'Do you notice how the number dips significantly around the time of each red flash? We did the maths. On average, give or take, three SSG guys go off-grid about ninety minutes before a terrorist attack, then come back online about ten minutes after.'

Voss looked doubtful. 'SSG guys will tend to go off-grid all the time. They travel with the Council members, and they can't be tracked then.'

'That's true, sir. But the key fact is the statistical link between the dips and the terrorist attacks. I told you we did the maths. The chance of that pattern appearing by chance is about one in seventy-two million.'

Voss watched for a while longer. 'I'm no mathematician, but OK. Suppose I forget that there are lies, damned lies and statistics, why would Tilkian do that? What's in it for him? Are you really suggesting that one of our most senior Guardians is an Insurgent sleeper? That he's responsible for planning and setting off the worst atrocities?'

'I don't know, sir, I really don't. But he's involved somehow, and you said yourself that we had a mole reporting back to the Insurgents. Suppose it isn't just Tilkian but most, if not all, of the SSG?'

Voss was still sceptical, to say the least. 'If the Special Support Group support the Insurgents, then why don't they just assassinate the entire High Council? I mean, they are their bodyguards, for heaven's sake. They have round-the-clock access and state-of-the-art weaponry. Not that it's even needed. It doesn't take much effort to wring the neck of some venerable sixty-year-old.'

'Maybe there aren't enough traitors in the Special Support Group to take out all the High Council? The moment it was known that one or some of the High Council were being attacked, wouldn't security around the rest be quadrupled and the rest of the High Council just lie low until the threat was over?' Kaspar was floundering. At Voss's increasingly dubious look, Kaspar added, 'I know I'm just speculating on that one, sir, but Tilkian is definitely up to his eyebrows in this. And it was Tilkian who assigned Mendel to investigate the attack on Loring School.'

'Mendel is a moron, I'll grant you that. But your mathematical theory is still light years away from being proof. What else have you got?'

'Brother Simon told me that Tilkian dopes our water supplies with antiviral medication and the antidotes for nerve gas. Well, one thing us hydroponic melon farmers know how to do is water purity analysis. The chemistry is so simple a school kid can do it. There are no drugs like that in the water. Whatever Tilkian is doing at the reservoir, it isn't what Brother Simon thinks he's doing.'

'Oh, hell, Wilding. Is there nothing you won't snoop into?'

Kaspar let that one go unanswered.

'Sir, we don't treat the Insurgents according to Council policy either. They don't go to a secure prison after medical treatment. We *torture* them. We put them in drawers and keep them for years at the old North Wing of the Clinic. I've seen what the staff there do. It's barbaric. And there is a constant SSG presence there.'

'OK, you can stop right there. You may have a point about the bombings and terrorist activity – we'll need to check that out with proper analysts – but let me set you straight on the other stuff.' Voss paused, unsure how to continue. 'The High Council believe that Insurgents have a trick, a mental ability . . .'

'You mean some of them are touch-telepaths? I know, sir. They can share thoughts when they touch you.'

'How the hell did you find that out?'

'From my first contact with the Insurgent in the desert, sir. Sometimes I see some of her memories. Nothing useful. Just bits of her childhood, and her taste in pastries.'

'A little something else you forgot to put in your report?' frowned Voss.

Kaspar decided not to answer that one.

Voss looked severely constipated. He had something to say but was having real problems working out how to say it. 'Wilding, what I'm about to say is not to leave this room. D'you read me?'

'Yes, sir,' Kaspar replied.

Voss's mouth moved like he was chewing on the words before spitting them out. 'It's not touch-telepathy. We do know that much. It's more like a form of touch-*empathy*.

They can't talk to each other using thoughts alone. The High Council's many experiments have proven that, at least. What some of the Crusaders have is more like a deep, acute sensitivity, on a scale never recorded before. Those who have it only need to touch others with the same ability to establish a link, a connection that enables them to share memories and emotions without the need to explain or justify. But like I said, not all of them have it. Just a few dozen Crusaders, if that, as far as we can tell. And no one in the Alliance has that capability, or so we thought. Until you.' He paused, then added coldly, 'What makes you so special?'

Kaspar inwardly flinched at the barely disguised contempt in Voss's last question. It wasn't his fault that Rhea seemed to be able to stroll around in his memories. And he could certainly do without the regular visits to her grandma's cottage. Besides, surely empathy alone, no matter how acute, didn't explain this ability to share memories?

'I don't know, sir,' he mumbled. 'But that still doesn't explain what goes on in the North Wing.'

'According to the High Council, when the Insurgents die, their souls or spirits, or whatever you care to call it, float off to their version of the afterlife and chat with other dead people.'

'Huh . . . ?' Kaspar blinked like an owl. Was Voss even serious?

'Yeah, I know,' scoffed Voss. 'It's all bollocks as far as I'm concerned, but that's why we don't kill the little

273

shits. The Council in its wisdom is worried that the ghosts of dead terrorists will emanate or resonate or urinate off some higher plane and pass on their intel via séances and the like to those Insurgents who are still living.'

The whole idea was preposterous. Surely no one in their right mind would believe such a thing? And yet . . .

'I suppose that might explain why ninjas kill themselves,' said Kaspar slowly. 'Maybe they believe the same thing? That once they get some vital information, if they commit suicide the data will get passed on to . . . who exactly?'

'Don't look at me. Like I said, it's all bollocks. But our spiritual masters have a real bee in their bonnet about it – so no killing. Just permanent storage at the Clinic's North Wing. We paralyse them with an injection of some shit into their necks, then we plumb them in to monitors, stick tubes in every orifice and bung them in a refrigerator.'

'Why cut their eyelids off?'

'Each storage drawer contains a holo-emitter. When the drawers are closed, nonstop looped images and clips play right in front of their faces – the most barbaric, messed-up stuff you can imagine. Their eyelids are removed so that they can't shut their eyes. It's supposed to be "neurally disruptive", not just to the ones in the North Wing but to any other Insurgents who may have some kind of mental, empathic link with them. Personally, I suspect it's also fun for the sadists who run the North Wing.'

'I don't follow, sir.'

'Guardian, switch your brain on! You said it yourself.

274

You came into direct physical contact with the terrorist you fought in the desert and now you can see her memories. It's like a faulty tap. Once it's switched on, it's very hard to switch off again, especially in times of great stress or pain,' said Voss impatiently. 'The Insurgents who are still at large have been in close contact with those in storage at the North Wing. We show horrific images to the ones we have in storage so they will pass on those horrific images to the Insurgents we haven't managed to round up yet. It gives us an edge and keeps them off balance.'

Kaspar glared at Voss. 'And you're OK with that? With the way we treat them?'

Voss's eyes narrowed. 'Remember who you're talking to. I warned you, Wilding. This is what happens when you poke your nose into things that don't concern you. You find that the truth is a lot uglier than the carefully constructed fiction.'

'So what was Tilkian doing at the reservoir?'

Voss sighed again. 'This is classified, OK? The touch-empathy thing is genetic. Apparently most people have the appropriate gene.'

'So . . . ?'

'I'm not just talking about the Insurgents, we in the Alliance have it as well. We have a natural ability to live in each other's heads. To share feelings, perceptions, ideas, emotions. All of us can wallow around in a sea of other people's mental shit. Imagine that. No privacy, no secrets, no surprises. Total frickin' anarchy.'

'And the reason we in the Alliance can't use it is . . .?'

'Tilkian's monthly trip to the reservoir. He adds a chemical to the water that stops the gene in question from being expressed and suppresses empathetic brainwave activity. And I bet you didn't detect *that* with your secondary-school chemistry set.'

Kaspar sat stunned. The last five minutes had over-turned everything he thought he knew. They had told him since birth that he was a member of a great society that valued the sanctity of life above everything. But the society he loved was built on lies, torture, cruelty and a permanently drugged population.

He forced himself to focus on the most immediate problem. 'What do we do about Tilkian?'

'First of all, *we* do nothing. I need to get all your amateur analysis checked by professionals. I want all your research material, full reports on *everything*. Every bot you ever launched – every person you even remotely suspected. We're going to have to get someone from the Council involved too. Your mate Brother Simon, probably. This is going to be a bitch. I'll need to talk to Mackenzie too. Did you have any other helpers?'

'No, just Mac. She . . . she won't get into trouble, will she?'

Voss gave Kaspar a studied look. 'Maybe you should've thought about that before you dragged her into this mess.'

Kaspar nodded his agreement. 'Even so, if it turns out I'm wrong, I don't want her to get it in the neck because of me.'

'Don't worry. I'll make sure she doesn't,' said Voss.

Something in Voss's tone reassured Kaspar that he was telling the truth. Mac was safe. That was something at least. 'What happens if the analysts agree with me?'

'*If* they agree – and it's a big if – then my vote would be to kill Tilkian and all the traitors,' Voss replied. 'We'd have no other choice.'

Kaspar's glare was back. This wasn't what he'd signed up for, not even close.

'What do you want? A trial? Get real, kid. If you're right about Tilkian, those evil sods have been running around blowing up things, killing Guardians and gassing little kids. Personally I'd execute the scum just for Loring School, never mind anything else. What are we supposed to say to the civilians? Oh, sorry, I know we were meant to be protecting you but, oops, the worst terrorists are actually *us*.'

Kaspar could see the logic of that, but the idea of executing Tilkian and his group just didn't sit well with him. At all. He'd signed up to protect and serve, for a noble cause. This cause was rancid. Kaspar felt unclean, like he was trying to defend the indefensible. And he still didn't understand why he could share Rhea's memories. She might be a touch-empath but he certainly wasn't. Unless . . .

Of course! The well on Uncle Jeff's farm.

For years, that had been the only water he'd ever consumed. Certainly none of the chemically treated water that the High Council had had doctored. Was that why Rhea's memories had become his own? Touch-empathy as a two-way street? He'd only started drinking the same water as

277

everyone else once he'd joined the Academy, by which time it was probably too late to suppress that ability within him. What was it Mac had said? *It's a latent tendency that only kicks in during puberty.* On the farm, then. But Voss was right about one thing at least – it had severely messed with his head.

Voss sighed. 'If you're right, then the Insurgency aren't the evil threat that we made them out to be. You think all the really bad stuff was done by the bloody SSG. And if you're correct, it would serve them right if we stuck them all in refrigerated filing cabinets like we've been doing to the Insurgents for years. But all that is way above my pay-grade. We'll leave major policy decisions to the High Council. In the meantime, you and me do what we signed up for. We round up terrorists, whoever they are – Insurgents, Crusaders, even Guardians if necessary – and we deliver them. The rest is philosophy.'

'So what happens now, sir?'

'For now, we do nothing. If you're right, we wouldn't want to tip our hand to Tilkian and his crew. There are a couple of guys in the Analysis Division that I can show your homework to before we do anything else.'

'How do you know you can trust them?'

'Because I've used them before. Chin and Akinyeme are absolute nerds. The kind of geeks that never go outdoors and get orgasmic about mathematics and computers. The kind of guys that Tilkian absolutely despises.'

'And then? Assuming they agree with me?'

'And then it'll get really crappy. There's a lot more to

the Special Support Group than just table manners. They're hard bastards and Tilkian has them well trained. And because they have to protect the High Council, their security clearances are higher than ours. If we kick this off, it's going to get rough. If it gets down to it, are you ready to kill someone?'

'I already have,' replied Kaspar. Every detail of that day in the desert was burned into his mind.

'I don't mean self-defence against some thug who jumps you and tries to beat your brains to a pulp. And I don't mean when you're howling mad at seeing your best mate murdered. I mean, could you stick a knife in another Guardian's ribs for the public good?'

There was a long silence.

'Because if you can't . . .'

'Yes.'

'Yes what?'

'Yes, sir, I could kill traitorous Guardians. People who can pump nerve gas into a school? I can kill every last one of them.'

Voss looked carefully at Kaspar, gauging his resolve. Finally he seemed satisfied.

'All right, kid. First we get someone to mark your homework. Then it's us against the frickin' world.'

40

The next few days were just weird.

'I don't want you doing anything different,' Voss had said. 'No clues that anything's changed, so keep to the routine patrols and keep your mouth shut.'

So the next day, Kaspar attended roll call with the rest of his squad and then waited for the inevitable general alarm. They sat around, they patrolled, and Kaspar waited.

And waited.

And waited.

Nothing.

No alerts, no attacks, not even so much as a false alarm.

'Maybe the Insurgency have all gone on holiday?' said Mikey.

If so, then it wasn't just a day trip. The next day was the same, and the next, and the day after that. There was an unnerving complete calm across the city. Kaspar stripped down and reassembled his rifle so often he knocked almost two seconds off the record he'd set in training.

After six days of absolutely nothing, Mariska's birthday party promised to be a good opportunity to let off steam.

Kaspar watched quietly from the sidelines as his friends got seriously out of order.

'Penny for 'em,' said Janna as she joined him in propping up the wall. She passed him a plastic beaker full of what tasted suspiciously like plum-flavoured rocket fuel.

'They're not worth that much,' Kaspar replied.

'Kas, are you still upset with me?' asked Janna. At Kaspar's blank look she continued, 'Because I asked you to explain the Insurgents' actions. I really wasn't trying to imply anything. I'm sorry some of the others took it that way.'

Kaspar blinked in surprise. Janna really did look contrite. 'Janna, forget it. I already have.'

'So what's the matter?'

'Nothing,' Kaspar denied. 'I'm fine.'

'Come on, hotshot. I know you better than that. Are you still brooding about Loring School?'

'No, I'm . . . Well, yes, I suppose I am,' he acknowledged. 'Every time I close my eyes, I can see them. In fact, I don't even have to close my eyes. I visited that school, Janna. I *met* them. I can't forget any of their faces and a little girl called Gnea haunts me. Doesn't what happened get to you at all?'

' Course it does. You have to ask? But I've got someone to talk to about it.' Her eyes drifted off across the pool to where Mariska was playing a drunken game of 'king-of-the-castle' on the diving board. 'Why isn't your girlfriend here? She's obviously into you and you need someone. Especially after . . .'

Dillon. She didn't actually say his name, but then she didn't have to. Thinking about Dillon made something ache deep within Kaspar. The guy's endless conspiracy theories used to be hilarious, but now shadowy plans and sinister plots seemed to be a reality rather than a diverting fiction.

'She had to work tonight,' he said. Kaspar had given up on denying a romantic link to Mac. Partly because it was a useful cover, and partly because deep down he kind of wished it was true. Actually, tonight Mac was locked in a basement with Akinyeme and Chin, Voss's two tame geeks, no doubt describing her parasitic bot-searches and her theories of co-relational analysis, and cross-checking every shred of computer-based evidence against Tilkian and the Special Support Group. Kaspar had been there too, but the second time he'd nodded off, Voss had put his foot down.

'You're useless in this state, Wilding. Take the rest of the night off. That's an order.'

'I can't, sir.' Kaspar was determined to go on, to do his part, even though he was exhausted. The previous night, they had given him psych-hypnotic drugs and made him eat mellisse croissants to enhance his recall. Mikey had caught him sneaking back to barracks at four in the morning looking wrung out and with crumbs on his uniform. There was now an official rumour doing the rounds that Mac was a secret sex-mad pastry chef and Kaspar was a lucky dog.

'Which part of "that's an order" don't you understand?'

Voss had snapped. 'You're no good to anyone if you're too shattered to stay awake. Or worse, too addle-brained to keep your mouth shut! Go to Mariska Toth's birthday party and then get some sleep. Tilkian can wait one more night.'

Gina ran across and grabbed Janna's arm. 'C'mon, guys!' she begged. 'You gotta help us get the little psycho off the diving board. We're getting owned. It's embarrassing.'

'I'll be right there,' replied Janna.

As Gina ran back to lend support to the others against Mariska, Janna turned again to Kas, concern turning down the corners of her mouth. 'Seriously, Kas, are you OK?'

Kaspar took a deep breath. Everything had gone wrong – and it was going to get much, much worse. Society's 'Great Ideal' was a sick lie that concealed institutionalized torture, and he and Voss were practically taking blood oaths to kill their fellow Guardians. Where Voss had spoken of one leak in the Guardian ranks, now there seemed to be several.

Was he OK? Suddenly one of Dillon's ridiculous sayings came to him – 'If you fall from the top of the Museum of Light, the last few centimetres are really gonna mess you up, but while you're falling – you might as well enjoy the view.'

'Yeah, I'm OK,' he replied finally, forcing a rather less than convincing smile. 'Let's go chuck Mariska in the pool. You take your top off to distract her and I'll go grab a stun rifle.'

41

The Insurgents' vacation lasted exactly one week and then ended with a bang; a lot of bangs. Kaspar was just coming off another uneventful evening shift and heading to the mess hall when the general alarm sounded.

'C'mon guys, let's go,' shouted Mikey from the Liaison desk. 'The bastards are back big-time.'

'What's the target?' asked Kaspar, a sense of dread enveloping him. He'd known about Tilkian for days and done nothing about him. If this was another Loring, then it would be his fault.

'It's the power grid. They're hitting everything. Two generating stations have been scrammed. They've blown up three feeds from the geothermal fields in the Badlands, and we're getting reports of minor explosions at distribution substations all over the place. I hope you lot can see in the dark?'

Right on cue, the lights went out, leaving only the battery-powered exit signs. The emergency generator kicked in almost immediately though, and the lights flickered back on.

'Any casualties?' Kas crossed his fingers.

'No reports so far. Most of these power-grid nodes are automated.'

Kaspar felt an enormous sense of relief. So this was a ninja job, the genuine Insurgency. But then Tilkian would probably already have something in place, some contingency plan ready to go. Within a couple of hours, there would likely be some new atrocity as the Special Support Group Shadow Insurgency brought the terror.

Voss came into Ops. 'Why is everyone still in here?' he barked. 'Get out there. You know what you're meant to be doing. Hit your assigned sectors. I want everyone except the Duty Comm team on the streets five minutes ago. *Move!*'

The yelling wasn't really necessary, as everyone was already deploying, but it didn't seem advisable to mention that. Kaspar headed for the door.

'Not you, Wilding.'

'Sir?' Kaspar turned and ran back to Voss.

'You're not going with them, kid. You're coming with me. We have an appointment.'

'With who, sir?'

But Voss was already heading out the other door. Kaspar had to jog after him.

'Sir, where are we going?'

'We're going to piss on someone's fireworks.'

42

Kaspar jumped into the hovercar and Voss slewed it out of the vehicle park and down Academy Approach.

'Where are we actually going?' Kaspar asked again.

'We are going to 242 South Herdjis Lane.'

'Which is . . . ?'

'A delightful bungalow in the sleepy suburb of Hemms-on-the-River. It has a beautifully manicured lawn, a wonderful view of the lake . . .'

Kaspar wasn't sure what was more scary – the Insurgency, rogue terrorist Guardians or Voss in this happy, whimsical mood.

'. . . and an en-suite auxiliary backup for the Power Grid Statistical Analysis department.'

Kaspar wasn't really sure what that was and he wasn't keen on displaying his ignorance. 'It's another camouflaged data node like the one on Wissant Avenue?'

'Yep!'

'Why are we going there?'

'Because it turns out that you and Mackenzie are geniuses. I knew she was, but you're a surprise!'

'Sir?'

'My two tame nerds finished their analysis of your analysis and their conclusion is that you and Mac were both spot on. They reckon that the chances of Senior Commander Tilkian being one of the good guys are about one in a billion. They expanded on your work and found so many anomalies in Tilkian's deployments that their computer had a nervous breakdown from counting them.'

Kaspar was stunned. Part of him had hoped that he was wrong, that this was all just some huge misunderstanding, that the bots had been misprogrammed or that Tilkian was doing some undercover work for the Council. But to know his suspicions were accurate . . .

'Turns out that Mac's approach to information mining is real cutting-edge thinking. It could revolutionize data analysis. I should be proud as I recommended her for the job, but you and her have been gigantic pains in my battle-hardened buttocks. And it seems that you in particular have a real talent for working the bots. Must be all the practice you've had.' Voss's pointed look made Kaspar's face grow warm. 'When this is over, the geek squad want to work with both of you on a series of projects in all kinds of areas – history, physics, meteorology. Who'd have thought it, from melon farmer to data-mining superstar?'

Kaspar's face grew warmer. 'So why are we going to . . . wherever it is you said we were going?'

'Because we got a tip-off.'

'From who?'

'From the lady in black who gave you such a kicking in

the desert or, if you prefer, the lady in white who gave you such a kicking in the massage parlour.'

'It was a gym.' Kaspar was really starting to miss the Voss who screamed and shouted. This new jovial one was winding him right up. 'You got a tip-off? From a ninja? No way.'

'Well, not directly. Through you. It seems the problem with touch-empaths is that once they've established physical contact with you, their emotions can sort of leak out. You've been exceptionally receptive to the one who's been handing you your butt.'

Kaspar chose to ignore that.

'I did wonder, because of the dreams I've been having,' he said. He decided to keep the well at his uncle's farm to himself, not wanting to get his uncle into trouble. 'But wouldn't it be fairly stupid for a touch-empath to work as a masseuse then?' he said.

'Maybe not. Don't forget we use chemicals in the water to suppress that ability, so none of the Alliance are supposed to be receptive to that kind of mental connection. Maybe the leaking only happens when the true empaths get emotional, lose control. You met her when you were both – let's say – "excited". First time, she'd just killed your buddy and you'd just killed hers. Emotions were definitely running high. Second time, you strolled into her place of business, blew her cover wide open and said, "Hello, I'm a Guardian!" Must've spooked the hell out of her.'

'OK, but how did that turn into a tip-off?'

'Because the nerds took all the images that they got out of you under the hypnotics and ran the world's biggest bot-search on them. If you said you saw a tree they built a database of trees. If you said croissant . . .'

'They built a database of croissants?'

'Yep. Then they did something called Recursive Symbolic . . . Signifier Deconstruction-ism . . . or something equally obscure. Basically they cross-referenced everything. And I mean everything. One cohort of bots actually worked out the address of the massage parlour without being told.'

'Gym.'

'Whatever. Anyway, it turns out that your pal from the "gym" had something on her mind. Something to do with power, and blackouts and tunnels.'

'I don't understand. You think that they're going to hit this Power Grid Statistical place tonight? Why is this particular one special? They're blowing up power installations all over. Power plants, cable distribution nodes . . .'

'Because according to the geeks she spent ages studying this place. And besides, it isn't an active node. It doesn't control anything. You can't hurt the grid from there. So this isn't just a quick bomb-and-run mission. No, she's going to be there, doing that ninja computer shit. Only this time we're going to be there too. Except that after we zap her, we're not handing her over to Tilkian's mob so that they can lobotomize her and stick her in a filing cabinet to cover their tracks. We are going to do some interrogating of our own.'

Kaspar's thoughts swung all over the place on hearing that. Rhea captured and interrogated . . . How was he meant to feel about that? She'd saved his life. But it was thanks to her and her partner that his best mate Dillon was dead. He owed her nothing.

Except that she'd stayed with him through the night when he'd needed someone desperately. But she'd probably only visited him in the first place to mess with his head and to obtain intel from him. Right and wrong were never meant to be this confusing, this contradictory.

'Sir, about Rhea . . .'

'Yes?' Already a frown had produced a line between Voss's eyebrows as he regarded Kaspar.

'Nothing, sir.'

Though Kaspar might not like it, Voss was right. Rhea could provide vital information about the Insurgents and their ultimate objective, and she'd also be able to shed light on Tilkian's involvement with the Insurgency, if any. That was the top priority now. Lives were at stake. If Tilkian wasn't involved with the real Insurgents – and Kaspar was now convinced that he wasn't – then it would prove once and for all that he and the others in the SSG were the real phantoms. Every time an Insurgent got caught, the results of their interrogation were faked and they were silenced for ever and put in cold storage. Or maybe they weren't even interrogated at all? Tonight might be the first time that anyone actually asked an Insurgent meaningful questions and was truly interested in getting meaningful answers.

'So what does this node do if it doesn't actually help run the grid?' asked Kaspar after a lengthy silence.

'Apparently, it's the backup of a backup for a utility that analyses demand for electrical power. It produces charts and histograms that allow better load-balancing and future planning for power stations. It is the world's most boring computer node. It's a nerdy lump of statistics of no importance.'

'Then why is Rhea interested in it?' frowned Kaspar.

Voss raised his eyebrows. 'Don't go all civilian on me, Wilding. You ask that like you think I should know the answer.'

'Sorry, sir,' said Kaspar. 'I don't get it, though. Why expend all that time and energy on statistics?'

'Tell you what, once we fry her arse I'll be sure to put that at the top of my list of questions.'

'Won't she have the usual support team?' said Kaspar. 'There's just the two of us.'

'I don't think she will. This place is way down everyone's list of priorities. It doesn't even make it onto our list of secondary targets. And because I'm a careful man, I've already got a unit responding to a substation alert just across the river. We do a target recce. If she's alone – we go in. If she has support – we can whistle up reinforcements in under two minutes.'

Kaspar nodded. Finally this was coming together. He checked the emitter on his rifle, popped the power pack, wiped the terminals and slammed the battery back home, waiting for the maximum charge to build. Then he did the same for Voss's weapon.

'Time for answers,' said Voss. 'It's payback time.'

Kaspar nodded grimly.

The rock in the pit of his stomach told him that tonight was going to change the course of the rest of his life.

43

Voss stopped the hovercar in a side street about two hundred metres away from the node and both men put on their tactical helmets, adjusting their multi-function goggles and respirators. Desperate Insurgents had been known to launch knock-out gas attacks, and occasionally worse, when cornered. Rhea was a formidable enemy – it would be incredibly foolish to underestimate her. Kaspar needed to stay sharp and focused. But his major concern wasn't so much Rhea as Tilkian and the rest of his murdering crew. If they had got wind of what Rhea was up to, they might feel it was an ideal opportunity to cause more devastation and blame it on the Insurgents.

Kaspar and his commander stepped out into the evening chill. Kaspar inhaled deeply, welcoming a last lungful of cool night-time air into his lungs before snapping on the respirator. In the distance he could see the blue and yellow lights of the skyscrapers at the centre of Capital City. Round the corner, South Herdjis Lane was totally deserted.

Both men advanced slowly up the street, covering each other. At any moment Kaspar expected to come across an Insurgent lurking behind a bush, but there was no one. They both bypassed the bungalow and checked as far as the next junction, but there was no sign of an Insurgency support team. No vehicles, no signs, no noises, no infrared signatures, nothing. Kaspar wondered how Rhea had arrived without a vehicle, but she could have parked two clicks away and run in. Or she might not be there at all. The two Guardians stealthily retraced their steps until they reached the node.

Voss held up his hand and they stopped, one either side of the front door. Voss pointed at himself and then sliced the air with his hand at neck height indicating that he would go in high, then he pointed at Kaspar and made another slice at hip level, telling Kaspar to go low. Kaspar nodded. The street was so quiet. All Kaspar could hear was the faint whine of his rifle in his headset and the sound of his own breathing into the respirator.

Voss signalled – GO!

Kaspar leaned in and unlatched the door, Voss kicked it wide open and fired a wide-focus stun beam into the hall just in case there was anyone standing there – but there wasn't. Kaspar stayed in a crouch, covering Voss, who stepped past him and advanced as far as the door that led into the main area where the computers were housed. As soon as he reached it, Voss fired another wide beam into the computer hall. His rifle hadn't built to full charge yet – but then he didn't want full charge. He didn't need it, nor did he want the electro-magnetic pulse to fry the computer equipment. The shot was just to get anyone's head down while Kaspar followed by lobbing in three rapid-dispersal gas grenades. They exploded together and the room was instantly filled with a dense cloud of luxothane-G gas that would incapacitate anyone for a couple of hours.

Once in the room, Kaspar headed left, while Voss turned right. They both had their goggles set to infrared mode so that they would be able see any heat signatures, but there was nothing. The tall cabinets that housed the computers partitioned the large room into half a dozen narrow aisles that would have to be checked one by one. Kaspar worked his way to the end, sweeping each aisle. Nothing. When he turned, he saw that Voss had found nothing either. As they both started to move back towards the door, the powerful computer-room air conditioning had already started to disperse the gas.

A warning tone in Kaspar's headset and a small light in the peripheral zone of his goggles indicated that the room was now bright enough to see without infrared filters.

'Go white,' Voss ordered into his throat microphone.

Kaspar clicked off infra-red mode. Looking left, up the alleyway between two cabinets, Kaspar noticed something that he hadn't seen in IR mode. Lying on the floor, in the centre of one of the big floor tiles, was a vacuum-lifter, a handle with two big suckers attached. When applied to a floor tile, the vacuum-lifter stuck like glue and allowed the attached tile to be lifted out so as to allow access to the underfloor cabling. A valve on the handle let air back into the suckers to break the seal. It was standard equipment in a computer installation, but this one had just been left in the middle of the floor. The maintenance guys were usually really anal about tidying stuff away. This looked like someone was still working.

Voss opened his mouth to speak, but Kaspar put his fingers to his lips to stop him, then signalled that Voss should look at the floor. Voss nodded and a few more silent signals were all it took to make their plan.

'I told you this was a stupid idea,' Voss shouted. 'There are bombs going off all over and we've just wasted our time on a fool's errand. Let's get out of here and do some proper work instead of investigating your psychic hunches.'

The guy should have been an actor.

'Sorry, sir,' replied Kaspar. He pulled off his headset and throat mike and placed them on a nearby computer cabinet.

The two Guardians stomped noisily out of the computer room, leaving the door open, and headed along the hall. Voss opened the front door, before slamming it shut again. Both men then crept as stealthily as possible back to the computer room. With his headset off, Kaspar could hear nothing but the throb of the air conditioning, but Voss listened intently, his head cocked to one side and his finger pressing the earpiece deeper into his ear.

For a couple of moments there was nothing and Kaspar started to have doubts. Then Voss looked up at Kaspar and gave a quick thumbs-up. Both men slipped back in, rifles raised and ready, and started creeping back to where they knew they would find her emerging from the floor. Voss had the lead, and was nearly there when Kaspar heard a noise behind him.

Shit, he thought. She *does* have help. How did we miss that?

Now they were sandwiched, and he couldn't alert Voss because he had no headset. Kaspar turned round to face the door and cover their rear. There was a commotion behind him, and he knew that things weren't good.

There should have been a crack and a single flash of blue light as Voss stunned the unsuspecting ninja.

Instead?

Damn it! He was surrounded. Nobody had appeared at the door yet, so he risked turning away for a second. He whirled round just in time to see Voss kick the dagger from Rhea's hand; then a secondary kick had her flying backwards up the aisle. He was trying to get enough distance between them so that he could bring his rifle to bear again, but she closed the gap between them with lightning speed. She twisted her upper body and her left leg spun out behind her, impossibly long, incredibly fast, looping around in a great arc. Her heel struck Voss on his left temple and he went down hard.

Kaspar sighted over Voss, but he had no clear shot. He swung the rifle round to check the door. No shot there either. Just then, he spotted someone in the hall. He nearly fired, but he recognized the toe of a Guardian's boot and the emitter of a stun rifle.

Yes! Reinforcements! Voss must've sent for backup after all.

Relief flooded over him as he spun again to face Voss, moving swiftly towards him. He had to get to Rhea before she could kill herself. The fact that her dagger was lying on the floor would help, of course, but she probably still had a gun.

When he reached Voss's body and peered round the cabinets, all he could see was her foot disappearing over the top of the cabinet.

'Damn, you're fast!' Kaspar fired, but all he hit was the ceiling. Then he was in pursuit, running back round Voss to head her off before she could reach the door. There was a blue flash. Kaspar was just in time to see Rhea collapse. Her fall to the floor was the only thing Kaspar had seen her do that wasn't graceful.

He kept running to her, and knelt to check her pulse. She was alive, but her pulse was thready and weak. He turned to the door to see who his unexpected backup was. It was a Guardian, of course, but Kaspar didn't recognize him straight away. He was heavier-set and older than most of Kaspar's colleagues, but he was familiar. Then the Guardian removed his HUD and Kaspar recognized him at once.

Tilkian.

Instantly Kaspar knew what had happened. They had been betrayed. Probably by one of the nerds. Even nerds could be bribed or blackmailed, or just plain threatened. Tilkian knew that he was suspected and had followed them here to make sure his secrets remained just that. Kaspar knew there was only one thing he could do.

Hesitation would be fatal. He was younger, fitter and quicker – and Tilkian's rifle wouldn't have recharged yet. He threw himself backwards like a swimmer starting at backstroke, and while still lying on his back he took a snap-shot at Tilkian. The bright blue flash lanced out and struck the older man dead-centre. Tilkian didn't move. In fact, he hardly blinked. He just stood there.

'Wilding,' said Tilkian. 'Drop the weapon and stand up.'

Kaspar felt a little foolish. He had never known a person stay conscious after being hit by a charge from a stun rifle. Kaspar's mind scrambled to think of something else – fast.

'Guardian Wilding, apart from the fact that I'm wearing an electric-grounding mesh that makes me immune to your Mark Six light-show weapon, I'm also armed with the new Mark Seven stun rifle. During development, I believe they named it "electric napalm". And on its highest setting it does more than stun. A lot more.' Tilkian swung the rifle lazily towards Kaspar. 'Now drop your weapon and stand up, unless you want to share your friend's painful fate.'

Electric napalm – that didn't sound good. 'You've got it on its highest setting?'

'Of course.' Tilkian raised an eyebrow. 'I knew who I'd be dealing with. Drop your weapon. I won't ask you again.'

Kaspar reluctantly let go of his rifle and stood up. 'Is Rhea going to die?'

'Rhea? You're on first-name terms with Insurgents now, are you? Don't worry, she's not going to die. That would be too easy. But the Mark Seven will ensure that she's in constant agony. An agony from which she'll never wake. A fitting end, don't you think?' Tilkian patted his rifle. 'This baby is going to save us all that medical faffing around at the Clinic. Get hit with a blast from one of these, and once you go down you stay down and your body is racked with an intense pain from which there is no cure and no escape. Magnificent, eh? Now pick up the girl.'

'Why?'

'I will have to stage-manage this scene to an extent.'

'I meant, why should I help you?'

'Because I am offering you a gift.'

At Kaspar's puzzled look, Tilkian smiled unpleasantly. 'The gift of a rapid and relatively painless death.'

Thanks for nothing.

'Why the generosity?' said Kaspar, desperately searching for an escape route.

'Because it suits us both, Guardian Wilding. My own selfish reasons are many. I won't have to kill you myself, I won't have to get your blood on my just-cleaned uniform, I won't have to conceal that a Guardian was stunned with a stun rifle and committed to the North Wing. It just works all round.'

'And why should I help you avoid a little blood?' Kaspar said bitterly. 'You're already up to your ears in it.'

'Would you really prefer to linger in a drawer in the North Wing, watching high-definition films of rape and torture and mutilation and murder for the rest of your miserable, painful, artificially prolonged life? If you like I could arrange for you to have the drawer next to your mother.'

Kaspar's whole body froze momentarily as he realized what the commander was telling him. He lunged forward just as Tilkian took a step back, and swung his gun up to point directly at Kaspar's head.

'That's far enough,' said Tilkian.

Kaspar struggled to keep the revulsion off his face. His mum was at the Clinic . . . Or was Tilkian just playing with his head? 'Is my mum really in one of the drawers in the North Wing?'

'Of course. Traitorous bitch! I put her in there myself.' Tilkian smiled.

'I'm going to rip your heart out,' Kaspar hissed.

'You're welcome to try.' Tilkian shrugged.

It took every gram of restraint Kaspar possessed to hold back, but he knew Tilkian would own him before he'd covered even half the distance between them.

Think, Kaspar, damn it. Think!

'Pick up the girl,' Tilkian ordered, his smile fading. 'I'm getting tired of telling you that.'

Kaspar moved slowly towards Rhea. 'Why do you do it?'

'What?'

'Why do you murder your own? Are you part of the Insurgency, committed to their cause – or are you just a mercenary scumbag looking out for number one?'

Tilkian laughed. 'I thought you were the research genius. I was led to believe you had uncovered all our little secrets. I'm disappointed.'

'So educate me then.'

'Don't insult me by supposing we're a part of the Insurgency, with their namby-pamby attitude to casualties.' Tilkian spat contemptuously towards Rhea's body. 'Surely you didn't think someone like *her* could have planned all those bombings? It seems that people have severely overestimated your intelligence. Now pick her up.'

Kaspar bent and picked up Rhea. She hardly weighed anything. As he straightened up, he said, 'Just tell me one thing. Why?'

Tilkian sighed, as if he was being pestered by a child. 'Why did the Insurgency start, Guardian Wilding? Do you know your history?'

'Yes, I know my history,' snapped Kaspar. 'I know that you are tearing apart a society you swore to protect by gassing school children and bombing innocent people. I'd just like to know *why*?'

'I think we'll have her over here, near the door. Paralysed, while fleeing the scene of your murder.' Tilkian moved back a step. 'As you're so good at history, Guardian, tell me about the origin of the Badlands.'

Kaspar frowned.

'Keep working while you speak. You have a choice. If you don't want to work, we can always just skip ahead to the dying part.'

Kaspar bit back his bitter retort. He started carrying Rhea past where Voss's body lay.

'Generations ago,' he said wearily, 'the misguided technical geniuses of the east planted nukes deep in the Earth so as to change the way that the tectonic plates moved and to create more land for themselves. It all went horribly wrong, their entire country was turned into a lava lake and about ninety per cent of them died.'

'Actually, no. The death toll was more like sixty-eight per cent – but go on.'

Kaspar's brow furrowed. 'So they lived as nomads for years until they built up their numbers and recovered to an extent. That's when they started up the Insurgency, to take our land away from us because they'd destroyed their own.'

'Wrong.'

'Wrong?'

'Very wrong, Mr Wilding. Your grasp of history is as tenuous as your grasp on everything else. After the volcanic cataclysm, the survivors were homeless and starving. There was a huge exodus and millions of refugees streamed west to escape the lava.'

'West? To where? There's just . . .'

'That's right. Here. Millions of refugees came here, to the place we call home – and they were allowed to settle in the south, near the Voren Lakes. A remarkable act of generosity, don't you think? And they flourished. They became a nation within a nation.'

'That's not what I was taught. I don't understand.'

'No, of course you don't. They rebuilt their scientific infrastructure really quickly. Secretly, of course. They weren't trusted, and their access to nuclear materials was prevented. But they weren't really interested in that kind of science any more. They had learned their lesson. Trying to manipulate the planet had been hubris, so in future their plans would be . . . more manageable. They started to develop a biological weapon. A binary virus, genetically engineered to be harmless to them but lethal to their enemies – their enemies being anyone who wasn't one of them. And when the weapon was ready, they released it.'

Even preoccupied as he was, Kaspar listened avidly to what Tilkian was saying, though he was revolted by it.

'The refugees repaid their hosts by unleashing a plague. Within a year, seventy-five per cent of their enemies were destroyed and the rest were fractured into tiny pockets of survivors, sick and demoralized. The binary virus ravaged their bodies and altered the DNA of a significant number of them. And when they were too weak to fight back, there was no more need for secrecy. The survivors were simply hunted down and killed. Only a few thousand escaped across the border into the Badlands.' That was the true War to End All Wars – one-sided, brutal and mercifully short.

Behind Tilkian, Voss was stirring.

Kaspar's head swam with the enormity of it. Tilkian had to be lying. How had he not heard any of this before? And yet it all sounded so plausible, backed up by Tilkian's smug tone. Voss was silently rising to his feet behind Tilkian. Kaspar had to keep Tilkian's attention away from his boss.

But how?

'That can't be right,' said Kaspar. 'If we were nearly wiped out and driven into the Badlands . . .'

'Not *we*, Guardian Wilding. Not *us*. *We* weren't driven into the Badlands. *They* were.'

'*They?* Who? Talk sense.'

Voss got up and started walking softly forward. Tilkian was oblivious.

'The original inhabitants of this country, Guardian Wilding. *They* were driven out. *They* were forced to live in the Badlands. And ever since, *they've* wanted their country back. *That's* what the Insurgency is about.'

'But . . . that would mean that we . . .'

'He finally gets it,' Tilkian said with contempt. '*We* are the "misguided technical geniuses of the east" as you so colourfully put it. *We* stole this land. *We* came within a whisker of annihilating the people who lived here. The society you are so proud of is built on a genocide.'

Kaspar couldn't speak. He couldn't think what to say in any case. He tried not to give Voss away by looking at him. He stared at Tilkian and forced himself to say something to keep his attention.

'What's the problem, Wilding?' smiled Tilkian. 'Having trouble working out whose side you should be on?'

Voss moved up and stood next to Tilkian. Tilkian turned to look at him.

'Abel.' Tilkian nodded. 'You've looked better.'

'Grigor,' replied Voss. 'Still making speeches.'

Tilkian turned back to Kaspar. 'I was just enlightening our young friend here about—'

Voss's right hand shot upward towards the back of Tilkian's neck and drove a thin steel spike between the base of the skull and the first cervical vertebra. Tilkian's eyes widened in shock. His head reflexively tilted back as

305

the steel penetrated the medulla of his brain, where his heart and breathing functions were controlled. The strike was almost certainly fatal, but Voss made sure by plunging the thin-bladed dagger that he held in his other hand into the left side of Tilkian's neck, and then slicing the blade forward, all with a single stroke.

It was as if Tilkian dropped through a trap door. His legs crumpled and he went down, vertically. His lifeless body pitched forward to land face down. A halo of blood started to form around his head.

Kaspar stood stunned. He'd seen plenty of dead bodies by now, but this was only the second time he'd seen someone die. Compared to this, the death of the guy in the desert and the suicide of the ninja at Wissant Avenue had been positively sterile. Even when he'd seen that Voss was conscious he hadn't expected the end to be so brutal, so bloody. He wasn't sure how he felt. Tilkian had given him so much information to process. But right now he had to focus.

'Sir, we have to get Rhea out of here,' Kaspar urged. 'If Tilkian is here, the others of the SSG can't be far away. We have to leave before his backup arrives.'

'I'm afraid not, kid,' said Voss, swinging his rifle to point at Kaspar. '*I'm* his backup.'

'What?' The look on Kaspar's face was now beyond confusion. He was still supporting Rhea, like someone trying to dance with a partner who'd drunk too much, but Voss's words brought him to a sudden standstill.

Voss pointed the rifle about a metre to Kaspar's left and

fired. The main stun beam hit the cabinet, but Rhea and Kaspar were caught in the peripheral charge. It was like being hit by a train. Kaspar fell back and slumped, sliding down the cabinet until he sat on the floor with Rhea on top of him.

'It's a good trick that — shooting to miss. They don't teach that one at the Academy,' said Voss. 'You get a partial stun, but because you didn't get the main beam, no after-effects that will show up in a post-mortem.'

Kaspar was tingling from head to foot. He tried to get up but his body was no longer his own.

'I warned you that curiosity had to be kept on a leash. But thanks to you it has all worked out for the best.'

Kaspar's mouth moved, but nothing came out.

'Old Grigor here was getting sloppy, making too many mistakes. So now Commander Tilkian and you will both have died heroic deaths at the hands of the evil terrorist you're currently grappling with. You will become a hero, posthumously of course, and I will get a promotion to head up the Special Support Group. Everybody wins.'

Kaspar's voice returned, weakly. 'You can't get away with it. People know now. Your people at the Analysis Division, Mac, Brother Simon.'

Voss smiled. 'Those two losers at the Analysis Division are already dead. They were killed earlier this evening in a tragic fire in their office. Probably terrorist arson. I take care of business.'

Kaspar's blood ran cold. Mac . . . would she be next? Or had Voss already taken care of her?

'Have you gone after Mac too?' he asked, almost afraid to hear the answer.

Voss regarded him, before shaking his head pityingly, his eyes cold.

'Don't you touch her. Keep her out of this,' Kaspar hissed. 'If you harm one hair on her head, I will kill you, even if I have to come back from hell itself to do so.'

Voss roared with laughter. 'Oh, how touching. You're in love with her,' he said with amused contempt. 'Rest assured, Wilding, I wouldn't dream of harming Mackenzie. She'll do exactly as I tell her and keep her mouth shut.'

Kaspar disagreed, but he kept his opinion to himself. The last thing he wanted to do was persuade Voss that Mac was a potential threat. Glaring at Voss, he at least had the satisfaction of knowing that Mac wouldn't keep quiet. She'd go to the authorities. Even if he failed, Mac would make sure that Voss paid.

'Wilding, you still don't get it, do you?' said Voss. 'Mackenzie is my daughter. D'you really think she'll choose you over me?'

Kaspar stared at Voss. Mac was Voss's *daughter*? She couldn't be. Voss had to be lying. He searched Voss's expression for any hint of deception but there was none. His boss was telling the truth. Mackenzie really was his daughter. No wonder she'd kept her job after the databot fiasco. Had she been reporting every conversation and every move he'd made back to her dad? If so, then Kaspar had never stood a chance.

'So Mac has been telling you everything I've said and

done and I didn't suspect a thing,' Kaspar said bitterly. 'God, I'm stupid.'

'My daughter refused point-blank to tell me what you were up to. The two of us are going to have a full and frank discussion about that when I get back home tonight,' said Voss, his words clipped with anger. 'She's been far more questioning and far less accepting of my role in the Alliance since she started hanging around with you. Something else I have to thank you for.'

'Well, Brother Simon knows of my suspicions,' Kaspar tried to bluff. 'And in the event of my death or disappearance, a full report will be sent straight to him.'

Voss shook his head, looking at Kaspar with pity. 'Wilding, who do you think Tilkian and I report to?'

'Well, the other Council Members will—'

'Do absolutely nothing. It's amazing. All that talent, all these brains, and you know bugger all. The Council knows everything. The Council plans everything. Do you think I just decided to kill Tilkian on the spur of the moment? I killed Tilkian because there was a Council resolution to kill him. Passed unanimously, twenty-one votes to nil.'

'But why? Why do the Council . . . ?' Kaspar couldn't even frame the question.

'Those in the Council have had their positions and status handed down to them, and they'll be handing on their legacy to their children and their children's children. What they have works for them, so what's their incentive to change it? Not all of us are content to live in barracks and eat melons for the rest of our lives. The Council live very well in their armoured mobile palaces and their underground retreats. They have servants, riches, power. And when I'm head of the Special Support Group, I'll live very well too.'

Kaspar felt like he'd spent his life asleep and was only just waking up to a world he didn't recognize and didn't want any part of. The whole Alliance was rotten from top to bottom. A whole society of genocidal bastards, Kaspar included, living in a stolen country, led by a Council of amoral overlords, supported by a devoted army of torturers who murdered and terrorized their own people just so they could wear silk suits and drink expensive wine. The only decent people in the whole world were the Insurgents. At least they were fighting for a cause, not just fighting for themselves.

'And the slaughter of innocent people, innocent children, means nothing to you?' whispered Kaspar.

'Why should it?' frowned Voss. 'The only one that matters to me is my daughter. And as for Loring School, most of the pupils there were the children of Crusaders who've chosen to live and work in Capital City. Why should I care about them?'

Kaspar just sat there, looking up at Voss and cradling the unconscious body of the only person he knew who was actually morally entitled to be on this entire damned continent. Voss walked back to the door and picked up Rhea's dagger, and still Kaspar couldn't move. He wasn't even sure he wanted to, that he deserved to.

He realized something else too. The High Council were

terrified that anyone in the Alliance might develop the same skills as some of the Crusaders. Empathy meant shared fears and feelings, memories and emotions outside the scope and control of the Council. And they would never tolerate that.

Heartsick, Kaspar closed his eyes. He asked softly, 'What's wrong with peace? What's wrong with no more war between the Alliance and the Crusaders?'

'Kid, where's the profit in that?' Voss answered.

Kaspar stopped fighting to open his eyes, to rise. He had failed. Every truth he'd ever believed in was a lie. So what was the point of anything any more? He gave in to his pain and despair and allowed himself to fall into unconsciousness, knowing he'd never wake up again.

44

Kaspar was falling, falling into blackness. But it was good because he wasn't afraid any more.

He didn't hurt, not physically, but he knew intense, bitter regret. If he had just one wish . . .

But he didn't.

Wishes were for the living.

Kas saw his parents, and Grandma . . . though it was kind of weird to see someone else's life flash past your eyes, but in a good way it was fair. It was the least he could do, to give Rhea some kind of death. She wouldn't be allowed one of her own. Instead, she was permanently paralysed, and her body would be abused by sadists before being trapped in a living hell at the Clinic. How many like Rhea had there been over the years? How many Crusaders had tried to get back their own land and failed? How many more would there have to be?

The sense of falling slowed. It was replaced by a softness, a warmth. He felt like he was being laid to rest on a bed. And the bread . . . he could smell the bread again. Oh, it was so strong now. How could you be dying, or even dead, and still be hungry? And it wasn't quite so dark now. He could hear a voice getting louder, a little girl's voice. Kaspar slowly opened his eyes. Above him, the sky had been painted with magenta and cyan and amber as well as pale blue. The air was so sweet, not just with the aroma of mellisse bread but with a ripe freshness Kaspar had never experienced, not even when he had visited this place before.

'Hello, Kas.' A little girl sat beside him, peering down into his face. She must have been about eight and she wore a blue dress decorated with tiny, vivid, blood-red poppies. Her bright green eyes were vaguely familiar. She sat with her legs tucked beneath her on the dry, springy grass. Kaspar tried to sit up, but found he couldn't so he immediately stopped trying. He tried wriggling his fingers. His left thumb could move. None of his other fingers stirred. He tried to move his arms, his legs. Nothing doing.

'Hi,' he replied. It was so pleasant, so peaceful to be on this grassy hillside, watching the sun rise. 'Where am I?'

'You know where you are. On the hill above my grandma's house. That's her down there.' The girl pointed.

Kaspar turned his head and saw the cottage at the foot of the hill, and at the door an elderly woman, with flour on her hands. OK, so his head was now working. He tried moving his arms again. The fingers of his left hand were beginning to work, albeit stiffly. The right hand didn't even twitch.

Still, no rush.

'What is this place?' he asked. 'I searched the datanet for

this location but got nowhere in a hurry. None of these landmarks were recognized.'

The girl sighed. 'All this is gone now. You built your Capital City over it.'

Kaspar was stunned. 'You're joking.'

'Why would I joke about it?' the girl said seriously.

'What's your name?' Kaspar asked, though he suspected he already had the answer.

'Rhea.' She frowned. 'Are you having a silly day?'

'A silly day?'

'A day when your brain doesn't work,' said Rhea. 'Grandma doesn't like those. She tells me off if I have one of those.'

A silly day? Try a senseless life. A meaningless existence.

'Rhea, I'm so sorry. I didn't know . . . I really didn't. I thought your people were evil. I thought I was doing the right thing.'

'I know that.' Rhea shrugged. 'I know you're different.'

'How d'you know?' asked Kaspar.

'Because I saw your mum.'

'What? When?'

'The first day we met, in the desert. While I was carrying you, I had a vision of you and your mum.'

'What vision?'

'Of the day you nearly died in the forest when the wolves were chasing you. Your mum saved you. My grandma used to tell me about your mum so it wasn't hard to recognize her when I saw her.' Rhea turned and pointed over his shoulder. There, about twenty metres away by a tree, stood Kaspar's mum, but she wasn't looking at him. She was looking with sorrowful eyes towards the cottage. Kaspar immediately tried to sit up but his body still wasn't his own.

'She's always here,' shrugged Rhea.

'I've never seen her here before,' said Kaspar.

'That's because you haven't been looking.'

'Mum? It's me, Kaspar,' Kaspar tried shouting, but his mum never once turned her head.

'She can't hear you,' said Rhea.

'Why not?'

'Because you're sharing my memories, not the other way round. Your mum was a good person. She tried to help us. She was like you.'

'Yes, she was a Guardian too.'

'Much more than that.'

'What d'you mean?'

'She was on our side.'

'How d'you know?'

'Because she's here, still trying to reach my grandma's cottage.'

So Tilkian was telling the truth about his mum. Waves of helplessness swept over Kaspar as he turned towards her again.

'You and your mum can only be here because you share our abilities. We thought it was only us Insurgents who could share knowledge until your mum. She must have found out something. She must have made real contact with one of us and tried to help,' said Rhea.

'I was told my mum had died. Many years ago.'

'But she didn't. You know for a fact that she didn't, otherwise she wouldn't be stuck out here like me. She'd be inside talking to Grandma. I can't talk to my grandma for real again until I die. Then I can give her this.' Rhea held out her hand.

'What is it?'

'Something she really needs.'

Kaspar lifted his head for a closer look. 'A necklace?'

Silver-, gold- and pearl-coloured over-sized beads adorned what looked like a long thin line of black rope.

'That's nice,' said Kaspar faintly. 'A bit long and heavy for you, though.'

'It's taken so long to make this. And it was really expensive.' Rhea didn't speak with pride or awe. Instead, her voice held a profound sadness. They regarded each other. What was Kaspar missing? With a frown, he turned his head to look down at the cottage, then across to the valley beyond.

'Where has your grandma gone?'

Rhea didn't even bother to turn round. 'Back into her cottage. She knows there's not much time left. I've never been inside Grandma's cottage but I need to get in there to see her.'

'Hang on, you told me all about the inside of your grandma's cottage. How could you know about it if you've never been in it?'

'Grandma used to tell me all about it when we were

living in the Badlands shelters among the lava lakes. She used to tell such beautiful stories, about streams, and lakes, hills and trees.'

'So this was her home before you had to live in the Badlands?'

'Oh no. Grandma was born in the Badlands. She just told beautiful stories gathered from handed-down memories.'

'So this isn't real?'

Rhea gave him a pitying look, the one reserved by children for when an adult has just been unbelievably stupid. 'Of course it's not real. You *know* it's not real.'

'OK, I mean, it's not a real memory.'

'It's a memory but from a long, long time ago. Many decades ago. A memory of a place we once called home, but was taken from us,' said Rhea. 'This was the land we Crusaders owned before we were forced to live in the Badlands.'

'So you share memories, then?'

'When we die – yes,' smiled Rhea. 'Then all our memories and all the things we know are passed on as common knowledge to the ones still living who are able and willing to receive that knowledge.'

So much for séances, and emanating off a higher plane. All that had been nonsense. The Insurgents died and passed on their knowledge to the living who possessed the same gene; it was that simple. Kaspar took a moment to try and take in what he was being told.

'I get that I'm here because you're a touch-empath,

but . . .' He glanced over his shoulder and then back to Rhea. 'Why is my mum here?'

'She's here because Grandma told me about her.' Rhea smiled. 'She's knowledge passed down to me. If you were talking with your mother right now, you wouldn't see a cottage and a stream.'

'What would I see?'

'I don't know. Your dad, maybe? A happy memory from her childhood? The end of the rainbow? Wherever she needs to be.'

'And you need to be down there with your grandma?'

'Yes.'

'To give her that necklace?'

'Uh-huh. A very special necklace. It has twenty-one beads.'

Kaspar peered closer. Each bead had a long number etched around it. 'What's the significance of the numbers?'

Rhea smiled and cocked her head to one side.

'Oh . . . twenty-one beads. I get it. One bead for each member of the High Council?' Kaspar stretched out his now-working left arm and took the necklace from Rhea's unresisting hand. Resting the necklace on his chest, he twisted each bead round for a closer look, using the fingers of his left hand. His right hand was still useless. 'These numbers . . . are they . . . are they sets of coordinates? You have the coordinates of all the twenty-one High Councillors? How on earth did you get that?'

'Well, from the backup for the Power Grid Statistical Analysis department, of course.'

'I don't understand,' said Kaspar, handing back the necklace.

'I get it, and I'm only eight.'

'You're cheating!'

'Am not!'

'You're not really eight. You're the same age as me.'

'And a lot smarter.'

'I'd be smart as hell too if I had the knowledge and experience of all my ancestors rattling around inside my head,' frowned Kaspar, sitting up. He could sit up! His body was slowly becoming his again, though his right arm was still a useless lump hanging off his shoulder.

'That's a bit snotty, considering most of them died because of the Alliance,' said Rhea.

'Sorry.' Kaspar grimaced. It was such a little word but it was all he had.

'Common knowledge is how we evolve,' said Rhea. 'Our way of making sure we don't make the same mistakes as our ancestors.'

'Huh?' Kaspar tried to stand but his legs still weren't his own.

'I told you; when one of us dies, all our memories, everything we know and everything we are passes as common knowledge to those left behind,' said Rhea.

Kaspar shook his head. 'How is that possible?'

'Certain animals can do something similar. Sheep and blue tits and some other birds, I think. Have you never heard of communes of animals where one animal is taught how to overcome an obstacle, say to find food, and then all the others know how to do the same thing without having to be shown? Well, it's the same with us. We can share our knowledge, but only when we die. And not all of us can do it. Only a few, like me. All those who can pass on knowledge volunteer to fight to get back what was once ours. We're the elite of the Insurgency. There aren't very many of us left now, though.'

'All of you who can pass on knowledge, you're the ones I call ninjas,' Kaspar realized.

Rhea nodded and continued to skip around him, her bare feet shining with the early morning dew from the grass.

'Most of us live in Capital City using fake IDs and living fake lives. That's why we have to use masks when we break into places, to protect our identities. You blew my cover when you came into my gym. I was very cross with you.'

Kaspar exhaled sharply when he remembered how to breathe. It all made so much sense now, the *real* reason why the Council were desperate for none of the Insurgents to die. 'That's why you're kept alive in drawers, so that none of your knowledge can ever be passed on.'

'You're not very clever, are you?' said Rhea. 'Your mum figured it out all by herself.'

'How the hell is any normal person supposed to figure out that you and the other ninjas have that capability?' said Kaspar, stung.

'Your mum did.'

'Am I going to be stuck here for all eternity listening

to you tell me how stupid I am?' snapped Kaspar. 'Because if it's a choice between you and living in a drawer, I'll need to think seriously about it.'

Rhea stopped skipping to stare at him. She sniffed, her lips turned down, her eyes sparkling with unshed tears. 'That's not very nice.'

Kaspar closed his eyes briefly before exhaling on a sigh. 'I'm sorry. I didn't mean it. I'm just angry and frustrated and I'm taking it out on you.'

'You wouldn't like it if you were shut up for ever in a drawer without ever being allowed to die and pass on what you know.' Rhea was one wrong word away from bursting into tears.

'I'm really sorry,' said Kaspar. 'I . . . it's all been a bit of a shock. And the worst part is, I can't do anything about it now.'

Rhea knelt down next to him, her expression now serious. 'What happens when there's a major power cut?'

Kaspar blinked at her sudden change of subject, but her expression told him that what she was saying was important – at least to her.

'Well, the backup power kicks in.'

'And if it's a *really* big power cut?'

'The backup power is prioritized.'

'To . . .'

'Hospitals, military headquarters?'

'All of whose locations we know. And . . . ?'

'And . . . other high-priority places?'

'And what are your most important high-priority places?'

321

'I don't know. Key industries, computer nodes. Oh, wait! The mobile shelters of the High Councillors. They're self-contained but they all tap into local power. I get it now. Anyone accessing the power-usage statistics can ignore fixed locations and concentrate on power drains in out-of-the-way places to locate the mobile headquarters of all the Council members. That's why you needed the real-time power usage statistics, to find the Councillors' current locations. And now you have the coordinates of all their locations. That's brilliant.'

'I like it,' smiled Rhea. 'It was my idea, actually. It's ironic really. It only works because your High Council are so paranoid about security. If they parked their shelters near to factories or hospitals or major computer hubs, we wouldn't be able to spot them. But they go and hide them in the middle of nowhere, so the power drains show up as anomalies. We can now locate all the High Councillors of the Alliance to within one hundred metres.'

Kaspar nodded slowly.

'You get it now?' asked Rhea.

He nodded again.

'Rhea, why didn't you just tell me this face to face? At the gym, or the night you came to my room?'

'Would you have believed me? Besides, trusting any of you doesn't come easily to us. The last time we trusted you, you stole everything from us and tried to wipe us out into the bargain. Besides, I didn't come to tell you anything: I came to find out what you knew and how you knew it. But we never wanted to kill people. And we had nothing to do with what happened at Loring School or any of the bombs that killed innocent people. We've only ever killed Guardians, and only then when we had no other choice.'

Kaspar nodded. 'I know. By the way, how did you get into my room at the Academy that night?'

'You could see some of my secrets so it's only fair that I could see some of yours. I peeked into your memories to learn the layout of the Academy, guard patrol positions, passcodes to the doors and the exact location of your room.'

Oh God! She saw far more than Kaspar had thought possible.

Rhea stood up and faced him, her hands on her hips. 'Two things. First, you should train more seriously. I kicked your bottom. Twice.'

'Yes, you did,' Kaspar agreed ruefully. 'Thank you for not killing me.'

'You're welcome. Don't make me regret it.'

'And the second thing?'

'Always check for hidden weapons. For instance, you didn't suspect this, did you?'

Rhea fingered the chain around her neck and pulled out a pendant from beneath her dress. She held it out and Kaspar looked closely. It was a smaller version of her black dagger, barely ten centimetres long, in a snug little scabbard.

'This belonged to my mother,' she said. 'I always keep

it close to my heart.' She tucked the knife back into her dress. 'I need you to use this on me.'

No way.

'I can save you,' said Kaspar.

'No, you can't. That SSG Guardian made sure of that,' she replied. 'I thought you said you got it now?'

'I do. It's just . . . maybe our medical people could try to find a cure.'

'It's too late for that,' said Rhea gently. 'And we both know it.'

'But what you're asking me to do . . . You're not my enemy, Rhea. How can I kill you in cold blood?'

'I know I'm asking a lot, but I'm also asking you to help me stop this war. I'm asking you to help me save hundreds, maybe thousands of lives. I need you, Kaspar,' she said softly. She threw the necklace up into the air and caught it again. 'It's pretty, isn't it? It really was *very* expensive.'

'Yes, I know.'

Rhea gave him a significant look. 'No, you don't.'

Kaspar couldn't look away. She was right. He had no idea how many of her friends, her family, had been tortured or were now living in stasis hell in the Clinic's North Wing to enable her to get the information she had on the necklace.

'It's getting chilly.' Rhea wrapped her arms round herself against the morning air, which was beginning to have a bite to it. A strange, icy breeze was beginning to blow around them. 'It's time for you to go back.'

'Voss will be waiting for me,' Kaspar protested.

'You have surprise on your side,' said Rhea.

'Suppose I fail?' said Kaspar desperately.

'If you fail, we all do. So don't!' Rhea smiled. 'I have to go to sleep now. I need you to promise me something.'

'Anything.'

'Promise me you'll make sure I don't wake up.'

45

Kaspar slowly opened his eyes. He tried to move, to stand, but his legs were still not accepting messages from his brain. Voss was standing seven metres away holding Rhea's dagger. The unconscious girl still lay slumped across him, face down. His left hand was round her shoulders and his right was trapped between her stomach and his thigh. Kaspar shook his head to clear it. He needed to do this. He had one shot at getting it right. Voss wouldn't give him another. But how could he do this when his body still wasn't working properly?

Voss started towards him.

'There's still something I don't get . . .' Kaspar began. Hidden from Voss by Rhea's body, he wriggled the fingers of his right hand. Thank goodness. They were finally working. His right hand crept up the front of Rhea's chest and hooked into the zipper of her costume.

'And what would be the point of telling you now?' asked Voss.

Six metres.

Kaspar slowly pulled down the zip. 'Don't you want to explain . . .?'

Five metres.

His hand reached between her breasts, and found the scabbard.

'No, I don't. I'm not Tilkian. Time to die, kid.'

Four metres.

Kaspar slid the knife from its sheath. It was small, but it was heavy.

'Not even . . .'

Three metres.

Heavy blade, minimal handle. Perfect for throwing.

'Oh, shut up, Wilding,' Voss hissed.

Two metres.

'You've been a pain in my arse for the last time.' Voss leaned forward and raised the dagger to point at Kaspar's throat. Kaspar let his right hand drop slowly to the floor.

'Goodnight, kid.'

One metre.

Yeah. Good night, you bastard! And rot in hell.

Kaspar brought the knife up smoothly in a rapid underhand throw. Kaspar was still weak, but over such a short distance he really couldn't miss and Voss had no time to react. The knife caught him just under the sternum and lodged deep in the right ventricle of his heart. Voss made a little sighing noise and collapsed, first to his knees, and then face down on the floor, dead before he fully hit the ground.

Kaspar gently rolled Rhea off himself and then carried her a couple of metres further into the room, mainly to get her away from Voss. He walked back and prised Rhea's long-bladed dagger out of the hand of his dead boss, wiping it carefully on his sleeve. He didn't even want Voss's sweat on Rhea, much less his blood.

Outside, he could hear sirens approaching in the distance. He knew that in a couple of minutes the goons of the SSG would arrive looking for their boss, Tilkian. Kaspar knelt down and instinctively felt for her pulse. She was still unconscious from the effect of the neuro-paralyser, and according to Tilkian that was the way she'd stay, locked in her head, screaming silently in agony until the day she died. He took her hands in his, then stopped. He quickly went back to Voss's body, rolled him over onto his back and pulled the little throwing knife out of his body. He wiped off the blood on Voss's tunic before slipping it back into the scabbard on the cord around Rhea's neck. He then zipped up her costume.

And yet he hesitated. Kaspar knew what was at stake, but could he do this? Cold-bloodedly cause the death of someone who wasn't his enemy? But if he didn't, nothing would ever change. The truth would never be known. And after tonight, when the Brothers and Sisters of the Council moved to new positions, the information on the necklace would be useless. The beaded necklace Rhea had held in her hands during his vision was just a dream-state representation of the knowledge she held in her head. If he didn't do as she'd requested, he'd be failing her, and everything they'd both been through would've been for nothing.

It was the last thing she had asked of him.

He placed Rhea's long-bladed knife in her right hand. Curling his fingers around hers, he held the point of the dagger pointed towards her abdomen, just like he'd seen the other ninja do.

'I hope Grandma likes your present,' he whispered.

And Kaspar pushed the knife inwards and upwards to the hilt. He owed Rhea a swift death, if nothing else. It took less than five seconds for Rhea to stop twitching. Tears in his eyes, Kaspar leaned over her to kiss her warm lips. He stood, stepped over Voss, walked past Tilkian without a backward glance and slipped away into the night.

46

In the Badlands, about a hundred and twenty kilometres from the city, a lizard scuttled away as a crack suddenly appeared in the hard-baked sand. A second parallel fissure opened up, and both lengthened and widened until a strip of sand about thirty metres long and four metres wide had been raised a few centimetres above the desert. Then the strip started to rotate along one edge, tilting up like a capsizing raft until a deep trench was revealed. But the trench wasn't empty. In it lay a large truck with an armoured cab. The huge wheels were completely deflated and the engine was beyond repair, but on the back of the truck lay an immaculately maintained missile and its support equipment. As soon as the oblong piece of fake desert that had camouflaged it for so long was clear, the missile started to rise, the launch rail rotating smoothly until the missile pointed vertically.

About fifteen kilometres away, quite near the burned-out wreck of a hovercar, another trench opened up, revealing another missile.

Over the next two minutes, all across the Badlands, a total of twenty-one missiles, each with dual warheads, broke cover and were bathed in sunlight for the first time in over twenty years. Then, at a single coordinated command, their solid rocket motors ignited. There was a second's pause as the missiles strained against the hold-down clamps, and then all of them rose swiftly into the air and climbed vertically for a while before gently tilting over and heading west and south.

In the city, a Guardian Civil Defence Supervisor had just decided to ignore a report from the seismograph warning network.

DIFFUSE LOW-INTENSITY SEISMIC ACTIVITY: BADLANDS NO THREAT.

But then a second, more urgent alert came in from the Air Defence network.

TRACKING TWENTY-ONE INBOUND MISSILES ON DEPRESSED TRAJECTORIES.

The supervisor's heart rate tripled by the time he had confirmed the launches and passed the word up the chain of command, but ten seconds later, as he watched the computer display the predicted impact points on his screen, he started to laugh and laugh hard.

The missiles passed the high point of their trajectories and deployed their warheads as they started their final supersonic plunge towards their targets.

As the impact points were confirmed, the supervisor laughed louder and louder.

'They've launched missiles. They're going to kill us all!' His assistant was frantic.

'No, they're not,' replied the supervisor, wiping tears of mirth from his eyes. 'Look at the targets. They've finally used their ultimate weapon, but all they're going to do is kill a few sheep and some trees. All those missiles and the fools won't hit a single military installation or a population centre. None of our Alliance citizens will even be injured. What a bunch of morons. Ha ha! One of their missiles is going to land in Calliston Water. That's in the middle of nowhere, for God's sake. And look at this! Another is going to hit Pelham Forest. Even the insects have abandoned that godforsaken place.'

Twenty-one intermediate range missiles, each carrying two one-megaton nuclear warheads, streaked through the evening air towards twenty-one anonymous locations scattered throughout the countryside. Only those members of the High Council who were watching their screens in their luxurious mobile underground retreats understood the importance of the ludicrous trajectories. A glass of vintage wine fell from Brother Simon's hand and smashed on his hand-woven silk rug as he sat frozen in his plush leather wingback chair. He could only watch helplessly as the warheads designated 'track fifteen' converged on a remote hillside thirty-seven kilometres from the capital. He was powerless to act as the warheads struck, penetrated ninety metres beneath the lush pasture and detonated within one hundred and fifty metres of their intended target. The resulting explosion created a huge underground cave, collapsed all the tunnels under the hill, crushed the luxurious mobile centre as if it was paper, and buried what was left of Brother Simon under a million tonnes of earth.

Within a couple of seconds all twenty-one members of the High Council, who had believed themselves invulnerable in their mobile underground retreats, were dead.

47

On his way back to the Academy, Kaspar checked to see if Voss had been bluffing about the fate of his two 'tame nerds', as he liked to call them. A fire had indeed raged in an office at the Analysis Division of the Academy. It had been so ferocious in its intensity that the authorities were still trying to confirm the IDs of the two fatalities. Kaspar didn't need to wait for confirmation. Voss had been telling the truth. And the worst thing of all was that Kaspar couldn't for the life of him remember their names. He found himself choking on regret that he'd inadvertently set in motion a chain of events that had cost so many lives.

And what would he say to Mac? Should he tell her the cruel truth about her dad or tell a kinder lie? How was he supposed to tell her that Voss had died by his hand? She'd never forgive him. Kaspar knew this wasn't about him but he was desperate not to lose Mac from his life.

But that had to be her decision, not his.

Mac wasn't at her usual desk at Library Services, but then again, Kaspar didn't expect her to be. He contacted her via his CommLink, using a channel that was supposed to be for Guardian tactical use only. The moment she saw who it was she beamed at him. Kaspar swallowed.

'Hey, Kas. Glad to see you're all right. There have been some really strange, powerful rumbles felt right across Capital City for the last hour or so. It felt like underground thunder. Any idea what those are?'

Kaspar had a pretty good idea but he was going to keep his ideas to himself – at least for the time being. It hadn't taken the Insurgency long to act on Rhea's information. Kaspar still couldn't process how he was supposed to feel about that. Too much had happened in a short space of time and his brain was on overload.

'Can I come to see you or can we meet some place?'

'What? Now? It's after midnight.'

'I know. I'm sorry, but it's important.'

Mac's smile faded as she took in Kaspar's sombre expression. 'OK. I'll meet you in the recreation room in ten minutes.'

Kaspar nodded and disconnected the call. He had ten minutes to work out what he was going to say and how he was going to say it.

Kaspar stood up when Mac entered the rec room. He'd taken a seat away from everyone else in the furthest corner away from the door. What he had to say was for Mac's ears only. He watched as she made her way over to him, curiosity written large across her face.

'Hi, Kas.' Mac smiled.

Kaspar nodded and waited for Mac to sit down before he did the same, choosing to sit next to her after an awkward moment spent standing and wondering if he should.

'So what's the problem? Akinyeme and Chin are still working on the data we gave them, but it's looking good so far,' said Mac.

So she didn't know about them either. Oh, God!

'Kas? Why did you want to see me this late at night – not that I'm complaining.' Mac winked at him.

'I . . . it's about your dad.'

Mac sat back, her eyes never leaving Kaspar's face. Her lips turned down with disappointment. 'Oh. So you've found out who my dad is. I guess it was only a matter of time.'

'Mackenzie, I—'

'Look, I'm sorry I didn't tell you that Voss is my dad, but I didn't want you acting all weird around me just because he happens to be your boss,' Mac interrupted. 'People either run for the Badlands when they find out or they're all over me like a rash 'cause they think they can impress my dad through me. It drives me nuts. But I never—'

'Mackenzie, I've got some bad news.' Kaspar had to break in. He couldn't let her carry on assuming that he was there to accuse her of something.

'Bad news?' Mac repeated sharply. 'What kind of bad news?'

Kaspar took a deep breath. 'I'm so sorry, Mac, but it's about your dad. He . . . he died tonight.'

Mac's eyes widened in horror. Her mouth fell open. 'Dad . . . ?' she whispered.

'I'm so sorry,' Kaspar repeated.

'But how? I don't understand. I spoke to him a couple of hours ago. He was fine.' Mac's eyes glistened as she stared at Kaspar. 'How can he be dead? How did he die?'

Silence.

The truth? A lie? Right or wrong? Which was it going to be?

Choose, Kaspar. Choose.

Only at that moment did Kaspar realize Voss had been right about his feelings for Mac. Somehow, sometime when he wasn't paying attention, he'd fallen for her. And this was the moment when he was going to lose her.

'How did my dad die, Kaspar?' Mac's voice was choked with tears.

Kaspar's gaze dropped to his lap but he forced himself to look Mac in the eyes as he spoke. 'I killed him.'

48

Early the following morning, Kaspar visited the North Wing of the Clinic. He was ready to take out anyone and everyone who got in his way, but the place was deserted. Had the rats felt the ship sinking and fled?

There was a sense of subdued panic in Capital City. When the daily early morning multi-media address by one of the High Councillors didn't happen, rumours began to abound. When no one from the High Council stepped forward to refute the rumours, speculation took hold of Capital City like some kind of virus. The explosions the night before . . . Could it be . . . ? But that was impossible. Surely the Crusaders couldn't have targeted all the High Councillors in one night? No one knew quite what had happened, but there was a general feeling of the calm before an enormous storm.

What with the rumours and gossip circulating, and most people glued to their TV sets and the datanet news, no one paid much attention to a lone Guardian walking through the Clinic's North Wing.

It took Kaspar over four hours to find her. He wasn't

exactly sure of the precise date and location of her 'death', only the month and year, so he had to laboriously search the North Wing room by room, floor by floor, and drawer by drawer until he found his mum.

He almost didn't recognize her. He was about to shut the drawer when some instinct made him take a closer look. He thought he was prepared for the sight of her, whatever she might look like, but he was wrong. Kaspar remembered her as toned and athletic – but now she was small – mere skin and bones, wasted away by years of inactivity. He covered her naked body with his regulation Guardian overcoat, before looking into her eyes. He brought his face close to hers, wondering if any part of her could recognize him, but the lidless eyes just oscillated crazily. She was long gone, driven mad by over eleven years of watching unspeakable horror while trapped in a paralysed shell.

'I love you, Mum,' he whispered. Then he switched off the life support to her cabinet and held her dry, leathery hand until her breathing ceased and the crazy eyes stopped moving. Only then did he wipe away his tears with the back of his hands.

Where was she now?

Was she in the cottage? With his dad? The end of her rainbow?

Had she finally found her voice? Or was she at last dreamlessly sleeping?

Kaspar had brought her a dress uniform, but he

couldn't bring himself to put it on her. It didn't seem right. With Janna and Mariska already out on patrol, he called the one other person who could help, the one person who hated him the most in the world. He called Mac.

The moment his call was connected, Kaspar could see that Mac had been crying. Her eyes were red and sore, her hair combed down and smooth against her head instead of the wild, spiky style she usually favoured.

'Why are you phoning me? I have nothing to say to you,' she said coldly.

'I understand that you never want to see me again. Believe me, I get it. And I wouldn't be troubling you if I had any other choice. But I . . . I need your help.'

Mac's eyes narrowed as she regarded Kaspar. She certainly wasn't making this easy for him, but then, why should she? The previous evening Kaspar had tried to explain the what and the why, but Mac had been in no mood to listen. He'd tried to explain that the political tracts written by the High Councillors over the years were nothing but lies. Mac refused to believe him. When he tried to tell her about Tilkian and her dad, she had raised her hand as if to strike him across the face. Kaspar had braced himself for the blow but made no attempt to stop her.

They had both stood frozen, captured images in an artist's painting. Seconds passed before Mac's hand had dropped to her side. An expression Kaspar had never seen before settled over her face, a look that made him flinch.

It hurt worse than any physical blow ever could. Without saying a word, Mac had turned and left the rec room, her movements stiff and jerky like a puppet's. She had been trying desperately to hold it together, at least until she left the room.

And Kaspar could do nothing but let her go, feeling utterly helpless.

From that moment, he had waited for the knock on his door or the CommLink call to report immediately to his new Commander's office at the Academy. Mac held his future in her hands. One sentence from her when the officials came to tell her about the death of her dad and Kaspar knew he'd be locked up, never to see the light of day again – if he was lucky.

That's why he had to take care of business while he still had the chance.

And the first order of business was to take care of his mum.

'Mackenzie, I really need your help,' he repeated.

The silence between them stretched unbearably taut.

'With what?' Mac asked at last.

'My mum is one of the inmates of the North Wing,' said Kaspar. 'I need for her to rest in peace. She needs to be washed and clothed and I . . . I . . . can't do it by myself.'

Silence.

'I'll be right there,' Mac said, disconnecting the call before he could thank her.

Kaspar went down to the ground floor to stand just inside the entrance. He paced back and forth continuously, worried that Mac would bring the military police with her. She had every right.

Less than thirty minutes later she arrived. Alone. The two of them regarded each other as Kaspar searched desperately for the right words to say.

'Thank you,' he said softly.

'I'm doing this for your mum, not for you,' Mac informed him.

Kaspar led the way up to the eleventh floor and into the third storage room off the corridor. Mac looked around, confused.

'Is this what you were trying to tell me last night? Is this place full of tortured and paralysed Insurgents?' she asked, aghast.

Kaspar nodded. 'Not just Insurgents. My mum is in here too. And she's not the only one of the Alliance to end up here. Anyone who challenged the High Council's right to rule or the way they governed ended up here as well. I recognized a few of the faces while I was searching.' He opened the drawer containing his mum. He didn't miss the way Mac gasped at the sight of her. She was still covered up to her neck with his coat, and the bag containing the military dress uniform he'd brought sat self-consciously on the floor beside her drawer.

'Is she . . . is she dead?' asked Mac.

'Yes,' Kaspar whispered. 'She is now.'

'Are the others dead too?'

'Not yet. But they will be if I have anything to do with it.'

'Can't they be revived? At least some of them?'

'No. The stuff they inject into them makes sure of that,' said Kaspar.

Mac nodded slowly. 'I'll call you when I've finished.' Her expression full of compassion, she looked down at his mum, reaching out her hand to stroke her hair.

With tears pricking at his eyes, Kaspar left the room. He paced outside, ready for anyone who tried to question his presence or turf him out of the building. But no one came along. The building was eerily silent. He glanced down at his hands. What would happen to him if he touched each and every living corpse in the North Wing? How many would he need to touch before the shared memories and the horrors they were constantly subjected to drove him insane? That's what Rhea and the other Insurgents had probably had to live with for years. Kaspar couldn't understand why she and the others like her hadn't wanted to wipe out every single member of the Alliance in revenge for the North Wing alone. They had to have a strength of mind and depths of compassion that Kaspar could only just begin to imagine.

Finally Mac called him back. Her faint smile told him it was OK to look now. Kaspar viewed his mum and breathed a sigh of relief. She looked a bit more like herself, except for the lifeless, staring eyes. It was traditional to close the eyes of the dead, but even that was denied to the victims of the North Wing. Kaspar took out his sunglasses and put those on her.

In a moment of awful black humour, Dillon's voice played in his head: '*A corpse in shades? Your mum looks totally cool, man.*'

Kaspar smiled. He didn't know if Dillon got an afterlife. He hoped so. He hoped that a lifetime of drinking chemically-laced water every day hadn't robbed him of that. He bent and kissed his mum on the forehead.

'Bye, Mum,' he whispered. Then he closed the drawer that contained her body for what he knew would be the last time. He straightened up to find Mac watching him.

'Commander Martinez came to see me this morning to tell me about my dad,' said Mac.

Kaspar forced himself to look at her even though her eyes were once again giving him ice burns.

'He saw that I'd been crying and wanted to know how I knew about Dad before the news had been officially released.'

'What did you tell him?' asked Kaspar quietly. He needed to know how long he had to finish what he'd started. Had Mac told the commander where he would be when he'd phoned her earlier to ask for her help? No. If that were the case, they would've already arrested him.

'I told him I had a premonition that something had happened to my dad,' said Mac.

Kaspar frowned. 'And he believed that?'

'He had no choice.'

'Does that mean that maybe someday you'll forgive me?' asked Kaspar.

Mac regarded him. 'I don't know, Kas. I truly don't know.'

'Fair enough,' Kaspar replied. At least it wasn't a straight-out 'no'. It wasn't all that he wanted, but it would have to do.

They left the North Wing together, but apart.

There was only one further atrocity attributed to the Insurgency. It happened the night after the missile strikes. The blowing up of the North Wing of the Clinic was without doubt a job of skilled precision. North Wing was obliterated but the implosion was designed so that no other part of the Clinic was damaged apart from a few broken windows. As the North Wing of the Clinic only housed the morgue, and a skeleton staff who were evacuated due to a fire alarm sounding just before the implosion, losses were minimal. News reports were grateful that the Insurgency seemed to have missed their target, which must surely have been the entire Clinic and not just one wing.

CCTV cameras picked up the image of one lone, masked figure entering the North Wing with a rucksack on his or her back, only to leave about thirty minutes later minus the rucksack. The perpetrator's face was obscured but new reports assured the populace that it was only a matter of time before the person responsible for such a heinous act was brought to justice. Kaspar watched the news and hoped fervently that they'd never find the person responsible. He really didn't fancy spending the next umpteen years of his life in prison.

He took charge of the disposal of Rhea's body personally. Those supposedly in authority had far too much on their plates to give him any kind of static about it. He found the perfect place to bury her, on a hillside overlooking a lake. He wanted to do that much for her. She deserved more but he had nothing else.

49

A week after the missile strikes, Kaspar walked into Library Services. A man in his early forties sat behind Mac's usual desk. That's how Kaspar had come to think of it – as Mac's desk. Kaspar took a quick look around but he couldn't see her anywhere so he headed over to the reception desk. Glancing down at the man's amber security pass, Kaspar said, 'Hi, Edwin. I'm Guardian Wilding. Is Mac working today?'

'Hello, Guardian. Mac's up in the reference section this evening. That's up on the second floor,' Edwin replied.

'Thanks.' Kaspar forced a polite smile, already heading for the escalator.

'Er, Guardian? D'you mind if I ask you something?'

'Go ahead.' Kaspar turned round.

Edwin was nervous, almost uncomfortable, but he looked Kaspar in the eye and asked, 'Is it true? About the High Councillors and most of the SSG? Are they really dead?'

Silence.

'Yes, it's true,' Kaspar replied at last. 'Most of the SSG

347

were protecting the High Council at the time of the strikes so . . .'

Edwin gulped. 'Oh God! So why haven't the Crusaders aimed their missiles at us in Capital City? Surely we're the next obvious target?'

Kaspar shrugged. 'I don't think they'll do that.'

'Why not? That's what I'd do in their shoes.'

Kaspar studied the man before him. Just a few short weeks ago, it would've been like looking in a mirror. 'Let's hope, as the shoe is on the other foot, that the Crusaders find our Alliance shoes a bad fit,' he said.

'So what's going to happen now?' asked Edwin.

Kaspar shrugged. 'No idea.'

'Guardian, aren't you scared?'

Kaspar smiled. 'I'm terrified. I don't have a clue what tomorrow may bring, but I'm hoping it'll be something new and different.'

'That's a good thing?' Edwin's tone was highly sceptical.

'Compared to the prospect of the old way of thinking and more of the same, it's a very good thing.'

'I disagree.' Active belligerence was now present in Edwin's voice.

Kaspar shrugged.

'You're wrong, Guardian,' Edwin told him. 'The past has a way of clinging on. Don't be so eager to dismiss it.'

'Life is about change. And change will arrive whether we want it to or not,' said Kaspar. And with that he headed for the escalator.

It took him over five minutes to find Mac. She was

sitting cross-legged in an alcove, wearing gloves to examine an old book resting on the wooden floor before her. Kaspar hadn't seen her in so long he took a moment to watch her as she pored over the pages of the book. Her purple, spiky haircut was gone, replaced by a jet-black, sleek-cut hairstyle. The army boots and outlandish clothes were also no more. She wore a white collarless shirt, black trousers and black trainers. As if she knew she was being watched, Mac froze momentarily before turning her head.

'Hi, Mackenzie,' said Kaspar.

Mac got to her feet without saying a word, her gaze never leaving Kaspar's.

'I . . . I wondered if we could have a talk, in private?'

Mac indicated the alcove they were in with one hand. 'You can't get much more private than this.'

'I needed to see you . . . to tell you how sorry I am about your dad,' said Kaspar quietly.

Mac frowned. 'You've already done that. Why are you here, Kas? Seeking absolution? D'you want me to forgive you and tell you that what you did to my dad was OK, and then you can get on with your day, your year, your life?'

'No. I know it doesn't work that way.'

'Then I don't understand what you want from me.'

'I-I need someone to talk to,' Kaspar admitted.

Mac raised an eyebrow. 'And I'm the best you could come up with?'

'You're the only one I came up with,' said Kaspar. 'You're the only one who knows everything I've done. I guess I need someone to tell me that I'm not the devil.'

'And you think I'm the one to do that?' Mac said, incredulity lending a sharp note to her voice.

Kaspar regarded her for a moment. He sighed. 'You're right. This was a really bad idea.'

He turned to leave, calling himself all kinds of a fool. What the hell was he thinking? But a week of uncertainty, incapacitating guilt and a lack of sleep had obviously dissolved what little sense he had left.

'Kas, wait,' Mac called after him.

He turned round but didn't attempt to move closer.

'You're not the devil, OK?'

Kaspar sighed again. He didn't feel any better for hearing it, and he suspected Mac didn't feel any better for saying it either. 'I shouldn't have come here. You've got things to do and I've already taken up too much of your time.'

'I'm not that busy. I'm hunting down the truth but it can wait for another few minutes,' said Mac. 'After all, it's not going anywhere.'

Hunting down the truth? What did that mean? Kaspar decided not to ask. He didn't want to push his luck.

'Kas, d'you ever regret becoming a Guardian?' asked Mac.

Kaspar immediately shook his head. 'No. It's what I was born to be. And I'm sure it's what my mum planned for me. I just didn't fully appreciate that until I saw her lying in a drawer in the North Wing of the Clinic. I'll never regret what I did there.'

'But you do have some regrets?'

'Oh yes. Loads of them.'

'Like?'

'You wouldn't understand,' sighed Kaspar. 'I don't mean to be patronizing, but you're a civilian. You don't have to make split-second decisions or even long-term choices that will affect the fates of countless others.'

'Don't give me that,' Mac countered angrily. 'You sound just like my dad.'

'Your dad was a great soldier and he may have got some things wrong, but he got that one right,' said Kaspar, warming to his theme. 'Voss used to say the definition of a civilian is someone who lets others do their dirty work. Mac, with the best will in the world, you don't know what it's like to risk your health, your freedom and maybe even your life. How can you? You deal with books and know-ledge. Your world is safe. Mine isn't.'

'Books and knowledge don't make for a safe world. Just the opposite. Books and knowledge are facets of the truth and the truth can be very dangerous,' Mac argued. 'You of all people should know that.'

'Yeah, the truth is dangerous and worth fighting for,' said Kaspar. 'But that's where I and the other Guardians step in and take over. That way you get to sit in your alcove and carry on reading.'

At the look on Mac's face, he clamped his lips together, but too late. Damn it! That wasn't what he'd come here to say at all. Well, Mac wasn't chucking books at him or launching herself across the alcove in his direction; at least not yet. Time to retreat.

'I'm sorry, Mackenzie. Every time I open my mouth, I put my foot in it.' He sighed.

'What else did my dad get right?' Mac asked.

Huh? Kaspar regarded Mac in surprise. The warmth that used to be in her eyes wasn't there, but neither was the ice.

'A lot of things actually,' he said. 'He was my mentor. I looked up to him.' He could feel his face begin to burn. Nothing was coming out of his mouth the way he'd planned tonight.

'Have you had dinner yet?' Mac surprised him by asking.

Kaspar shook his head.

'My break is about to start and I was thinking of heading over to the mess hall for a meal,' said Mac. 'If you've got nothing better to do . . .'

'You want me to come with you?' Kaspar asked, astounded.

'It'd be nice to talk about my dad with someone who knew the real man, but who hasn't forgotten all the good things he did. But if you're too busy or about to go on duty, then no worries,' shrugged Mac.

'No, I, er, I'd love to have dinner with you,' said Kaspar. 'I'd really love that.'

Mac frowned. 'It's just a meal, Kaspar. It doesn't mean we're engaged or anything.'

'Yeah, I get that,' said Kaspar, his face warming.

Mac smiled. Kaspar smiled back. She bent to pick up her book and put it back on the shelf before they headed out of the alcove together. Kaspar kept stealing glances at her. She had a real knack for doing the unexpected, but he kind of liked it. And for the first time in too long, some of the guilt that had been sitting on his chest and slowly suffocating him began to ease – just a little.

But a little was good.

A little was a start.

I'm posting this on the datanet because I have something to say.

Like a phoenix rising from the ashes, the truth has finally arisen in Capital City. We in the Alliance have been betrayed, not by the Crusaders but by our own High Council. For decades we have been taught their vision, their extracts, their version of history.

It was all lies.

Buckle up, because here comes the truth.

We in the Alliance were the ones who almost destroyed our planet. Capital City is built on the land, the blood, the bones, the tears of the Crusaders. This land was theirs long before it was ours. We took it by force and exiled them to the Badlands. Our High Councillors were corrupt. Our Special Support Group were the ruthless lackeys of the High Council.

Never underestimate the value of fear. It is a powerful weapon of control. The High Council instilled within all of us a fear of the different, the unknown, the truth. We were taught to fear the Crusaders. We were told they were out to destroy us. How many of us challenged that view? I know I never did. How many of us had the courage to question what we had been taught and told?

The SSG were the ones responsible for the Loring School outrage and countless other attacks that were then blamed on the Insurgents. Such attacks focused our attention, our fear and our hatred away from the true perpetrators.

Each and every Alliance citizen is as guilty as those in the High Council for how we have treated the Crusaders in general and the Insurgents in particular. We stopped thinking for ourselves because it was easier to let others do our thinking for us. Will we allow those with a thirst for power to rise up to fill the vacuum left by the High Council and to once again suppress freedom of expression and thought? Will we continue to digest the lies of old simply because they are easier to swallow than the inconvenient truth? Or will we seize this new day and ensure that never again do we place our lives, our thoughts, our destinies in the hands of unworthy others?

The choice is yours and mine.

So, who am I?

Just an average Alliance citizen who has had access to confidential data in the past, but was too complacent to scrutinize it until very recently.

For those who still doubt my words, I've posted datanet links at the bottom of this screen to a number of now-unlocked sites containing top-secret information that confirm that every word I've said so far is the truth.

What we do with that truth is up to each and every one of us.

But as I once read, there are none so blind as those who refuse to see. It is time for all of us to open our eyes.

A friend of mine recently accused me of letting others do my dirty work. Well, this is me raising my head above the parapet. I've posted this message and the links to all the corroborative evidence on every news and social networking site I could think of.

I don't know what will happen next. Maybe it'll go viral, maybe it won't – but at least the truth will no longer be hidden away. It's out in the sunlight for all to see. I don't know what kind of trouble I may bring down upon my head for doing this. But I've thought long and hard about it, and if I do get my head handed to me, then it's a price I'm willing to pay.

To any remaining authorities out there, posting this was my decision and my decision alone. I had no collaborators and it was all my own idea. If you're so afraid of the truth that you decide to come after me, I'm easy to find.

My name is Mackenzie Voss and I have one wish for you, for me, for all of us.

Peace.

www.mackenzievoss.net

www.alliancehighcouncil.net/classified/historical_documents

www.alliancehighcouncil.net/classified/crusader_threat/
containment